INCUBUS

INCUBUS

by
Michael R. Davidson

INCUBUS

Legacy Publishers
PO Box 62442
Virginia Beach, VA 23466
www.legacypublishers.net
info@legacypublishers.net

Library of Congress Control Number: 2012954586
ISBN 978-0-615-73579-5

Contact author at info@michaelrdavidson.com

Cover design by M. Davidson
Printed and bound in the United States of America.
First printing 2012

DEDICATION:
TO THE MOLE HUNTERS WHO GUARD OUR FLANKS

In the development of this novel the author was inspired in part by actual events connected with the dissolution of the Soviet Union and its aftermath that have been amply reported in the press and literature.

Having made this clarification it is important to emphasize the fact that this is a work of fiction and the situations described, as well as the characters and their actions are totally imaginary.

Having reviewed the manuscript, as required by law, the CIA required the following disclaimer:

TABLE OF CONTENTS

CHAPTER 1 15

CHAPTER 2 19

CHAPTER 3 24

CHAPTER 4 34

CHAPTER 5 36

CHAPTER 6 45

CHAPTER 7 54

CHAPTER 8 57

CHAPTER 9 64

CHAPTER 10 72

CHAPTER 11 83

CHAPTER 12 87

CHAPTER 13 91

CHAPTER 14 97

CHAPTER 15 103

CHAPTER 16 109

CHAPTER 17 121

CHAPTER 18 125

CHAPTER 19 131

CHAPTER 20 137

CHAPTER 21 141

CHAPTER 22 145

CHAPTER 23 150

CHAPTER 24 155

CHAPTER 25 160

CHAPTER 26 165

CHAPTER 27 168

CHAPTER 28 174

CHAPTER 29 178

CHAPTER 30 193

CHAPTER 31 196

CHAPTER 32 201

CHAPTER 33 205

CHAPTER 34 210

CHAPTER 35 215

CHAPTER 36 220

CHAPTER 37 224

CHAPTER 38 237

CHAPTER 39 241

CHAPTER 40 245

CHAPTER 41 252

CHAPTER 42 257

CHAPTER 43 265

CHAPTER 44 270

CHAPTER 45 277

CHAPTER 46 281

CHAPTER 47 293

CHAPTER 48 297

CHAPTER 49 304

CHAPTER 50 307

CHAPTER 51 310

CHAPTER 52 319

CHAPTER 53 330

CHAPTER 54 334

CHAPTER 55 338

CHAPTER 56 344

CHAPTER 57 348

CHAPTER 58 354

CHAPTER 59 357

CHAPTER 60 362

CHAPTER 61 366

CHAPTER 62 371

CHAPTER 63 373

CHAPTER 64 378

CHAPTER 65 386

CHAPTER 66 389

CHAPTER 67 399

ACKNOWLEDGEMENTS

Thanks are due to my family, especially my long-suffering wife, Alma, for their patience and support. I can be sometimes difficult to live with when I'm in the throes of research and writing.

The original inspiration for the title, INCUBUS, was the testimony of former Director of Central Intelligence Richard Helms before a House Select Committee in 1978. Excerpts from this testimony can be found at the end of this book. Richard Helms was still the DCI when I joined the Agency and was a man we looked up to and admired for his strength of character and his dedication to insuring that the CIA became and remained a professional and respected intelligence service. He came up through the ranks of OSS and CIA, and I doubt that we will ever have another experienced intelligence professional of his caliber as DCI. The nomination of a career CIA officer to the post would in these mistrustful times be considered politically incorrect.

The affair at the center of the INCUBUS plot was extremely painful for the Agency and is still the subject of controversy. I will not reveal the plot here in the hope that the story will be read without preconceptions, but for those interested in the best account of actual events I have seen to date, I recommend SPY WARS by Tennent "Pete" Bagley (Yale University, 2007).

My sincere appreciation goes to Author Robert O. Morris and his wife Maka and to Legacy Publishers for helping me bring INCUBUS to print.

Michael R. Davidson
New Market, VA
October 2012

"(The question)... hangs like an incubus in the air."

Richard M. Helms
Director, CIA 1966 - 1973

CHAPTER 1

Ballston – Northern Virginia

The General wished his condominium provided a parking area. The two block walk from the space he rented by the month in a public garage was beginning to tax him and his daughter nattered at him constantly about it. What was he supposed to do? Hire a chauffeur? He chuckled softly to himself as the thought crossed his mind that at his age he should consider himself fortunate to be able to walk two blocks at all. He'd just returned from a small gathering of friends organized by his daughter to celebrate his 80th birthday, which would be tomorrow.

He was a man accustomed to cooler climes so the evening drop in temperature was a relief from the heat of the day. He had led a full life, a successful and above all *interesting* life, and in that he was more fortunate that most or more cursed. Like other men the General also had done things that upon reflection now caused him shame, but soon he would rectify at least one those mistakes so that he might meet his Maker with a 50/50 chance of escaping Hell.

He shook his head at the irony. Advancing age, like foxholes, abhors atheists.

He considered the implications for an old atheist as he turned from the bright lights of the main thoroughfare into the side street where he lived and the final half block to his building's entrance. The lighting here was not so good, with pools of relative gloom between the evenly spaced street lamps, but he knew the way well.

The dead end street was only a block long and lined with look-alike red brick condos whose residents seldom ventured outside in the evening to socialize, preferring instead to remain within the electronic bubbles created by the glow of flat screen TV's and five channel sound systems. The General found such voluntary isolation curious and wondered if it were a phenomenon caused by the infestation of modern society by electronics, or if there were something deeper within urban dwellers that rendered them antisocial.

*****

Given the slow pace of the old man it would cost only a few seconds for the dark figure following to catch up. John Buchalter wore a baseball cap that placed his face in shadow, and a loose shirt with the tail outside his jeans.

He reached beneath his shirt for the snub nosed .38 he carried stuffed into his waistband. It was a cheap gun, a 'Saturday night special,' for which he had paid a man he knew in Northeast DC an exorbitant $300.

Buchalter had been waiting for the old man in the parking garage and considered killing him there, but had discarded the idea almost immediately. The garage was too public and too close to the main thoroughfare. He didn't want to have to kill any innocent witnesses. The dead-end street on which the General lived would serve his purpose well.

He closed the distance quickly, the rubber soles of his athletic shoes silent against the concrete, drawing the .38 as he moved. Buchalter was a big man, and he could have overpowered the aged General easily. But his orders were to shoot him with the cheap gun. Within seconds he was directly behind his quarry who sensed his presence and had just begun to turn his head when Buchalter extended his arm so the pistol was within inches of the General's head and pulled the trigger. His victim dropped like a bundle of rags to the sidewalk. Death was instantaneous.

Buchalter waited, listening. There was no reaction to the crack of the single shot in the night, no windows opened, no alarm raised. This July was oppressively hot in Washington and its suburbs. Air conditioners were pumping tons of cooled air into hermetically sealed apartments and houses, isolating their inhabitants from the outside world.

Satisfied that he had attracted no attention, he knelt quickly to go through the dead man's pockets, removing the wallet, the man's watch, everything of value. This was supposed to look like a common street crime. But for Buchalter, the most valuable find of all were the keys to the General's condominium. They would be used later to make a surreptitious entry and search, but not tonight. The body could be discovered at any moment. Best not to push his luck.

Buchalter turned away back toward the main thoroughfare. The near–by Metrorail Orange Line would drop him at Farragut West, only a few short blocks from the White House, where his boss waited.

CHAPTER 2

The Arlington Police Department is housed along with the county jail and the 17th Judicial Court in a modern, white building at 1425 North Courthouse Road, across the Potomac River from the District of Columbia. The Washington area's legendary heat and humidity, even at this early hour, leaked into the lobby as Detective Krystal Murphy entered through the big, glass double doors. She wore her usual work clothes consisting of a blue polo shirt emblazoned with the Arlington Police shield, blue jeans, and sneakers with her badge, service pistol, extra clip, and cuffs at her belt. Her shoulder-length auburn hair was pulled back and held behind her head with a scrunchy.

Sergeant Bernice Williams, a perpetually bored, stocky woman who claimed to have "seen it all," waved at Murphy from the reception desk. It was eight AM, and Bernice was sucking caramel-infused coffee from a cardboard Starbucks cup.

"Krystal, Lieutenant Jefferson wants to see you."

"What's up?"

"There was a robbery/murder in Ballston last night."

Murphy felt a twinge of excitement. Murder was rare in Arlington. "Who was it?"

"Dunno. Some old Russian dude?"

"Russian?"

Bernice shot her a look that said she couldn't care less because it wasn't her department and her coffee was getting cold. Murphy took the hint. "I'd better get to Jefferson's office."

"Good idea."

Murphy rode the elevator to the fourth floor and wove her way between the gray metal desks toward Marty Jefferson's glass walled office at the rear of the common area.

Charlie Cogburn, her partner, waited for her at a desk that was littered with the remains of an Egg McMuffin and a packet of hash browns. He looked up when she entered and gave her his usual once-over, his eyes lingering on her breasts and then sliding downward. It was a daily ordeal that Cogburn inflicted upon her because he just couldn't help himself. She figured the Arlington Police now had the perfect politically correct balance for their small squad of detectives: an African-American, a woman, and a dumbass.

In his fifties, short, grizzled hair going thin on top, expanding belly exploding against a short-sleeved rayon shirt that overlapped his belt, with a tie of some dark, indeterminate color dangling loosely from his unbuttoned collar, Cogburn was a sterling representative of society's shockingly large dumbass element.   Maybe he had been a good cop once, but time and cynicism had taken their toll. When she'd made detective and was assigned as Cogburn's partner she'd been incredulous. Her promotion, she knew, was too recent for her to make waves, and detective slots in the small department were few, but the man was insufferable. Whatever unnamed cretin in Human Resources had assigned her to the antediluvian misogynist that was Charlie Cogburn must have had a sick sense of humor.

"'Bout time you got here," Cogburn drawled, grunting as he lifted his bulk out of the chair, showering the tiled floor with biscuit crumbs. "Jefferson's been waiting."

"Well, then, we'd better go see him. I understand we have a murder."

Lieutenant Marty Jefferson was a trim African-American in his mid-forties. Today he wore an immaculate tan summer suit, electric blue shirt, and a red power tie. Somehow he managed to look cool all the time. Jefferson had earned a Masters in Criminology at Ole Miss and was a man who had learned the correct way to ride the bureaucracy on the way to the next promotion. Always the gentleman, he rose when they entered. "Take a seat, but don't get too comfortable. You'll be out on the street at the crime scene as soon as we're finished here."

Despite herself Murphy was excited. Serious crime, especially murder, was uncommon in Arlington County where crime had been dropping in small increments for several years. There had been only two homicides in all of the previous year, and this year there had been only one until now. Murder found a more propitious environment across the Potomac in D.C.

"This will have to be handled carefully," began Jefferson. "The victim was a former Russian KGB General named Pavel Kondratiev." He stumbled slightly over the pronunciation and Murphy could see that the imperfection embarrassed him. "He's a bit of a celebrity here in Washington. I Googled him this morning, and there's a ton of references to him on the Internet. It would probably be a good idea if you did the same." He looked at Murphy when he said this. Computer research was not Cogburn's strongpoint, although Murphy was certain the man knew enough to navigate to porn sites.

Jefferson continued. "The victim was discovered on the street around five this morning, only a few hours ago, by a newspaper delivery guy. CSU is over there now, and I want you two on the scene before the body is moved."

The Crime Scene Unit was represented by Jeff Headley who in Murphy's opinion was not exactly the sharpest scalpel in the drawer.

"He was an important man in Russia until he was forced into retirement and charged with treason. He somehow made his way to the States and eventually became an American citizen. He made a name for himself on the lecture circuit. He's even been invited to participate in seminars at the CIA. Last month he published his memoirs, and the book was pretty well-received. That's all I can tell you for the time being. Right now, you need to visit the crime scene and interview his daughter."

"He has a daughter here?" Murphy asked.

"She lives over in Falls Church. You'll have to notify her of her father's death."

CHAPTER 3

They were submerged in nearly liquid mid-July heat as soon as they stepped out the door into the parking lot and Cogburn's armpits immediately blossomed dark with sweat. It was the kind of heat that can take your breath away and shorten tempers. Things didn't improve when Murphy's feet crunched on the discarded fast food cartons and wrappers that littered the floor of Cogburn's unmarked Ford. The inside of the car smelled like a burger joint's grease pit at the end of a long day, and she rolled down the window as soon as he started the engine.

"Hey, roll that up. I'll get the A/C going."

"How do you stand it? Why don't you clear the trash out of here once in a while?"

He grinned evilly as he backed out of the space, enjoying her discomfort. "S'matter, sweetheart? I thought the Army made you tough."

When she was first assigned to Cogburn, his reaction had been completely archetypal of the male superiority syndrome all too familiar to Murphy. Men had a hard time seeing past her Irish good looks and she purposely dressed down to minimize them. She'd attracted a lot of male attention in her rural Indiana hometown, but high school boys were just a distraction, not that she had anything against them. As she was fond of putting it, she spent the first eighteen years of her life plotting her escape from the anonymity of vast Midwestern corn fields.

During her second year in junior college, an Army recruiter visited the campus and she recognized in the military the possibility of realizing her ambitions. She enlisted immediately. Six months later she found herself assigned to a military police unit in Wiesbaden, Germany.

The military was an eye-opening introduction to the real world that solidified her self-reliance and brought out a toughness that surprised even her. One night at the enlisted club, a combat division sergeant who had somehow managed to wrap himself around the better part of a bottle of Jack Daniels made a clumsy pass at her that she brushed off good naturedly. The Sergeant belatedly spotted her MP unit insignia and became abusive. She managed to ignore him until he stood weaving behind her and breathily declared, "You can't spell 'wimp' without 'MP.'"

It wasn't a "fair" fight – the sergeant was drunk, after all, but he outweighed her by about a hundred pounds. She stood away from the bar where she had been nursing a Coke and faced the leering drunk. "Sergeant," she said in a clear voice, "You are obviously intoxicated. You need to go somewhere and dry out or it's the brig for you."

It became very quiet as everyone's attention

turned to the confrontation. The sergeant laughed nastily.   "You   need   an   attitude   adjustment, sweetheart," he said.   "A good fuck from a real soldier should take care of you." Then he made the mistake of reaching out and touching her shoulder.

She sidestepped around him, slipped her arm under his armpit, and kicked the back of his knee hard with the heel of her combat boot, causing him to crash to the floor. It was really too easy for her then to immobilize his arm in a hammer- lock and cuff him to the wild cheers of the other patrons. He spent the night in the brig.

She'd briefly considered a military career, but when her enlistment was up she decided to complete a university degree in criminology on the GI Bill instead. After graduation, she found employment with the Arlington Police where she worked her way steadily up the ranks, interrupted only once by a six-month stint with a Reserves MP brigade in Baghdad.

They arrived at Utah Street where the victim's condo was located, a quiet dead-end just around the corner from the Ballston Metro Station. The street was lined on both sides with mid-rise red brick condominium buildings, apparently built with an eye to the *faux* colonial sterility common in the Washington suburbs. Murphy guessed the area would be quiet at night with little foot traffic – just the right environment for a mugging. The killer could have doubled back the half-block to Fairfax

Drive and been out of the area via Metro train within minutes.

The crime scene was easy to spot. The morgue wagon was already there with two body retrieval guys leaning against its side, undoubtedly anxious to be on their way. The uniforms had the area cordoned off with yellow crime scene tape. She didn't see Jeff Headley and this annoyed her. He should have waited until the investigating officers arrived.

She was out the door as soon as Cogburn pulled to a stop, only too happy to escape the noisome atmosphere inside the car. "Where's Headley?" She directed the question to one of the uniforms.

"He was here earlier, looked things over and left. Said there was nothing beyond the obvious. The vic was killed sometime after midnight. He took a liver temperature and said he'd get more samples at autopsy."

Headley preferred to avoid the heat and work in the air-conditioned morgue. She couldn't blame him, but it was not exactly the proper protocol.

Once Cogburn had joined her they raised the blanket that had been placed over the corpse. The vic was an old man, probably in his late seventies, dressed in a nice suit and tie now spattered with blood from a bullet wound that shone redly in the white hair on the left rear side of his head. His pockets had been turned inside out. There was no jewelry.

"Looks like a hit and run," said Cogburn, straightening up from the corpse. "Probably some homeboy from across the river that we'll never catch."

Murphy winced at the comment. They'd not even begun the investigation but Cogburn had already come to a conclusion and dismissed their chances of success. "What makes you so sure?"

"Experience, baby, experience. Unless we get real lucky and some bonehead steps forward and volunteers information or the mugger makes a stupid mistake, we're not gonna find any clues to his identity. I've seen too many of these things to expect anything else."

"We still have an investigation to complete."

"OK, Shirleylock, let's investigate."

The uniform snickered and she skewered him with a venomous glare she had perfected while still an MP. "You call Headley and tell him to get his ass back here and do his job before the body is removed."

The uniform removed his cap to wipe sweat from his forehead and appealed to Cogburn. "It's hot as hell out here. Can't we clear up now?"

"Do as the detective says. We gotta go inform the vic's daughter." Cogburn wasn't showing solidarity, Murphy knew. He didn't give a damn about protocol, but he was just sadistic enough to derive satisfaction from the uniform's discomfort. She almost regretted losing her temper.

The daughter lived a few miles away in Falls Church in a modest townhouse near the city center. They knew only that her name was Viktoria Kondratieva. It was nearly ten AM by the time they drew up at the address and Murphy wondered if they would find the woman at home.

But she answered the bell promptly. Murphy guessed her age somewhere in the early to mid-forties. She was petite with short black hair in a pixie cut framing a face with sharp features and large, brown eyes. She was neatly dressed in what Murphy guessed was an Ann Klein suit with a skirt that was just a tad too short for a woman of her age.

Murphy took the lead, displaying her badge and introducing themselves as Arlington Police officers, and the woman's eyes widened in what looked like fear. She was Russian. A visit from the police was something to be feared there.

"Ma'am, I'm afraid we have some bad news. Could we please come in?"

Kondratieva backed away from the door and they followed her inside. The place was neat and nicely furnished in a modern, Scandinavian motif – lots of blond wood. Murphy noted a rich, colorful carpet in the tiny living room that she thought looked Persian and was probably worth a lot of money.

"Ma'am, I think it would be best if we sat down." This wasn't the first time since joining the force that Murphy had notified next of kin of the death of a loved one, but it was the first time that the cause of death was murder. She could feel a quiver of apprehension, or maybe it was excitement, in her chest.

Kondratieva sat uncomfortably on the edge of the sofa and stared at them with fearful intensity. She had spoken hardly a word since greeting them at the door. Cogburn was hovering behind Murphy, and before she could speak, he asked, "Is your father Pavel Kondratiev?"

"Yes. What is this about?" She spoke with a strong accent, a tremble in her voice.

Cogburn bumbled on. "Your father was murdered this morning near his home."

"What did you say?" The woman struggled to understand the words.

Murphy was incensed. This was not the way to break the news to this poor woman. She shot Cogburn a reproving look over her shoulder before turning back to Kondratieva. "Your father was discovered early this morning. I'm so sorry." She knelt and took the woman's hands.

Kondratieva sat perfectly still for a long moment as she struggled to make sense of the words.

She squeezed her eyes tightly shut and began to tremble, like an autumn leaf ready to drop from the tree.

"Charlie, go to the kitchen and fetch a glass of water."

Cogburn headed reluctantly out of the room.

"I know it's a terrible shock. Should I call someone?"

"There is no one. I had only my father here." Murphy assumed that by "here," she meant outside of Russia.

Cogburn returned with the water. Kondratieva took a sip and placed the glass on a crystal coaster on a side table. She was struggling to control her emotion.

"Did your father have enemies, anyone who might wish him harm?" asked Murphy. She heard Cogburn snort behind her.

Kondratieva nodded, again squeezing her eyes shut, before answering. "They finally got him."

"Who got him?"

Kondratieva opened her eyes as the tears finally escaped down her cheeks. "The Russians, of course. The Russians finally killed my father."

Cogburn snorted again, and Murphy shushed him.

"Can you tell us more? Why would the Russians have done such a thing? Do you mean the Russian Mafia, something like that?"

"No, not the *Mafiya*. It was the government. They wanted to keep him quiet. He'd just published his book."

"I don't understand."

"They wanted to keep him quiet, to protect their secrets."

"Ma'am," rumbled Cogburn, "it looks like this was a simple robbery and murder. Sorry about your dad, but we don't see any big international conspiracy here."

Can't the oaf just keep quiet? His words startled Murphy. Kondratieva had been on the verge of telling them more, but her jaw snapped shut at Cogburn's interruption. Kondratieva's expression as she looked from one to the other of them was somewhere between disdain and sad resignation.

After making certain there was no one they could call to be with Kondratieva, Murphy promised to let her know as soon as it was possible to make arrangements for her to identify her father's body.

Back in the odiferous Ford she turned on Cogburn. "Why did you do that? She was providing information."

"Sure, about some cockamamie international conspiracy bullshit."

"Maybe there was something to it.   You heard what Jefferson said about her father."

He engaged the gears and drove away, throwing the air conditioning onto maximum as he did so. He steered toward East Broad Street back towards Arlington. "Look, Murphy, I've seen a hundred cases like this. You saw the scene. The guy was robbed. Russian boogiemen aren't going to go through a vic's pockets. Like I said, this was some homeboy from DC out to get some money for blow."

She decided not to argue, but why wouldn't a Russian hit man go through the vic's pockets? Cogburn was her superior and nothing she might say would change his mind at this point. Maybe Headley's CSU would turn up something useful.

But Headley didn't, other than to identify the bullet that killed the General as a .38 caliber round.

And the next day when Murphy went to fetch Kondratieva to formally identify her father's body, nobody answered the door. Another week passed and it became clear that Viktoria Kondratieva had disappeared. According to the neighbors she had not been seen since her father's death.

Despite this, Cogburn's crime report concluded that the General's death had been incidental to a mugging. It was filed with the cold cases and there was nothing Murphy could do about it.

CHAPTER 4

Ewan Ramsay's day was about to be shattered by an echo from the violent end, nearly two decades earlier, of his association with the Central Intelligence Agency.

It was nearly mid-morning and a late summer's cloudless sky promised a fine afternoon for the west coast of Ireland when the car appeared on the narrow coastal road that hugged the rocky southern littoral of Cleggan Bay. It drew Ewan's attention through the kitchen window that faced inland and provided a clear view of the approaches to the white stone house that was his home. There were no trees or shrubs to block the sight lines. He had made certain of that.

Initially he paid only cursory attention to the car, a metallic blue Ford Escort, a common European model, but it slowed as it passed and then pulled off the road after a few hundred yards, just before it would have entered the outskirts of the village of Cleggan.

The double buzz of the phone interrupted his observation, and he had a premonition that the call was related to the car. When he lifted the receiver of the kitchen's wall-mounted phone, an American accented voice sounded over the line. "Mr. Ramsay?"

Ewan replied, "Yes. Who is calling, please?" Over the seventeen years he had lived in Ireland, he had acquired a lilting accent that approached but did not completely replicate the local dialect.

"My name is Robert Strachey. Would it be possible to speak with you personally?" The caller's voice was polite and friendly, and unmistakably American, but the name meant nothing to Ramsay.

The lilt disappeared when he answered. "What do you want?"

"I can't say over the phone, but I assure you it's important."

The evasive response triggered a red warning signal that flashed in his mind and Ramsay's muscles tensed involuntarily. "I'm afraid it would not be convenient, Mr. Strachey."

The line went quiet for a moment, then, "I'm afraid I have no choice but to insist. I'll be there in a moment."

Through the window he watched as the blue Ford made a U-turn and headed slowly back. He opened a drawer and withdrew a clunky looking automatic pistol, a Glock 17, and racked the slide back to chamber a hollow point nine millimeter round.

CHAPTER 5

The house was solid, built of native stone, and well maintained. It sat on a rocky promontory that jutted into the bay next to a deep inlet with a stone dock to which was moored a 26-fooot whale boat. The side of the house facing the road was protected by a knee-high, field stone wall through which an un-gated graveled drive led to a small parking area in front.

Bob Strachey pulled to a stop, switched off the engine, and took a deep breath before stepping out and crunching across the gravel toward the front door. In his nostrils, the briny tang of the sea mingled with the slight putrescence from the tidal flats. Beyond the house, the flats stretched toward the receding sea around a series of tiny islands, now exposed by the low tide and accessible by foot. He could see sheep on some of the islands.

The man who lived in this isolated corner of Connemara was legendary and dangerous, a known killer who played by his own rules. Halfway to the door, Strachey felt eyes upon him. He stood still and raised his arms above his head. He was dressed casually in khaki slacks and a blue polo shirt and had purposely left his windbreaker in the car. He turned in a complete circle to display that he was unarmed. After a minute he lowered his arms, continued to the door, and rapped his knuckles against it.

For a long moment there was no response other than the loud barking of a dog from inside. Then the heavy, planked door swung back to reveal a tall, lean man, his long brown hair liberally peppered with gray and swept back from a high forehead. He immediately reminded Strachey of the actor Clint Eastwood. He wore ragged jeans with a white cotton pullover and Sperry boat shoes with no socks. Had Strachey not known the man to be in his sixties he would have placed his age nearer fifty. In his right hand he recognized a Glock 17 that was pointed unwaveringly at his chest. Behind the man a small black dog snarled, baring exceptionally large, white teeth.

"I told you it would be inconvenient to meet," grated Ramsay.

In his youth Strachey had been an All-American football star at the University of North Carolina and in his mid-forties he retained his Tar Heel athleticism. Despite this and despite the difference in ages, he calculated his chances of disarming Ramsay at zero. In any event he had not made the journey to Ireland to engage the man in combat.

He had come seeking his help.

He ignored the gun and kept his eyes steady on Ramsay's. "I'm sorry to have disturbed you, but I have a personal message for you from Terry Stoddard." Terrence Stoddard was the Director of National Clandestine Services for the Central Intelligence Agency.

Ramsay's eyes narrowed when he heard the name. Otherwise the chiseled face remained cold and inscrutable. And the barrel of the Glock didn't waver from Strachey's chest.

"You've come to the wrong man," he said. "You'd best get back in your car and go back to wherever you've come from."

Strachey didn't budge. "The only way I'll leave is after we've had a chance to talk." With another glance at the Glock, he continued, "You can shoot me, of course, but I don't think you want that kind of trouble in Ireland." He reached slowly into his hip pocket and extracted between thumb and forefinger the slim, leather wallet that contained his Agency credentials, a nice photo ID with an official seal behind a plastic window, and held it up so Ramsay could read it.

Ramsay gave the creds a cursory glance. "That's the most pathetically useless piece of shite I've seen in a long time," then added, "If I were to shoot you, Mr. Strachey, no one in Ireland would ever learn of it."

"They would if Terry Stoddard informed the authorities that one of his people vanished after talking to a known fugitive from justice who lives in Cleggan."

Without removing his eyes from Strachey, Ramsay

signaled the dog to retreat and stepped back from the door. "I think you'd better come inside, after all, Mr. Strachey." He waggled the pistol back and forth to indicate he should enter.

Strachey passed through the doorway as his host stepped back well beyond his reach with the pistol casually aimed in his direction. Ramsay waved his free arm toward an arched door on the right of the entrance foyer that led into a spacious, comfortably furnished living room with a beamed ceiling and a large fieldstone fireplace. Most of the furnishings were in leather and on the walls hung several original oil paintings depicting local seascapes.

"Please sit over there on the sofa near the fireplace." Ramsay raised his voice slightly and said over his shoulder, "I think you should come in and hear what our guest has to say, Sasha."

A woman appeared from a door at the other end of the room. Like Ramsay, she carried a Glock, and Strachey wondered inanely if the pair had a matched set of pistols, like wedding rings. Strachey estimated her age at early to mid-forties although she retained the lithe shapeliness of a much younger woman. Her ash blond hair was pulled back into a ponytail, and like Ramsay she was dressed casually in jeans and a long-sleeved white cotton pullover with a boat neck. She was breathtakingly beautiful with large, hazel eyes. As she drew nearer Strachey detected a scarcely noticeable hairline scar that ran down from above her left eye and ended high on her cheek. She went to Ramsay's side, and the two of them stood together appraising their unwanted visitor.

The woman spoke to Ramsay, "I've looked around outside. It's clear."

The dog that he now recognized as a Scottish terrier joined them, taking his place proprietarily at the woman's feet, and gazed curiously at Strachey with brown, almond-shaped eyes. A surprisingly deep growl rumbled in its throat underscoring the tension in the room.

Ramsay broke the silence. "It's your dime, Strachey, if that's your real name. Say your piece." A pause. "Then we'll see whether you drive away in your little blue car or end up at the bottom of the bay."

Strachey had read Ramsay's file. This was no idle threat.

He had considered several scenarios and in the end settled on this open confrontation on Ramsay's home turf. It was the only way to guarantee a private audience. The really hard part of his mission was yet to come, and already he was in trouble.

Strachey returned their gaze evenly and controlled his breathing. "That seems a bit harsh, Mr. Ramsay. As I said, Terry Stoddard sent me here." Addressing the woman, he said, "And I came alone."

"I've learned never to hesitate to do what is required," said Ramsay, "and that name means nothing to me.

"You and he entered the Central Intelligence Agency at the same time and went through training together. You were good friends. Back then your name was Harry Connolly."

"You're not improving your situation. In fact, you just made it a whole lot worse."

Ramsay and the woman exchanged a quick look, and Strachey did not miss the woman's cocked eyebrow, like she was asking whether it was all right to shoot him now.

"You deny that you know Terry Stoddard?"

"I didn't say that. I said the name means nothing to me."

"I hope that's not true. Terry sent me to ask for your help."

Ramsay barked a sound that might have been a laugh. "Now there's an irony."

Strachey started to rise, but thought better of it when the woman raised her Glock. She looked like she knew how to use it. He settled instead for a perch on the edge of the sofa and leaned forward, hands on his knees, a posture calculated to emphasize his sincerity.

"Look," he said, "do you think I would have put

myself in this situation if it wasn't important?"

"I don't know," said Ramsay. "I don't know how much of a fool you are."

Silently asking himself the same question, Strachey gritted his teeth and said, "I don't like having guns waved in my face. Either shoot me or hear me out like civilized people."

Ramsay's demeanor remained unchanged. "Who said we were 'civilized?' But we'll hear you out before deciding whether or not to expend a bullet on you."

Strachey shrugged and looked down at the floor, repressing his anger. "All of this happened before my time, and I've been with the Agency since 1995. Your fireworks were a few years before that, and then you disappeared. They accused you of being a Soviet mole, a long-term penetration of the Russia Section, and that you'd gone completely rogue and murdered a bunch of people in Austria before disappearing. It was later proven that you were not the mole, but you never re-appeared."

"You've said nothing that is not already public knowledge or pure speculation."

"But you ARE Harry Connolly, aren't you?"

"Harry Connolly ceased to exist a long time ago."

"... and became Ewan Ramsay?"

No answer.

Strachey shrugged and continued, "A few years ago, when Terry Stoddard was still Chief of Station in Paris, he heard a story from one of his liaison contacts about a mysterious operative who had helped them on an operation involving the Saudis in the early '90's. The French apparently had good reason to believe this person was somehow affiliated with the Israelis – Mossad to be precise. Terry thought the description resembled Harry Connolly. He retired when his Paris assignment was over but was called back last year to take over the National Clandestine Services. He hadn't forgotten the French story, and now he had some powerful means at his disposal to investigate, specifically a data search and retrieval program that is second to none, and he put it to work. You can't have as many run-ins with the Russians as you have had over the years and not leave a trail. It led me to your door."

The man, the woman, and the dog had remained immobile throughout his recitation, but Strachey sensed a change, subtle at first, in the interpersonal dynamics that shot a crackle of electricity through the atmosphere of the room.

"That's an interesting story," said Ramsay carefully, "but even if it were true, you've still not said why you're here." He turned to the woman. "Sasha, why don't we sit down and listen to the rest of Mr. Strachey's story." He tucked the pistol into the waistband of his jeans and sat in a chair opposite Strachey. The Scottie bounded into his lap and settled there, keeping wary eyes on Strachey.

Relieved and hoping he wasn't showing it, Strachey settled back on the sofa. The hostility had retreated to be replaced by cautious curiosity, but it was still two guns to none. His mission would succeed or fail on the quality of what he now had to say and the conviction with which he said it.

CHAPTER 6

Strachey waited until Ramsay's attractive companion also took a seat. She reminded him of a panther ready to pounce on its prey. "Have you heard of General Pavel Kondratiev?" he asked.

"That's an antediluvian reference." Ramsay closed his eyes for a moment, digging for the relevant memories. "He was KGB, an old Washington hand, I believe. He served several long tours of duty there. He must be nearing eighty by now."

"Correct. He was a star in the First Chief Directorate, the youngest KGB general ever. You didn't get that far that fast in the KGB without some singular successes."

"That was the general opinion concerning Kondratiev."

"The General eventually became Head of the Second Chief Directorate, Counterintelligence, but he fell out of favor when he sided with the Yeltsin faction during the '91 coup attempt. He was forced into retirement, and eventually when Shurgin won the Presidency, he charged Kondratiev with treason. Ironically enough, the general made his way back to Washington, became an American citizen, and has been there ever since. He made a name for himself on the lecture circuit. He's even occasionally been invited to take part in seminars at CIA. In other words, he didn't bother hiding himself. Of course, the Cold War is an anachronism these days, viewed as ancient history by the newbies. We almost stopped chasing Russians altogether back in the nineties."

"Get to the point." Ramsay gave him a 'you're not telling me anything I don't already know' look.

Strachey cleared his throat and continued, "Kondratiev published a book of his memoirs last month. It was well received. In some circles it created a bit of a stir."

Ramsay still said nothing, just raised his eyebrows and waited for the other shoe to drop.

"The book provides accounts of most of the major Soviet penetrations of the US Government from the early sixties to the time Kondratiev left the KGB in '89. He, of course, takes credit for their recruitment and handling. It's all quite believable, and there's no reason to doubt what he wrote. The stir was created by the end of the book where he claimed to have in his possession proof of a major KGB operation that has not yet been uncovered, one that would astound the American public and cause America to seriously re-evaluate its relationship with Russia if revealed."

Opposite Strachey, Ramsay watched him intently while the woman sat with her arms folded as if she were sheltering herself from a chill wind.

Now came the tricky part.

"At a press conference last week Kondratiev said he would reveal the information out of gratitude to the American people for the safe haven the U.S. had given him. That stirred some excitement in the media and a lot more public interest in his book. Official Washington was on edge, especially the White House. The General scheduled a second press conference."

Ramsay broke his silence. "But . . . ?"

"Kondratiev didn't make it to eighty. He was murdered. It happened in Arlington, on the street near his house. The police think it was a mugging that turned into a homicide."

"What does this have to do with me?" Strachey was getting impatient.

"Nothing at all, yet."

Ramsay fell silent, waiting. The woman began tapping her foot on the floor in a staccato beat that told Strachey he'd best make his point soon.

"Terry Stoddard suspects it wasn't a simple mugging, especially in light of the alleged big secret he was about to make public. He, Kondratiev's daughter, and most of the right wing press and talk radio think the Russians may have been involved. Given the General's past as a KGB American Targets officer, Terry thinks he may have intended to reveal the identity of a penetration of some kind, maybe in the Agency."

"Another one? Is the FBI investigating?"

"No federal statute was broken, and the Justice Department is pretty selective these days about who they go after. President Shurgin will visit Washington this month to sign the new strategic weapons control agreement, and everyone is walking on egg shells. The Administration is leery of offending the Russians with a lot of inconvenient questions on the eve of the visit. They need the Russians to support sanctions against Iran, and soon we'll have to depend on them to get our astronauts to the space station. The Arlington police wrote the incident off as an unsolved street crime. There's not likely to be much more investigating unless new and convincing evidence comes to light."

Ramsay's lip had curled at the mention of Shurgin, a reaction for which Strachey had no explanation, but there was definitely some animus there beyond a generalized dislike of Russians.

"Get to the point," said Ramsay.

"To make a long story short, Terry Stoddard wants you to come to Washington, find out who killed Kondratiev, and determine whether or not he was telling the truth about the Russian skullduggery."

What happened next was startling and left Strachey feeling like the only person in the room who didn't get the joke. Ramsay and Sasha turned to one another for a second and then both burst out in peals of laughter. The dog woofed along with them, its short pointy tail wagging.

Ramsay wiped tears from his eyes and said, "Forgive us, but you have no idea of the absurdity of what you just said. The last time a CIA officer asked me to help solve a murder things went entirely off the rails. That's how I ended up here in Ireland." He glanced at the woman. "Nevertheless, despite everything that happened so long ago back in Vienna, things didn't turn out so badly."

This could be a hopeful sign. "So what do you say to Terry's idea?"

"I think it's probably best to let sleeping dogs lie. Kondratiev's exploits were far in the past. I'd have to be a fool to accept Stoddard's request to chase a wild goose. Harry Connolly is still a wanted man in the United States despite the passage of time, and from what you say, Washington is even more bollixed these days than it was the last time I was there and would not welcome anyone nosing about – least of all me. And given what happened twenty years ago, why should I care one way or the other? If Stoddard wants the matter investigated he can do it himself."

"That's the problem."

"What?"

"Have you followed what's been happening with the Agency since you left?"

"The Clandestine Services weren't in very good

shape even twenty years ago."

"Well, things haven't changed much except that there's a lot more emphasis on paramilitary ops, armed unmanned aircraft and the like, and all the emphasis understandably is on counter-terrorism, Iraq and Afghanistan. The Special Ops Group is the moneymaker these days. Other than that, we've become basically a liaison and analysis outfit. With the reorganization of the Intelligence Community, the establishment of a Director of National Intelligence, the DNI, and the growth of an incredibly complex network of private contractors, the CIA is now a notch lower on the totem pole. And now there's an 'intelligence czar' in the White House. Nobody salutes the DCI anymore."

"That's Washington for you," said Ramsay, "Pile one bureaucracy on top of another and expect things to work better. I believe that countries get the kind of intelligence capabilities they deserve, and the U.S. is no exception. I have no sympathy for bureaucrats and no desire to help them. If the CIA is helpless, then so be it. I'm Irish now, in case you've forgotten where you are."

Strachey like all CIA case officers had been trained to convince people to do things they didn't want to do. The strategies and techniques are prehistoric, and the trade deserves its nickname as 'the world's second oldest profession.' But put one good case officer up against another, and they'll fight to a draw. 'You can't bullshit a bullshitter,' as the adage goes. Strachey had no doubt that Ewan Ramsay AKA Harry Connolly was more than a match for him. If he couldn't convince the older man with reason, he would have to resort to threat, and he didn't want to do that.

"I don't believe you," he said, "I read your file."

"Don't be so sure. I still don't understand why Stoddard can't handle this himself."

"He can't. He's hemmed in by the lawyers, the Inspector General, and the DNI, not to mention the Hill. He was a major player in preventing a nuclear attack by terrorists in Spain last year. He was rewarded by being raked over the coals by the Congressional Oversight Committee that's now controlled by people who just couldn't understand why deadly force was necessary to save a nation of 50 million people from nuclear disaster. It was only the President's personal intervention that prevented his being sacked, and even the President was reluctant to get involved in Spain."

Strachey didn't mention the central role he himself had played in the deadly Spanish nuclear affair, the details of which remained highly compartmentalized.

He continued, "The constraints on CIA action inside the U.S. are comprehensive. There is little that Terry can do that would not be discovered immediately, and no other Government agency is going to do anything. That means Terry has to look elsewhere for help from someone not connected to the CIA. Not even the DCI knows what he's doing this time. He needs someone he can trust, someone off the reservation, and that's you. He risked his career sending me here." *And mine, too,* he thought.

"Screw Terry's career! He's put my wife and me in jeopardy by sending you here. How many people know?"

"Only four: Stoddard himself, the Deputy Director for Intelligence Harvey Grant, the technician who ran the computer program, and me."

"So it's in the system at Langley – that means other people can find it, too."

"Not for the time being. That doesn't have to happen."

"How can you be sure?"

"I'm very close to the computer tech who controls the information." In fact, Amy Strachey nee Larson was his wife.

"And if I don't agree?"

This was the conversation Strachey had hoped to avoid, but he had rehearsed the words, knowing it would come. He forced himself to hold Ramsay's glare. "If the information we put together is left in the system there is no guarantee that it won't be discovered by someone else. If you accept the job, we'll see to it that all traces are expunged –

permanently."

So there it was – the threat of exposure laid bare – sordid blackmail – and distrust laced with danger descended once again over the room, sucking the air out of it.

"You live down to all my expectations, Strachey." The lupine glint returned to Ramsay's eyes. He was a man accustomed to eliminating threats, but he had already realized that killing Strachey would solve nothing.

Regardless, Strachey had made an enemy.

Ramsay sat rock still, holding himself under control. "I think you'd better leave now while I'm still of a mind to let you," he said quietly.

His wife lacerated Strachey with a glare and seemed about to bolt to her feet, but Ramsay retrained her with a hand on her arm. Strachey received the distinct impression that this woman could be as dangerous as her mate.

As he held open the door for Strachey to leave, the older man said, "Come back tomorrow at the same time. I'll give you an answer then."

CHAPTER 7

When Ewan returned to the living room Sasha was curled on the sofa holding the dog, Angus II, close and biting her lip, her anger of a moment before now supplanted by anxiety. "What are we going to do?" This could ruin everything, the quiet life they had at last achieved, their sense of security, their plans to at last enjoy some of life's pleasures.

Ewan had first brought her to this house nearly nineteen years earlier when they had just become lovers and she was still his Mossad handler. At the time he was an emotionally damaged man, recently separated from his country through the machinations of a traitor who had burrowed deeply within the CIA. The house later served as a refuge where she could recover from cruel and defacing wounds inflicted by a Russian madman whom Ramsay had killed. He had nursed her back to health in this place and finally convinced her to marry him. The stones had absorbed their secrets and protected them against the ravages of the dangerous lives they led outside of Ireland. The house was home.

He finally answered her. "Our choices aren't great: go to Washington or disappear again. It's a Hobson's choice."

"It's blackmail!"

"Yep, it sure is. And this is something we can't take to the Mossad. The way things are between Israel and Washington these days, they wouldn't touch an operation on U.S. soil with a ten foot pole. We're on our own, unless life on a backwater kibbutz ducking Palestinian rockets and Iranian nukes suddenly appeals to you." As (now retired) members of the Mossad's ultra-secret *Kidon* unit, they had more than once been offered secure resettlement in Israel.

Sasha made a face. "We can't just sit here. That Agency bastard as much as said they'd out you if you refuse to cooperate."

"Yes, and the fact that they've found me after all these years means they could do it again. There's more to this than Strachey was telling us, something big enough to drive Terry Stoddard to such an extreme."

"It's a trap."

"I'm not so sure, but it could well be. So we'll have to be clever."

"It must be a trap. This is something the CIA surely could do on its own, on its own turf."

"You heard what Strachey said, and he was right. The CIA is more hemmed in than most people realize, and one thing is clear – they don't dare run an operation on U.S. soil. Too many people would know about it."

"There are plenty of other options."

"You heard what our visitor said on that subject, too. And there's another thing – Stoddard either does not or cannot trust anyone else in Washington with this. And it seems there are few in the CIA he can trust either."

Sasha knew he had made up his mind. He was like that, arriving at decisions quickly and forging ahead, heedless of the danger. She looked around the comfortable room, at the furnishings, the paintings (there were almost no photographs), at the life they had so carefully constructed, their refuge from the dangerous world they had known their entire adult lives. She would do anything to protect it. Ewan was fifteen years her senior: physically fit as he was at present, he would inevitably decline. She was determined to make the most of the time they had left, and she didn't want that time to be spent on the run. But she knew her husband too well. He was restless in retirement. Clandestine operations are addictive and leave their practitioners with little else that truly stimulates them. She recognized the signs.

"What's your idea of 'clever'?" she asked with a hint of sad resignation.

CHAPTER 8

Two weeks after the Kondratiev murder the Arlington Police received an unusual late morning visitor. The first Murphy knew about it was when Lieutenant Jefferson poked his head out of his office to tell her to go fetch Cogburn from the snack bar. "We have a foreign VIP visitor coming in to discuss the Kondratiev murder."

Jefferson was in his office talking with the visitor when she returned with Cogburn. Seeing them enter, the Lieutenant brought the visitor out to introduce them. She heard Cogburn's sharp intake of breath.

"Detectives Cogburn and Murphy, this is Major Vera Fedosova of the Russian Internal Security Service, the FSB. She'd like to talk to you about the Kondratiev case."

Major Fedosova was the reason Cogburn had almost stopped breathing. She was tall, with long, ash blond shoulder length hair, a perfect face with intelligent, hazel eyes that now betrayed a certain level of amusement. She might just have stepped out of the pages of *Vogue*. Murphy recognized the black MaxMara pant suit and Jimmy Choo's that clicked sharply on the tiled floor as she strode toward them, hand outstretched. *Quite an outfit for a cop. Do the Russians pay that well?*

Murphy stole a glance at Cogburn who still hadn't exhaled. He stood a little straighter and was making a vain attempt to suck in his gut.

The formalities complete, Jefferson retired to his office, leaving them seated with the Russian at the squad room's small, Formica-topped conference table.

"As I told your Lieutenant Jefferson, my name is Major Vera Nikolayevna Fedosova of the FSB." She flashed open a thin wallet to show a badge and ID printed in Cyrillic. "We are somewhat like your Federal Bureau of Investigation. I wanted to speak with the officers in charge of the investigation into the murder of former KGB General Pavel Kondratiev.

"You are no doubt aware that this case has raised questions and many spurious allegations, in the less responsible sectors of the American media and something you call 'talk radio,' of Russian involvement in his death. You also must know that President Shurgin has a state visit to Washington scheduled next week. My mission is to investigate the matter as thoroughly as possible in anticipation of the visit so that the President will be well prepared to answer any questions relating to General Kondratiev's death."

"But it was a common mugging, nothing more," said Cogburn.

"Yes," Fedosova sighed theatrically, "and I know this must be an imposition on you. We don't expect to turn up anything of importance, but it's a matter of being thorough. I'm sure you can appreciate why this is necessary in advance of the Presidential visit."

Cogburn swiveled his head toward Murphy. "Go get the file." He returned his full attention to the visitor and slumped back in his chair with a smirk as he undressed her with his eyes. He didn't seem to mind that she noticed.

Murphy fetched a cardboard file folder from her desk, which she placed on the table in front of Fedosova. The file was embarrassingly thin.

Fedosova listened impassively as Cogburn explained that serious street crime, especially murder, was uncommon in Arlington County. General Kondratiev's murder was an anomaly.

The investigation showed that Kondratiev had been accosted on the street near his Ballston neighborhood condominium most likely while walking home from the public garage where he kept his car. Death had been instantaneous from a .38 caliber bullet wound to the back of his head. The murderer had gotten away with the General's wallet, the contents of his pockets, and his wristwatch, clear indications that the motive had been robbery. The crime had taken place well after dark, and there had been no witnesses.

"Have you identified any suspects?" Fedosova asked.

"Nah," Cogburn didn't sound concerned. He was staring fixedly at the cleavage that showed where Fedosova's cotton blouse gapped open at the second button.

He licked his lips and continued. "This was a random robbery. Your guy was just in the wrong place at the wrong time and some punk off'd him. Without a witness there ain't a prayer that we'll ever catch the guy unless we get a tip or get very lucky."

"So the case is closed?"

"I didn't say that. It'll remain an open case until it's solved, but we got no leads, and we got no witnesses. Nobody even heard the shot."

"Have you checked on possible motives for the murder? Kondratiev had a daughter. What does she say?"

"Motives?" Cogburn snorted and rolled his eyes at Murphy. "The guy was robbed. That was the motive."

Murphy interjected, "Are you referring to the press conference Kondratiev had scheduled?"

Cogburn shot an annoyed glance in his partner's direction which Murphy ignored.

Fedosova's hazel eyes spotlighted Murphy with renewed interest.

"There has been some speculation in the American

press about that aspect."

Murphy returned the look with her own professionally suspicious eyes. "Do you think it's true?"

"You mean, do I believe that my government had something to do with it? No, of course not."

"Maybe you're here to make certain nothing is discovered. Maybe that's why you're asking about Kondratiev's daughter."

The Russian Major remained perfectly relaxed in the face of Murphy's insinuations.

"I am here to find out the truth, if it can be found."

"Maybe," said Murphy.

"And his daughter?"

"She moved back here from California last year – a divorce she wanted to get as far away from as possible – and was taking care of her father, managing his money and his papers."

"So you did question her?" The Russian woman had deftly slipped around Murphy's questions and returned to ask questions of her own.

"Briefly. She lives over in Falls Church, and when we notified her of what happened, guess what she said?"

"I'm listening."

"She said, and I quote, 'The Russians finally got him.' No one has seen her since then, and no one knows where she is. And now you're here. What a coincidence."

Cogburn rocked back in his chair with a wide grin like he was a spectator at a Jell-O wrestling match.

Fedosova again chose not to be provoked.

"Was a search made of Kondratiev's living quarters?"

The front legs of Cogburn's chair hit the floor with loud, twin thumps.

"We didn't have to," he cut into their conversation with surprising emphasis, "Like I said, this was a street crime. Nothing happened in his condo."

Murphy grimaced and added, "There was no legal justification for going after a search warrant."

She had disagreed strongly with her senior partner on this point, but he was, after all, the senior partner. She'd appealed to Jefferson, but all the Lieutenant wanted was a smooth ride.

"I see," said Fedosova. "So, if there is nothing more you can tell me, I'll be going. Thank you very much for your cooperation."

She offered up another dazzling smile as she stood.

Cogburn's pig eyes followed her as she walked back to the elevators, but Murphy thought she read something other than lust in them.

As soon as the elevator doors had closed behind the visitor, Cogburn shot from his chair and headed for the stairs. Over his shoulder, he said, "I gotta go somewhere. See you in a while."

CHAPTER 9

Sasha stepped back out into the oppressive Northern Virginia heat and headed for her rental car. Next stop was the murder scene. The cavalier attitude of the police was unexpected, but it should make the next step easier.

She eased behind the wheel feeling her carefully coiffed hair droop in the oven-like confines of the car. No wonder Americans were so enamored of air conditioning. Israel was hot, too, but drier and made more bearable by the nearness of the sea. For just a moment she was nostalgic for her sun-drenched homeland, so different from the storm-tossed, chilly Irish coast where she and Ewan now made their home. But she wished with all her heart that they were there now instead of chasing the chimera of an old man's secret.

She shook off the nostalgia and punched the address of Kondratiev's condominium into the GPS before droving away. In her rearview mirror, she didn't miss the unmarked police car that pulled out behind her in the noon hour traffic. She'd seen Cogburn's unkempt figure rushing to the parking lot beside Police Headquarters as she entered her car. Maybe the Arlington police had more interest in the case than they cared to reveal.

She found Kondratiev's condo on a quiet dead-end side street lined with trees planted with military precision at orderly intervals to lend an impression of shaded seclusion.

There were few spaces for parking, but the red brick condominiums themselves did not appear to have garages, thus explaining why Kondratiev had used one of several private parking garages Sasha had noted within walking distance. She pulled to the curb, got out of the car, and immediately spotted Cogburn's big Ford as it nosed into the intersection behind her. Cogburn would know the area well and not turn into a dead-end street. He would drive on and leave his car close by to approach on foot.

That was OK. She didn't plan to do any more right now than reconnoiter the spot where the Russian had been shot. She would return later under cover of darkness to enter and search Kondratiev's apartment. She reasoned that Cogburn had been sent by Jefferson to report on what she did at the scene, so she made a show of referring to her notes and pacing the murder site as it had been described in the file. Cogburn tried unsuccessfully to conceal his paunchy figure behind a tree a half-block away at the mouth of the street.

Her inspection of the area took no more than ten minutes, and she re-entered her rental and drove to the end of the street to turn around and head back toward Fairfax Drive.

*****

From his concealment Cogburn watched unhappily as the Russian female cop turned the corner and sped away. There was no way he could get back to his car in time to pursue. He wished he had some help on this one, but then the money would not be so good.

The appearance of the Russian policewoman had put him off balance. It was unexpected, and the people he was working for should have warned him, damn it! He had had the Kondratiev investigation under control and all but relegated to the cold case files.

Now this broad in her expensive suit and stiletto heels was nosing around. What a babe, he thought, even if her titties weren't as big as he preferred. She looked to him more like a high class hooker than a cop, and he'd bet that some FSB nabob was banging her on a regular basis. How else could a broad like that land such a job? Jefferson had introduced her as a Major.

She'd done what she said she was going to do – take a look at the spot where the Russian had been killed. Maybe that was the end of it. Like she said, just making sure there were no loose ends. But he didn't like her asking about searching the condo. One of his tasks had been to make sure that did not happen.

With any luck they'd never see her again, but she was on the loose on his turf, and he was being paid a lot of money to make sure the Kondratiev case remained another unsolved street crime and to convince everyone that it did not merit further investigation.

The Russian broad was a wildcard.

He decided he should report it at once. The people he was working for definitely would not like it if she upset the apple cart now. And maybe he could get another payday.

*****

Cogburn shifted his weight in an unsuccessful effort to find a more comfortable position. The car seat beside him was littered with McDonalds wrappers, and a large soft drink container sat three-quarters empty in the cup holder, the ice having long ago melted. Even with the windows down the interior of the car was sweltering without a hint of a breeze to ease his discomfort.

The river of perspiration running down his backside made him feel like he was stuck to the vinyl car seat, adding considerably to his irritation. Again he wished he had help, but the orders had been clear. Take care of it yourself. Involve no one else.

He checked his watch. Nearly nine P.M. He'd parked his unmarked cruiser at the dead end of Utah Street four hours earlier. He couldn't risk letting the engine run so he could have air conditioning. A parked car with the engine running would attract attention. Cogburn had stood enough surveillance watches in his time to expect discomfort, but the heat was damn near unbearable.

A slim female figure appeared in the distance walking on the same side as Kondratiev's condominium and Cogburn was instantly alert. The faux antique globular street lamps were widely spaced and the woman was still too far away for positive identification, but he thought he recognized that sassy walk. Cogburn grabbed a pair of binoculars from the top of the dash and focused on the approaching figure. He was parked half a block away from the building entrance, but as she drew even with the doors the two lamps affixed on either side provided enough illumination to allow a glimpse of her face and ash blond hair. It was her, all right. She entered the building.

Cogburn let loose a string of epithets. He waited several minutes before rolling up the windows and exiting the car. He took his time approaching the entrance and peeked inside before pushing through the double glass doors. There was no one in the lobby but a doorman seated behind a desk. The sudden blast of air conditioning was refreshing.

He walked up to the man and flashed his badge.

"Official police business," he said.   "A woman entered this building a few minutes ago. What did she want, and where did she go?"

The doorman was flustered by Cogburn's appearance and abrupt questions.   He was a bespectacled older guy of indeterminate age, wearing a baggy short-sleeved nylon shirt with a tie – one of life's failures with a dead-end job on a dead end street. Cogburn knew how to handle nonentities like this.

"Answer the question." Cogburn leaned over the desk until his face was inches from the doorman's.

"You mean the woman who just came in?"

"That's what I said, shithead. Now answer me."

Shrinking back into his seat to escape Cogburn's Big Mac with extra onions breath, the doorman said, "That was the daughter of one of our residents, I mean, one of our former residents."

"Yeah? What 'former resident?'"

"That Russian guy who was murdered out here on the street."

"She said she was General Kondratiev's daughter? Are you sure?"

"I guess. She called this afternoon and said she would be coming by this evening to pick up some of her father's effects."

"You guess?   How do you know she was his

daughter?"

"Well, she said she was, and she had I.D." There was uncertainty in his voice now.

"And you let her in?"

"Well … sure. I gave her a key to the apartment."

"She's up there now?"

"I think so."

Crap! This was not good. Clever bitch, pretending to be Kondratiev's missing daughter. Why couldn't the broad just leave well enough alone? And who the hell was she really? Cogburn had met the daughter, and this woman sure as hell wasn't she. Could there be another one?

He adopted a conspiratorial tone. Still leaning across the desk, he said, "Look, buddy. This is a top security matter. We have reason to believe that this woman is not who she says she is. I want you to give me another key to the apartment and stay down here. Don't say a word to anybody about this, not now, not ever. Got it?"

The man handed over a key that he had extracted from a metal lockbox in one of the desk's drawers. "Number 301 on the north side of the building."

Cogburn headed for the elevator. He knew exactly what he would do – flash his badge, tell the broad she was under arrest for breaking and entering, cuff her, toss her in back of his cruiser, and make a call to his contact number. He didn't expect to see her again after that. Simple.

CHAPTER 10

Cogburn stepped out of the elevator into a thickly carpeted corridor illuminated by sconces in tasteful art deco bronze holders mounted along both walls. There were two apartments at this end of the building, and he headed toward door marked 301. He put his ear against it but could hear nothing.

As quietly as he could he slid the key into the lock and turned it slowly until the lock clicked and the door opened a fraction. Drawing his Beretta nine millimeter, he carefully pushed the door and slipped across the threshold into a tiled foyer. The lights were on in the living room straight ahead, and he stepped cautiously forward. He crossed a short hallway that bisected the foyer with closed doors at either end, probably leading to bedrooms. He still heard nothing. Where was she?

There was a soft sound behind him, but before he could turn something hard slammed into the side of his head. His knees crashed painfully onto the hard, tiled floor, as points of light exploded behind his eyes. He struggled to remain conscious, but failed.

*****

He didn't know how long he had been unconscious. Probably not long.   He opened his eyes and cautiously raised his head. It was painful. He was immobile, bound to a chair in Kondratiev's kitchen with duct tape. The tape covered his chest in wide gray strips, his arms had been pulled behind the chair back and taped together, and if felt like his legs were taped individually to the chair legs. Also, he was naked except for his briefs. He'd chosen to wear the special tiger striped ones today.

The overhead light was bright and hurt his eyes, which only slowly came into focus on the two figures seated on the other side of the table.   When at last he came fully to his senses he recognized the female Russian cop and the damned doorman. The doorman? He looked somehow different now. The heavy black framed glasses were gone, the face seemed somehow to have filled out, and whereas he had been cowed by Cogburn in the lobby, now he looked like Clint Eastwood in a bad mood.

"Welcome back," said the doorman.

Cogburn was suddenly furious. "You're in real trouble now, motherfucker," he spat. "I'm a cop on official business. You'll go to jail for this. Where are my clothes?" He was not proud of his middle-aged body and was acutely embarrassed by the presence of the attractive Russian woman.

The doorman raised a hand in which he held Cogburn's ID wallet that contained his gold badge. "We know who you are, Detective."

"We met earlier at Police Headquarters.   Don't you recall?" chimed in the woman.

She smiled at him like someone might smile encouragingly at a slow-witted child.

"But," continued the doorman, "we don't think you're here on 'official business.'"

Cogburn shook his head to clear away the remaining cobwebs.

"I'm a cop.   I'm here on cop business.   And you'd better untie me right now. Who the hell are you, anyway? You're not a doorman." There was something about the guy's accent. "You sound Irish."

"You are partially correct: I am definitely not a doorman. The person normally on duty downstairs is probably busy at the moment counting the generous wad of money I gave him earlier today."

"Untie me right now!" Cogburn mustered all the bravado he could. "When I don't report in there'll be cops swarming all over this place."

"I don't think that's going to happen." The man observed him blandly.

"Where's your partner?" asked the woman. "If you were working a case, your partner, Sergeant Murphy, would be with you, right?"

"She's around," bluffed Cogburn. "You'd better untie me before she gets up here."

"No, Detective Cogburn," said the man, "there's no one with you. You sat alone in your car at the end of the street for hours. You got out twice to pee in the bushes because you couldn't break off your solo surveillance. There was no one to relieve you, no pun intended. Now, why don't you tell us the real reason you're here. Who sent you?"

"I ain't telling you nothing. You're trespassing. And you've assaulted an officer of the law. You're in real trouble."

Cogburn struggled against his bonds, but to no avail. The only result was to make him acutely aware of the sticky side of the duct tape pulling at his abundant body hair.

The man looked at him reprovingly.

"Nobody's coming to rescue you."

He stood and went to the granite kitchen counter where he retrieved something shiny. When he returned to his seat, he laid a straight razor with an ornate bone handle on the table. Cogburn didn't like the looks of it.

"Kondratiev was an old fashioned fellow. We found this in the bathroom. Tell me, Detective," he said, "are you familiar with the movie <u>Reservoir Dogs</u>?"

Cogburn had, in fact, loved the bloody Tarantino crime flick, but he said nothing.

The man shrugged and continued, "Well, if you

did see the film you will undoubtedly recall that famous scene in the warehouse where Mr. Blond duct tapes the cop, Nash, to the chair?" He raised his eyebrows in query.

Cogburn stubbornly clamped his jaw but he knew the movie's torture scene well – it was one of his favorites.

The man continued, "As I recall, Mr. Blond taped the cop's mouth shut, cut off one of the cop's ears with a straight razor, and then doused him with gasoline and set him on fire."

Cogburn's eyes strayed unbidden to the razor on the table.

"You wouldn't," he said.

There was a slight tremor in his voice.

"Oh, there aren't many things I wouldn't do, Detective."

The man reached under the table and produced a can of charcoal lighter fluid.

"General Kondratiev did not keep gasoline in his apartment, but he was apparently a devotee of the charcoal grill." He picked up the can and shook it so the liquid sloshed around. "This stuff doesn't burn as hot as gasoline, but it should do the trick." He smiled wolfishly at the detective. "Barbecue anyone?"

"You wouldn't dare," said Cogburn. The needle

on his personal danger scale arced into the 'oh, shit' zone.

The man turned to the woman.

"Should we do this here or take him into the bathroom. We could put him in the tub."

The woman seemed suddenly anxious. "Are we being too hasty?"

"We don't have a lot of time. He either gives up what he knows voluntarily or under duress. We get what we need either way, unless he dies before he talks."

"Maybe he'll talk to me," she said, casting an appraising glance in Cogburn's direction.

Cogburn knew what they were doing. He'd played the good cop/bad cop routine hundreds of times himself. He was usually the bad cop. These two were just role-playing. But did Russian cops play by the same rules as American cops? He'd heard stories.

"Well, Detective," said the woman, "will you talk to me?"

"Go fuck yourself."

The man clicked his tongue against his teeth and shook his head.

To the woman, he said, "You heard him. He doesn't want to talk. I'll just do him here. I don't feel like dragging him all the way to the bathroom and lifting his fat, ugly body into the tub. It won't make any difference after the fire anyway."

He stepped around the table behind Cogburn and pulled the chair back so there was space enough to stand in front of the detective.

The doorman said, "Last chance."

"Go fuck yourself."

"You need to expand your vocabulary. Let me explain how this is going to work. I'm going to begin cutting pieces off of you and tossing them into a pile on the floor. If you refuse to cooperate, the pile on the floor eventually will be larger than what's left tied to the chair. At that point, I'll douse the mess with the charcoal lighter and set it on fire. The lady and I will then find a nice restaurant for a late dinner."

His captor reached around Cogburn's head to a counter. When his hand reappeared it held a large roll of gray duct tape from which he pulled a long strip before tearing it off and wrapping it around the detective's lower face, covering his mouth. He pulled off another strip and wrapped it under Cogburn's chin and over the top of his head, effectively clamping his jaw shut.

"We wouldn't want your screams to disturb the neighbors."

The tall man picked up the razor and tested its edge against his thumb. Panic wrapped its fingers around Cogburn's heart and squeezed hard as it dawned on him that these people meant to do exactly what they said.

Cogburn saw the Russian policewoman avert her eyes as the man grabbed the top of the detective's right ear and yanked it painfully outward. He brought up the razor and held the gleaming blade before the detective's eyes.

These people are crazy! Alternating hot and cold waves washed over Cogburn's body. His vision blurred. Then he fainted.

*****

When he regained consciousness the tape had been removed from his mouth.

The man was once again seated across the table beside the Russian policewoman, but he still had the razor in his hand.

"This isn't going to work if you keep passing out on us," he said. "We need your full attention."

"All I have is a phone number." The words tumbled out of his mouth, driven by panic. He was having trouble breathing.

"What was that?"

"A phone number! That's all I have."

Cogburn was panting heavily now.

"Ah. Cooperation! You might live through this, after all."

"But I'm a cop," he protested weakly.

"You're a bad cop," the man replied. "You were paid to make certain that Kondratiev's murder was treated as a common mugging and to prevent anyone from searching this apartment. I imagine you were paid quite a lot of money for those services. Someone also ordered you to watch tonight. I don't think you intended to arrest this young lady when you came up here. You planned to kill her, and that makes me very unhappy."

The man flipped the razor open.

Cogburn shrank away trying to make himself smaller.

"No, that's not true! I was just supposed to take her somewhere."

His interrogator leaned across the table.

"Where?"

"I don't know. Like I said, all I have is a contact number. I call for instructions."

"Now we're getting somewhere." The man laid the razor back on the table. "Who is this 'someone'?"

"Just a guy. Really," Cogburn wailed. "He said he works at the White House."

He looked expectantly from the man to the woman, hoping his mention of the White House would have a salubrious effect on his situation. No reaction.

"Did you kill Kondratiev?"

"Hell no! I had nothing to do with that. Please. You gotta believe me!"

"Do you know who did?"

"No, I didn't even get the first call until the morning after the shooting."

"And . . ."

"This guy calls me and says he'll pay fifty grand if I make sure there is no big investigation. He said it was my patriotic duty. He knew I was the lead investigator."

"How would he know that?"

"I don't know."

"What did he want you to do?"

"Just what you said: make sure no one suspected it was more than a street crime and prevent anyone from searching this place."

"How were you paid?"

"I opened a new bank account, and someone made a counter deposit in cash the next day at a different branch."

"I assume that you used your contact number when the lady investigator from Russia turned up in your office asking questions?"

"Yeah."

"What instructions did you receive?"

"Watch this place, and if she showed up, detain her and call him."

CHAPTER 11

Neither of them was fond of torture, although they had been trained in multiple brutal but effective field interrogation techniques.   Sasha's own dreadful experience at the hands of sadists with sharp knives made her especially uncomfortable with threats of mutilation. But she and Ewan had been taught never to make a threat they weren't willing to carry out. She felt immense relief at the Arlington detective's capitulation. He escaped the pain and saved her the personal humiliation she would have endured had Ewan been forced actually to employ the razor.

Ewan addressed Cogburn.

"We're going to give you a little time to think now."

The cop looked like he was going to be sick.

Sasha went to the sink and drew a glass of water. She carried it to the bound man who gulped thirstily when she held it to his lips. She replaced the glass on the counter and walked out of the kitchen.

Ewan followed her out to the living room. His wife was a professional, capable of extreme violence, even mayhem, as a former member of the Mossad's deadly *Kidon* unit, but her own wounds eighteen years earlier at the hands of Russian rapists and torturers were not only physical. The scar on her face and the glass prosthesis that replaced her left eye were constant reminders of the experience. He could imagine what she was feeling and tried to explain.

"He's the only lead we have."

He regretted having succumbed to her insistence on accompanying him to the U.S., partly because he preferred to know she was in a safe place and partly because he knew the reason for her insistence was that she worried he was getting too long in the tooth for field operations.

Sasha brushed Ewan's arm from her shoulders.

"We should get started," she said. "We don't have much time."

She surveyed their surroundings. There had been little time to examine the quarters before Cogburn's appearance. Kondratiev's taste had been drawn to modern Scandinavian design, which both she and Ewan detested, but there was an expensive Persian carpet on the floor, and the walls were heavily adorned with Russian art and antique icons. The predominant color scheme was beige and white, beige carpeting, off-white walls and white drapes, relieved only by the deep reds and golds of antique Russian icons that must be worth a fortune. The bland colors suggested that Kondratiev the spy still preferred anonymity even though long retired from active duty.

Ewan started on the living room as Sasha headed back into the hallway to search the two bedrooms. He looked behind pictures, under cushions and in drawers, but found nothing.

Sasha's voice came to him from the hallway. "Back here."

He found her in one of the bedrooms. It had been converted into a study, its walls lined with books, most of them Russian titles. A large desk sat before a window and dominated the space. A low row of file cabinets stood against the wall beside it.

"There's nothing here," said Sasha, holding up a set of cables attached to the computer screen on the desk. The connectors dangled emptily from her hand. The computer itself was nowhere to be seen.

"Ah, the dog that didn't bark in the night. How about the file cabinets?"

"Haven't looked yet. This was so obvious, I spotted it right away."

Ewan stepped around the desk and opened the file cabinet drawers, one after the other. All were empty.

"That settles it," he said. "If the police had searched here they wouldn't be so convinced that Kondratiev's murder was a common street crime."

"And guess who was most upset when I asked

whether they had searched?"

"I wonder how many cops were paid off."

"From the way she reacted and the questions she asked me, I'm pretty sure that Cogburn's partner, Murphy, was unhappy about the way they wrote off the murder."

"Whatever the truth, we're not going to find anything here. That leaves us with Cogburn as our only lead. What do you think about his reference to the White House?"

Sasha didn't get a chance to answer because a loud crash suddenly interrupted them. They rushed from the room.

CHAPTER 12

Cogburn had tipped his chair over on its back, a result of his futile struggle to break his bonds. His white legs waggled helplessly in the air, and his tiger striped briefs were now prominently on display. Worse for him, he had banged his head against a countertop, as well as the floor.

Ewan lifted the chair upright and examined the now doubly pained detective. There was a sizeable lump growing on the back of his head, but he was still fully conscious. Ewan scooted the chair back to the table and took a seat on the opposite side with Sasha. He picked up the bone-handled razor and flipped it idly open and closed as he spoke.

"There's a chance you'll live through this, detective, but only if we believe you are cooperating. What do you say? Will you behave? Will you switch teams?"

Cogburn stared for a long time at the razor in Ewan's hands before he lowered his head and his chin slumped to his chest. He looked utterly deflated.

"Yeah." His voice was a whisper.

"Say it like you mean it."

The detective raised his head, defeated.

"Yes, I'll cooperate."

"Good. Now, are you up to making that phone call?"

"Huh?"

"You're going to call that contact number and tell them you have the lady detective in custody. You're going to ask for instructions."

*****

It was after eleven PM when the cell phone in John Buchalter's pocket vibrated. The caller ID told him it was Charlie Cogburn.

Before answering, Buchalter turned to his companion, "It's him."

He punched the button to accept the call and held the Blackberry to his ear.

"Is it done?" he asked.

Cogburn sounded weary when he answered.

"Yeah. I got her in the car now. What do you want me to do?"

"I'd almost given up on you."

"What now?"

Cogburn uncharacteristically was not in a talkative

mood.

Buchalter gave the Arlington cop directions to his present location and broke the phone connection. He estimated it would be over an hour at least before Cogburn arrived with his prisoner.

He turned to the man at his side.

"Well, he actually has her. They should be here sometime after midnight."

 "Are you clear about what to do?"

The man spoke with a definite accent. Buchalter was uncomfortable working so closely with a Russian, but his boss had suggested he look at it as a liaison operation between allies, and the boss was the boss. It wasn't Buchalter's place to ask questions.

"Yeah, I know exactly what I have to do."

"Just to be clear, you take care of the American, and I will take charge of this Russian woman he's bringing to us."

Buchalter removed his pistol from its holster, extracted the clip, and checked the action of the slide. This was no 'Saturday night special,' but a very expensive, finely tuned and accurate Sig-Sauer. It was his own personal weapon, and Buchalter was very proud of it.

His companion was annoyed.

"That must be the hundredth time you've played

with that damned thing. What's the matter? Are you afraid it won't fire?"

"No, not at all. It works just fine."

Buchalter was proud to have been chosen for such an important and highly compartmentalized assignment. This was becoming the kind of job he'd always dreamed about. He felt like James Bond. He had been given a license to kill, and he wasn't going to make any mistakes.

CHAPTER 13

Just after one A.M. Cogburn turned the unmarked police cruiser into the tree-lined drive that led to a farmhouse near Berryville, Virginia. Once a remote farming community west of Washington just off Route 7, Berryville was under assault by the constantly expanding ring of bedroom communities around the capital. This address, however, was still isolated and approachable only by a narrow dirt road. Ahead at the top of the long drive was a wooden farmhouse that might have been a century or more old. The windows were dark, and the only illumination came from the cruiser's headlights. There were thick woods on one side and in back of the house.

Sasha was in the rear seat. The detective was queasily aware that she held his own Beretta pointed at the back of his head.

Modern travel being what it is she and Ewan had arrived in the U.S. unarmed but confident that they could pick up whatever they needed along the way. Ewan had found some very well-made and appropriate knives at a cutlery store in Tysons Corner shopping center, and Cogburn had been kind enough to donate his Beretta to the cause.

Despite her protests Ewan insisted that she carry the gun. She didn't think she needed a firearm to handle the fat Arlington cop, but it did make sense. She would be exposed while Ewan would be concealed.

As they rolled to a stop, a blinding spotlight mounted in one of the windows on the upper story of the house blossomed into incandescence and turned the area around the car into daylight.

*****

Leaving Sasha in charge of Cogburn a mile before reaching the farm house, Ewan had made his way on foot across the open fields and woodlands that made up the property. The moon was waxing, but his jeans and black t-shirt made him difficult to spot as he moved from shadow to shadow.

Ewan reconnoitered the house for nearly an hour before signaling Sasha to make an appearance, grateful that at this hour of the night the temperature had dropped from the stifling nineties into the mid-seventies. A freshening breeze rustled the leaves and foretold a cooling high pressure system moving in across the Appalachians.

Experience suggested that whoever was waiting to meet Cogburn and his 'prisoner' would not expect trouble. Their operation was extremely sensitive, involving the murder of General Kondratiev, a high profile victim. That meant they would use the minimum number of operatives at the pointy end of their stick - maybe only one.

If it were the Russians they might have used one of their illegal operatives from Department "S" of the *Sluzhba Vneshney Razvedki*, or SVR, the Russian foreign intelligence service that had assumed the responsibilities of the now defunct KGB's renowned First Chief Directorate. At least one of their operatives trained in the art of assassination would surely have been assigned to the Washington, D.C. area to be available for just such a mission. The Russians had long ago discovered the permanent solution for political opponents and 'enemies of the state.' From what Ewan had seen the current occupants of the Kremlin had not changed their methods.

At the rear of the house, two cars were parked, one of them a large, black SUV, the other a non-descript Chevrolet. Two cars meant at least two people in the reception committee, but what caught Ewan's eye were the diplomatic license plates on the Chevy. The distinctive red and blue plates bore the digraph 'YR,' designating the car as belonging to the Russian Embassy.

Ewan discarded the notion that an SVR illegal was waiting for Cogburn and Sasha inside the farm house. Illegals don't drive cars bearing diplomatic license plates, and whoever was driving that car betrayed an excess of confidence in his operational security that would be unthinkable for any

Department 'S' operative. There was arrogance at play here.

When he checked the SUV he was startled to discover that it bore official U.S. Government tags. *Curiouser and curiouser*. Ewan's mood darkened. The SUV could carry a lot of passengers, but there were no sentries posted, as might have been expected in such a case.

Could this be an elaborate trap that Terry Stoddard and the CIA had set for him? But no one, not even Robert Strachey or Stoddard, even knew that he and Sasha were already in the country. They had flown out of Paris to Canada and driven a rented car down to Virginia where they had taken a suite at the Ritz Carleton at Tyson's Corner under the name DuPont. This was their little joke as 'DuPont' was the favorite French pseudonym for illicit trysts. Check any discreet hotel registry in France on any given weekend and one will find a plethora of couples named DuPont.

He hoped to avoid contact with the CIA inside the United States, if at all possible, do the job and get back out before reporting. Strachey had provided him with a contact telephone number, but he didn't want to use it.

Government tags could, of course, be faked, and he hoped that was the case here. He didn't want yet another serious collision with the U.S. Government that could re-awaken official interest in finding him.

For now, he and Sasha had the advantage of surprise. He hoped the coming encounter would not turn deadly. There were a lot of questions he wanted to ask.

He circled the farm house and checked the woods that lay on the other side. They were clear. Had there been a hostile stationed outside, Ewan would have found him. That meant everyone waited inside for Cogburn's arrival. He crept along the rear of the house and risked a peek inside through what turned out to be a kitchen window before continuing to the back door which was located inside a small, screened porch. He tried the screened porch door, wary of squeaky hinges, but they had been recently oiled and the door opened noiselessly. Two quick steps across the porch brought him to the kitchen door that led into the house.

If he were in charge of the house, he would have had someone guarding the rear entrance, but there was no one. More arrogance. He was right -- whoever it was clearly did not expect trouble. Idiots.

He tried the knob. The door was unlocked and swung silently into the kitchen where he caught the sound of conversation from the upper story. The words were unintelligible, but there were at least two men up there waiting in the dark. Not necessarily a good sign.

Treading lightly across the linoleum kitchen floor, Ewan went back outside and used his Blackberry instant messenger to signal Sasha to come ahead. When he received her confirmation he went back inside the house. It would take Sasha and Cogburn only a few moments to cover the remaining distance to the lane entrance.

CHAPTER 14

The interior was organized simply, with a kitchen, pantry, parlor and sitting room on the first floor and a flight of wooden stairs leading up to the bedrooms. The place was clean and sparsely furnished, belying its dilapidated exterior, and he caught the strong pine scent of floor cleaner. Someone was caring for the house. The farm's secluded location would make it a good safe site. Did they plan to hold the 'Russian policewoman' prisoner here? Interrogate her? Kill her? If that was their plan, it would not succeed.

Ewan strained to capture meaning from the on-going rumble of voices from upstairs but caught only stray words. The men were speaking English, but the presence of the diplomatic car outside strongly suggested that one of them should be a Russian. A light footfall was audible from the second story moving towards the front of the house. They would be watching to catch sight of Cogburn's car through the front windows.

A flash of light outside alerted him to the arrival of the detective's car as it turned in at the bottom of the lane. Almost immediately there were quick footsteps toward the head of the stairs. Someone was coming down. That left at least one man upstairs. Ewan backed into the shadows of the parlor and watched as a heavyset man descended the stairs and strode to the front door where he waited until Cogburn's car rolled to a stop.

There was a loud click and a hum, and the front of the house suddenly was awash with bright light as the man went out the front door.

Comfortable in the knowledge that his wife could take care of one man, Ewan headed for the stairs and started up, removing the Aegis Tanto SOG knife he had purchased earlier as he went and flicking open its three and a half inch serrated blade.

He was half-way up when gunfire erupted from the front of the house. He counted three quick shots.

Ewan raced back down the stairs and out the front door. The gunshots signaled that the advantage of surprise had been lost, and Sasha could be in trouble. But it was now quiet in front of the house, and two bodies lay still beside Cogburn's car, clearly visible on the floodlit drive.

"I'm OK! Go back," Sasha shouted at him. She was still inside the car. But if the person behind the light that shone from the second story was armed, she would be pinned down.

Ewan turned to re-enter the house just as the clatter of feet sounded on the stairs. Through the gloomy interior he glimpsed a figure rushing through the kitchen to the back door. Ewan followed but stopped at the door to survey the area behind the house. He could kill from five meters with a knife, but the Tanto was not made for throwing, and it would be no contest in any event if the man he pursued now waited for him with a gun. Regardless, Ewan did not intend to allow him to flank Sasha.

There was the sound of a car engine starting, and the Chevy kicked gravel in a wide circle as the driver swung it around. Ewan sprinted out the door and around the corner in time to see the car continue accelerating down the lane toward the road. There would be no fight from that quarter.

He re-entered the house and went up the stairs where he checked all the rooms, finding a spotlight mounted on a tripod in the open window of a front bedroom. There was no one there. He leaned out at shouted, "It's clear. I'll be down there in a second."

He found Sasha beside Cogburn. She had lifted the detective to a sitting position, with his back resting against the side of the car. The inert figure of the second man lay on his back on the ground a few feet away, mouth and eyes open wide in the surprise caused by violent, unexpected death.

"What happened?"

"He," she jerked her head toward the body, "told Cogburn to get out of the car, and as soon as he did, he shot him and took a step in my direction. He looked quite surprised when I fired at him, two shots, center mass. Cogburn is still alive."

Ewan knelt beside the detective. The bullet had hit him high on the right side of his chest, and he was bleeding profusely.

"Poor Cogburn," said Ewan. "The bastard's had a rough night. I think I can stop the bleeding, but he's going to need medical attention soon."

Sasha looked appraisingly at the bleeding detective and then switched her gaze to Ewan.

"What do we do, dump him in front of a hospital?"

"No. I think it's time to use the number Strachey gave us."

He pulled out his Blackberry and punched the speed dial, perversely enjoying the thought of awakening the CIA man from a sound sleep, probably in some tacky tract house in McLean.

When Strachey answered, however, his voice was clear.

"Ramsay?"

"Who else? I have a little problem."

"Where are you? Are you here already?"

"If 'here' means Virginia, yes I am. I need to see you – right now. And bring a doctor and a lot of bandages."

"Jesus! Are you injured? OK, where?"

Ewan could picture the CIA man sitting upright at

the edge of his comfy bed. He gave Strachey the location and GPS coordinates of the farm.

"We're OK, but you'd do well to hurry, Strachey. We need a medic. Otherwise just bring a couple of body bags."

"We? A COUPLE of body bags?"

"Or a shovel."

Ewan severed the connection.

Sasha was tending to Cogburn as best she could.

"We should get him into the house."

Between the two of them they managed to maneuver the moaning detective's bulky weight up the steps and into the house where they deposited him on a couch in the living room. Sasha found some towels in the bathroom and sat down to tend him. Cogburn had regained consciousness, a stricken look on his face, he kept repeating, "He shot me."

Ewan went to the door.

"I don't know how long we dare stay here. The Russian may have gone for help. But we can't move Cogburn on our own. Strachey said he should be here within the hour. If the Russian has to drive all the way back into Washington, we should have just about enough time."

He headed out the door. "I want to take a look at the dead guy."

"We'll wait right here, won't we, Cogburn?"

The detective seemed confused.

"He shot me," he repeated.

Ewan returned a few moments later muttering curse words culled from several languages.

"Uh oh. What is it?" asked Sasha.

"I think you killed a Fed."

CHAPTER 15

Bob Strachey drove like a madman from the house he shared with his wife, Amy, in McLean to the near-by CIA main campus, which he entered from Route 123. Several minutes later, he left via the same gate, this time driving one of the Agency's anonymous black Lincoln Navigator SUV's.   The location provided by Ewan Ramsay was several miles beyond Leesburg to the west of Route 7, but at this time of night, he could be there within forty minutes with luck. He boosted his speed once he passed Tyson's Corner and switched on the flashing blue and red lights concealed behind the SUV's grill.

Keeping one hand on the wheel he fumbled out his phone and hit the speed dial for Terry Stoddard's secure cell phone number.   The DNCS would be at his Georgetown townhouse. After several rings Strachey was rewarded with his superior's voice.

"Terry, it's Bob. We have a problem involving your erstwhile friend. Seems like he's here, and he's already in trouble – serious trouble. He needs some help."

Stoddard sounded instantly alert.

"Are you handling it?"

"Trying to. I'm on my way now, but I'm going to need some assistance of the medical and disposal variety."

"Is Ramsay hurt?"

"I don't think so, but someone else is. Didn't take him long, did it?"

The line fell silent for a moment before Stoddard replied.

"Ramsay is one of the best field men I've ever known. Unless the Mossad has changed him completely, he's not one to take foolish risks."

"We'll need a medic set up at a secure location. Can you take care of it?" asked Strachey.

"Call me when you're on the scene and can fill me in. I'll work on setting something up in the meantime. We're going to need a good cover, though, if we want to keep this thing compartmented."

"Roger that. Talk to you later."

Strachey ripped the SUV through the interchange at Leesburg. The road became hilly, forcing him to slow his pace as he left the gently rolling Virginia countryside behind and entered the foothills of the Appalachians. All the time he was thinking that it had been a major mistake to call on the services of Ewan Ramsay AKA outlaw Harry Connolly. The man played by his own rules and was thus uncontrollable. How could he have come to the U.S. without first letting Stoddard know? Evidently there was a severe deficiency of trust on both sides, and now the bastard might well have blown the entire operation.

Strachey patted his side to reassure himself that his Walther PP was securely in place underneath the loose tail of his shirt. He'd grabbed the old but extremely accurate German pistol, one of his favorites, from his bedside table before leaving his house. He hoped he wouldn't have to use it tonight.

He grabbed his cell phone again. It might be a good idea to forewarn Ramsay that he would arrive at the site within a few minutes.

*****

Strachey would have missed the turn into the lane had the SUV's GPS not warned him that he had arrived at his destination. There was a dim light in one of the windows of the lower story and a car parked in front of the house. As he pulled even with the car his headlights swept over the body of a man lying face-up on the ground. No one else was in sight.

Not good.

He slid out from behind the wheel of the SUV and reached under his shirt to place his hand on the grip of his pistol. As he approached the body, the farmhouse door opened and he recognized the figure of Ewan Ramsay striding across the porch toward him. He also noticed that that the damned man held a pistol pointed directly at him.

Strachey stepped quickly behind the cover of the car and drew his own weapon.

"What the hell are you doing, Ramsay?"

"Keeping safe. Step out from behind the car."

"Like hell. Put that gun away."

A female voice sounded behind him.

"Drop your gun, Mr. Strachey."

He froze. Ramsay had brought that predatory blond woman with him. The memory of facing their twin Glocks in Ireland flashed through his mind. He again wondered if their weapons were monogrammed 'His' and 'Hers.'

Ramsay called to him.

"Sasha is a crack shot, Strachey, as our friend over there on the ground would attest if he could still speak. Now, drop your weapon."

What had Terry Stoddard gotten him into?

Using only his thumb and forefinger he held his Walther at arm's length out to his side, knelt, and laid it carefully on the ground. If he got out of this he swore that he would deck this phony Irishman.

The phony Irishman spoke again.

"Very good. Now, come out from behind the car and walk towards me."

There was no choice but to comply.   He could think of no maneuver that would allow him to escape or counter-attack.

"I'm getting tired of you two pointing guns at me, Ramsay."

"And I'm getting tired of the CIA screwing with us."

Strachey now stood at the front porch at the base of the steps looking up at Ramsay's angular figure.

"What are you talking about now?   We're not trying to screw you."

"Maybe.   Maybe not.   That dead man on the ground out there was a federal agent.   Take a look."

Ramsay tossed him a thin, leather wallet. Strachey caught it in mid-air and looked inside.   There was just enough light spilling across the porch for him to make out the creds that identified their bearer as John Buchalter of the National Intelligence staff. *What the hell?*   But there was a plastic photo ID tucked into a pocket of the credential wallet that left him completely nonplussed.

Without looking up, he said to Ramsay, "Did you see this?"

"Yes."

"Do you know what it is?"

"Just what it says in big blue letters: it's a White House security pass."

Strachey suddenly wanted to sit down.

CHAPTER 16

"I need to call Terry Stoddard," said Strachey.

"I'll bet you do," replied Ramsay.

His gun had not strayed from the CIA man.

"So, what do you think, Ramsay? That we somehow set you up? We didn't even know you were in the country – that was your choice. Think about it. And stop pointing that damned gun at me. It's beginning to annoy me."

Ramsay tucked Buchalter's Sig Sauer into his belt and leaned against one of the lathed poles that supported the porch roof.

"I have thought about it," was his ambiguous reply.

Strachey looked behind him. Sasha still had her pistol covering him.

Ramsay asked, "Why were you armed tonight? CIA men don't usually carry weapons."

"This one does."

Ramsay considered this.

"A long time ago the Agency hung me out to dry and then tried to have me killed. It could be happening again. It's dangerous for me to be in this country."

"That was a long time ago. If we had intended to kill you, it would have happened in Ireland."

Ramsay contemplated him for a long minute, like a man trying to decide if a large dog he'd confronted in the street were vicious or benign.

"You might have tried," he said at last, and then to Sasha, "You can lower your weapon. We'll play along a little further."

Strachey retrieved his pistol from the ground and replaced it in his holster. Nothing made him angrier than having a gun pointed at him. It was a dangerous anger because it could rob him of caution, and it took a moment for him to bring it under control. He wanted to deck this tall, old guy who thought he had all the answers.

Ramsay turned back into the house and said over his shoulder, "Come on in, Strachey, and see what else we have."

Still fuming, he climbed the steps and went through the door into the living room. Ramsay waved at the sofa where a bulky man lay moaning, his chest wrapped in blood-soaked towels.

"Meet Detective Cogburn, one of Arlington's finest."

"You shot a cop, too?"

"No, Mr. Dead Fed out there shot the cop. My

wife shot the Fed."

Ramsay said this as though it were good news.

Sasha came through the door behind him.

"There was no choice," she said.

"Of course not." Strachey's voice dripped with sarcasm. "Have you shot anyone else tonight, or have you met your quota?"

He was seriously pissed off, and he didn't care if it showed.

Ramsay calmly shook his head.

"There was someone else here waiting for us, but he took off as soon as the shooting started."

The trace of a wry smile played around his lips as he paused then added, "He was driving a car with Russian diplomatic plates."

Strachey let this sink in: a wounded cop, a dead Federal officer with a White House pass, and now a Russian diplomat. By bringing Ewan Ramsay into this mess Stoddard had set a fox among the chickens.

"I think I'd better call Terry Stoddard now," said Strachey, his eyes on the wounded cop. "He's arranging the medical assistance you requested."

*****

An hour later they arrived at a CIA safe house near Winchester, Virginia, where they had driven in convoy from Berryville. Strachey led the way with Cogburn laid out in the rear seat of his SUV and the body of the dead Fed bundled into the cargo area. Ewan drove the dead man's SUV and Sasha brought up the rear in Cogburn's Ford.

The town was well known to Ramsay who had once had a cabin in the mountains some fifty miles to the south. He'd been an exile for so long that he was surprised at the nostalgia evoked by the familiar surroundings. He knew this part of Virginia intimately, and nothing much had changed except for the increasingly heavy traffic as more and more Washington bureaucrats populated the suburbs. The daily exodus began at a much earlier hour than he remembered, as if the need to escape the rarified atmosphere of Washington to gasp in the oxygen of the suburbs had grown more urgent. People dressed more casually in public than he remembered, slovenly in his opinion, and he wondered if this was indicative of general decline.

Stoddard greeted them at the door, urbane as ever and immaculately dressed in tan slacks, and a blazer, his tie knotted in a perfect Windsor, looking more like a man on his way to the country club than a spook welcoming this motley crew to a safe house after a shoot-out.

They had been close friends in the old days, and like Ewan, the DNCS had grown leaner with age rather than gaining a middle-aged paunch. The sandy hair had thinned only slightly and was liberally tinged with gray, as was the pencil moustache that reminded classic movie buffs of Errol Flynn.

Stoddard extended his hand and Ewan took it. He got a good vibe.

Cogburn had again lapsed into unconsciousness. They half carried, half dragged him to a room that contained a full complement of medical equipment where a doctor and a nurse waited. Ewan guessed that Stoddard had chosen this particular safe house for its location near the elaborate Winchester Medical Center and that the two medical personnel were CIA cooptees who worked there. This off-site medical facility had been set up for just such occasions as this.

Leaving the medics to their work, the group gathered in the well-appointed living room where Stoddard invited them to sit.

"It's early, I know," he said, "but I think we all could use a stiff drink."

Encountering no objections, Stoddard placed an unopened bottle of Lagavulin single malt scotch on the coffee table along with four glasses.

"I seem to recall that you favored this label," he said to Ewan with a slight smile.

Ewan was not in an especially convivial mood but the Lagavulin suddenly seemed like a good idea.

Its strong peaty flavor had made it possible for the whiskey to be imported into the U.S. during Prohibition labeled as a medicine. It was a true connoisseur's whiskey, the epitome of Islay scotch.

"You remember correctly," he said.

Stoddard poured generous measures all around before taking a seat.

"Please tell us how all this happened."

The DNCS'S voice was without a trace of hostility, and he appeared unperturbed by the situation. He was just as Ewan remembered – unflappable under stress. In contrast, Strachey's expression and body language clearly showed he was still smarting from his treatment at the farm, which along with the Lagavulin further improved Ewan's mood. Strachey's visit to Ireland and the threats he had made were the reasons he and Sasha were in the middle of this mess that promised to become even messier. Strachey might be working for Stoddard, but it was easier to dislike the errand boy.

As Ewan savored the whiskey, Sasha filled the others in on her visit the day before to Arlington Police Headquarters posing as a Russian police officer. Ewan took up the narrative from the moment Cogburn entered Kondratiev's condo, omitting the details of the detective's interrogation. When he had finished he tossed the dead federal agent's credentials onto the coffee table.

Stoddard flipped open the credentials and

groaned. Both the credentials and the White House ID had photographs of the dead man. Stoddard went very still for several heartbeats and his brow was creased in what might have been pain or consternation or both.

"I've seen this name before," he said quietly.

"What does that mean?" asked Ramsay.

Strachey's head swiveled toward his boss in surprise.

"His name was on a list of transferees. Buchalter was from the CIA Office of Security. He wasn't particularly good at his job, but his father, Frank, was an old hand in Security who was well-respected in his day, and there was some residual loyalty there. Buchalter was promoted to mid-level, but he and everybody else knew he wouldn't rise any higher.

"As part of the reorganization of the Intelligence Community after 9/11 the White House ordered all agencies to provide personnel to man the staff of the new Director of National Intelligence." A sour expression momentarily pinched his features. "Naturally, when we get orders like that, we don't volunteer our best and brightest. John Buchalter saw a chance to improve his lot, and we were pleased to let him go."

"So he worked for the DNI?" Ewan asked.

"As far as I know. He left the Agency several

years ago. We were glad to get rid of him, and no one expected to see him again."

"Well," said Ewan, "he did pop up again, but everybody's rid of him now for good."

Stoddard's urbanity failed him for a second.

"Shit!"

"Well put, Terry," said Ewan tipping the last of his glass's contents down his throat. He poured himself another. "Shall I summarize?"

Stoddard nodded gloomily.

Ewan raised his re-charged glass in Strachey's direction.

"Your prize spook here ruins a perfectly good summer morning by barging into our home in Ireland and blackmailing us into taking on this so-called job that the CIA is too pansy to handle itself. Being ever brave but somewhat dimwitted people, my wife and I take the bait and begin what should be a run-of-the-mill off the books investigation that incidentally involved some minor subterfuge and breaking and entering – but that's small potatoes.

"As we are peacefully going about our business breaking into Kondratiev's apartment, Detective Cogburn barges in all eager to snatch my wife and drag her off into the wilds of Virginia to hand her over to person or persons unknown.

"We gently convince said detective to take us

to his leader who turns out to be the gun-happy, not much lamented DNI operative John Buchalter who now rests peacefully in your tame spook's big black car. Worse, he's also somehow affiliated with the White House, and, oh by the way, the Russian Embassy apparently is working with the White House. What's wrong with this picture?"

Sasha kicked his ankle -- hard. She had a familiar 'why do you always have to be such a smartass' look on her face.

"You haven't lost your talent for acerbic summations," said Stoddard with a wry grin, or maybe it was a grimace. "We anticipated running into the Russians and tracing their operation out of the country, something we could handle quietly and one of your specialties, I believe, but not another federal agency, and certainly not the White House."

Strachey spoke up.

"Could it have anything to do with Russian President Shurgin's upcoming visit? It's only a few days away."

Any mention of former KGB General *Shurgin* who was now President of the Russian Federation inevitably put Ewan into a bad mood -- they had a history.

He said, "Vitaliy Mikhailovich Shurgin is a corrupt, evil bastard. Everything the man touches is tainted."

Ignoring Ramsay's interjection, Strachey pursued his thought.

"The timing would seem to connect the events. The odd thing is that from your description, it was the dead man, the American, who handled the wet work while the Russian remained inside. He may have been there only to confirm or deny Sasha's identity as a Russian police official or to take her into custody. We may be dealing with a high-level U.S. Government operation involving a conspiracy with the Russians. But why try to kill Cogburn? He was working with them."

"They paid him a lot of money to cover up Kondratiev's murder," put in Sasha, "but he wasn't really one of them."

Strachey said, "Right. Dead men tell no tales. He didn't know who he was really working for, and they didn't intend to leave any witnesses to whatever they had planned at the farm house."

Ewan had no doubts on that score.

"If things had gone the way they expected," he said, "there would've been two fresh graves at that farm this morning."

Strachey again took up his narrative.

"But witnesses to what? Unmasking your wife as an imposter? That wouldn't require killing anyone. She could have just been arrested and bundled off to jail, or at worst kidnapped and smuggled out of the country to Russia.

"No, there's something deeper here, and it's most likely connected with the information Kondratiev planned to make public. It's the only thing that makes sense, and last night's events are even stronger evidence that Kondratiev was murdered to keep him quiet. I agree that neither Sasha nor Cogburn was intended to leave that farm alive."

"So that brings us back full circle to Kondratiev's murder," said Sasha.

Strachey said, "And then some. It seems pretty certain now that the General's murder was not just a simple but terribly convenient street crime."

"It cost a man's life to confirm that," said Ewan.

"The real question," continued Strachey, ignoring him, "is what Kondratiev knew that could have driven both the American and the Russian governments to such extremes? Did tonight put us any closer to getting an answer?"

Ewan said, "Well, their neat little plan went seriously off the rails. They might want to back away now, but if we keep stirring the pot they'll have no choice but to come after us, and sooner or later that will expose them. They've already made one serious mistake, and they'll make another."

Strachey was struck by a thought, and he asked Stoddard, "Does Buchalter's past connection with the Agency give us grounds to get involved officially?"

"I don't think so," the DNCS replied. "He's not been on our payroll for a long time. We're still on our own."

CHAPTER 17

Stoddard poured himself another drink.

"Things like this seldom turn out well for anyone." He fixed worried eyes on Ewan. "We've already pushed you out onto a shaky limb, for which I sincerely apologize. I wouldn't blame you if you left now and didn't come back, and you needn't worry about how I found you. That information already has been destroyed."

Ewan cocked an eye at him and decided that the DNCS was telling the truth about destroying the computer files. Strachey was staring blankly into his empty glass, and Ewan wondered whether it was in shame or an attempt to mask exasperation because his boss had tossed away their only trump card.

Returning to Ireland was tempting and certainly the wisest course, but there was an element that gave him pause. If Vitaliy Shurgin were somehow involved, if resolving the mystery of Kondratiev's death could hurt the Russian President, he wanted in on the action. The thought of doing harm, real harm to Shurgin tapped into a deep reservoir of hatred. He knew Sasha would agree, and this might be his last chance to strike another blow against the man who had long been his nemesis, the man who had ordered that Sasha be tortured those long years ago in Geneva and cost her an eye. He'd killed everyone directly involved in that affair, but Shurgin had been far away, safe in Moscow.

When the Soviet Union came tumbling down, Shurgin, then a KGB general, was entrusted with control and safekeeping of the combined liquid assets of the KGB and the defunct Communist Party of the Soviet Union -- some fifty billion dollars in all. He usurped those funds to build an empire that controlled Russia's enormous natural resources and industry, political parties, and international criminal organizations. His ruthless tactics had finally won him the Presidency, and he intended never to relinquish control.

Ewan exchanged a glance with Sasha before saying, "We'll stay a little while longer. I'd like to find out exactly who we're fighting and what it is they're so anxious to keep hidden. But, Terry, are you sure you want to continue with this, given the players involved? As you said, nothing good is likely to come of it."

"Thanks for the concern." Stoddard sounded like he meant it. "But if the Russians are mucking around with the DNI and the White House, I want to know what it's all about, and you lack sufficient local resources to get the job done. Now, let's put our heads together and see where we go from here."

Ewan began. "We need more information on the dead fed, Buchalter, and what connection he had with the White House. It's the only lead we have right now. From what Terry says, it's doubtful that Buchalter was the brains behind all this. I've seen a lot of his type, and they're all the same, no matter what country they're from – fit to follow orders, but incapable of much thought. It makes them more useful to their betters."

Strachey protested, "When and if we find out, what then? We can't storm the White House with guns blazing."

Ewan didn't bother to hide his annoyance.

"We won't know until the time comes, will we?"

Stoddard intervened, "Harry, it's Bob's job to play devil's advocate, and he'll continue to do so. I trust him and so should you."

The use of Ewan's real name galled him. He would still be Harry Connolly had it not been for the CIA, but that had not been Terry Stoddard's fault. Right now, Terry was worried about retaining control of the situation and its possible consequences. Terry was worried about Ewan's well-known penchant for playing by his own rules and probably regretted having brought him here in the first place. The same was true of the Mossad, but they recognized his unique value and had given him plenty of elbow room, as was fitting for a member of the *Kidon* unit.

Realistically, there was little more that he and Sasha could accomplish without Stoddard's support, and that meant tolerating Strachey. So for the time being, the CIA was the only game in town.

Ewan shrugged. "If you say so, Terry, but please don't call me 'Harry.'"

Stoddard nodded and waited for him to continue.

"Here's what we have to work with," said Ewan, "Buchalter's SUV, the diplomatic tag number of the Russian's car, and Buchalter's credentials." He then paused for dramatic effect before placing the *piece de resistance* on the coffee table. "And finally, Buchalter's cell phone that might be chock full of useful information."

"Holy shit," exclaimed Strachey.

He snatched up the phone and said to Stoddard, "Terry, I'd best get this to Amy right now. As soon as they figure out that Buchalter's missing they could screw with the call records or just zap the phone. They might even be tracking it right now."

"I turned if off and removed the battery," said Ewan, and dropped the flat cell phone battery onto the table.

"Go," said Stoddard, and Strachey was already on his own cell phone as he headed out the door.

Turning to Ewan and Sasha, Stoddard said, "Now we wait. Shall we check on our patient?"

CHAPTER 18

His wife's voice was still fuzzy with sleep when she answered Strachey's call. He glanced at his wristwatch. It was five thirty AM.

"Baby, get dressed. I'll be there to pick you up in a half-hour. We have things to do, and we've got to do them pronto."

"Huh?"

"You may have noticed by now that there is no one in bed with you. I've just pulled an all-nighter, and we're only getting started. Pull on some clothes and be ready when I get there. I'll brief you on the way to the office." He ended the call and concentrated on the road. Once again he had the blue and red lights flashing.

Damn that old man! Ramsay should have mentioned the cell phone immediately and Amy could have been working it over hours ago. The expatriate didn't trust him or the CIA, and he had to admit there might be good reason for that. But damn it, they were supposed to be working together now. What had Terry Stoddard been thinking? The DNCS was running a risk bringing Ramsay and his wife on board. They were not team players.

As he hurtled ahead through the pre-dawn gloom this thought triggered a recollection of an interview with a personnel officer early in his Agency career. Ironically enough, the purpose of the interview had been to chastise him for not exhibiting the accepted traits of a 'team player.'

Strachey's independent streak was inherited. Raised in the small mountain town of Canton, North Carolina, he had starred on Pisgah High School's football team, the "Black Bears," eventually winning a football scholarship to the University of North Carolina at Chapel Hill. His father, Sam, the elder of two brothers, had served two tours in Vietnam and returned home, gratefully still intact, when Strachey was four years old in 1972. Sam Strachey had gone to work for the town's major employer, the Champion International Paper factory. There had been no spitting on Vietnam vets in this tightly knit, patriotic community. Sam had taught his son the virtues of patriotism and personal honor while the two spent countless hours fishing the mountain streams and hunting in the forests. Sam still loved to tell the story of how Strachey had killed his first buck when he was only eleven. Strachey was still an excellent shot.

Sam's younger brother, Harold, had escaped the war through deferment when he won a scholarship to Duke, and he had remained there to earn a degree in law and a job with a well-known Charlotte law firm. His trajectory had continued upward. He now owned a fine house on Queen's Road in Myers Park, as well as a townhouse in Washington, D.C., from which he conducted his lobbying work.

With a college degree and his uncle's pull, Strachey could have landed a cushy job after college, but his father's example led him to the Army as an enlisted man.   The Army had tried mightily to retain him in its ranks because his superiors liked his formidable analytical and language skills. They had also really liked the fact that his uncle was a powerful Washington lobbyist with heavy political connections.   Strachey had been an All-America tight end for the North Carolina Tar Heels, and they liked that too.   But after three years in military intelligence, Strachey had tired of the Army's rote methodology, strict discipline and narrow focus, as well as the amount of time he spent behind a desk. He wanted action. The CIA was more than pleased to accept his application. In the Agency he developed into a field officer with enough "imagination" to make his superiors slightly uncomfortable.

The previous year he had found himself twice-divorced at 41 and in a dead-end job in Madrid. He had been thinking seriously of finding another line of work when he'd discovered a terrorist plot of gargantuan proportions. Working with Stoddard's team and some brave Spanish cops, he had foiled a madman's plans to detonate a nuclear device in a Spanish city. Several people had died in the course of that operation, some of them at his hands. Impressed, Stoddard had called him back to Washington to become his executive officer, a new position with intentionally vague responsibilities answerable only to the DNCS.

When Stoddard first briefed him on his plan to recruit Ramsay for the Kondratiev operation, Strachey had advised against it.

"There's no way we can control a cowboy like him. Why don't I handle it instead?"

The conversation had taken place across Stoddard's desk in the DNCS's spacious office on the seventh floor. Stoddard had been in his shirtsleeves sipping tea from a fine porcelain cup. The view from his windows was partially blocked by the glassy bulk of the New Headquarters Building, which was touted to be totally impermeable to electronic eavesdropping. Old hands referred to the original HQS building as "regular" and the new one as "extra crispy." Cell phone use was banned in both buildings, but Strachey had surreptitiously used his in the new building. It had worked perfectly. So much for "impermeable."

The Kondratiev killing had set off vibrations that jangled the DCNS's Cold War sensibilities. "I don't doubt that you could handle it, Bob, but we need deniability on this. Harry Connolly was one of the best at what he does. And I'm sure he still is."

"From what I've heard he just kills people these days."

The statement had elicited a pained expression from Stoddard. "Maybe he has good reasons. The people he now works for lack the luxury of lawyers and Congressional busybodies looking over their shoulders and making operational decisions they are unqualified to make."

It had been obvious that old warrior Stoddard felt a kinship with old warrior Harry Connolly. Strachey was amazed that an unreconstructed CIA original like Terry Stoddard had managed to rise through the Agency's increasingly lard laden bureaucracy to such a position. But the man was a deft politician and accomplished at concealing his true feelings behind an upper class, polished veneer. Strachey counted himself fortunate to be part of this man's trusted inner circle and to be called his friend. He would do anything for Stoddard.

And he had to admit that Stoddard was probably right – if they tried to mount an operation like this on their own, they would be brought to a screeching halt before they could set a foot out the door. They needed a cat's-paw. But Harry Connolly AKA Ewan Ramsay was no mere cat's-paw -- he had a tiger's claws and a demonstrated capacity to use them.

He had reluctantly agreed to Stoddard's request to contact Ramsay and play the distasteful role of blackmailer. Now Ramsay and his trigger-happy wife had been in the States only a few days: one man was already dead and another had nearly died. All they had to show for it were some credentials and a cell phone that could well lead to more grief and the ends of careers, or worse, prison sentences. Despite all the deniability Ramsay provided, Strachey, Stoddard, and Amy were now wading neck deep into a polluted pool of intrigue, and some of the stink might stick.

CHAPTER 19

Thirty minutes after he called his wife Strachey pulled up in front of his house on Meadowbrook Avenue, just off of Chain Bridge Road, and found Amy waiting in the drive. He could tell she was excited as soon as she settled into the seat beside him. She wore her usual geek work 'uniform,' a dark Ann Taylor pantsuit, geeky black horn-rimmed glasses, and she'd pulled her hair twisted up with a matching black clip. But underneath the geek disguise was a willowy body that would make a model envious. Her *café au lait* beauty still took his breath away. Amy had been another member of the team that foiled the Spanish plot, and they'd been married now for five months. He leaned over for a kiss and caught the scent of *Amarige*, his favorite, lightly applied.

"What's up?" she asked.

"I'm not sure you want to know," he replied gloomily, the rush of pleasure at seeing her suddenly dampened by the thought of involving her in this mess.

By the time they'd reached the entrance to the CIA compound he'd filled her in, and she sat lost in thought beside him as he steered through the park-like grounds to the sub-basement garage entrance. One of the perks of being Stoddard's executive officer was an envied indoor parking space.

"So we're going rogue?" she asked.

"Looks that way. I don't like it either."

He maneuvered the big SUV into a parking space. Before he could open the door she put her hand on his arm. "Bob, last Christmas your friends in Spain did exactly the same thing, and they made a good call. I have a lot of faith in Terry Stoddard."

She was right. His Spanish friends had contravened the orders of their government; in fact, they had ignored the direct instructions of the Spanish President to do what they felt was required to save thousands of lives. But Strachey wasn't sure that the present situation rose to that level.

"I see your point," he said. "But Spain was entirely different. We knew who and what we were after there."

"So," she searched his face with those big brown eyes. "Are you going to go through with it? Terry won't force you, but he'll continue working with Ramsay anyway."

Strachey flipped a mental coin and it came up in favor of protecting Stoddard's back. It was a two-headed mental coin. Stoddard had stuck by him in hard times.

"Let's get you to your Bat Cave with this cell phone," he said. "You may regret this when you see what's on it."

Amy's office was a shielded vault, protected by an electronic keypad and an iris recognition protocol. She was the only occupant. A large work table sat against a wall upon which hung four huge display screens. Most of the light in the room came from the screens augmented by a single desk lamp that burned on one side of the work table. Strachey couldn't recall Amy ever having turned on the overhead lighting. If there were truly a 'Bat Cave' at Langley, this was it, and Amy was its mistress.

She was in charge of the top secret Palantir Program, an impressive position for someone in their mid-thirties, but graduating at the top of her class from M.I.T. lent her powerful credentials. She'd been heavily recruited by high tech firms offering her high paying jobs, but the CIA had more gadgets, including Palantir. Like Google or Bing but immensely more powerful, the super-charged search engine accessed the entire U.S. Government security database, a constellation of literally thousands of supposedly separate databases belonging to the various agencies of government: the military, intelligence, law enforcement, plus the foreign databases to which CIA and NSA had access, either overtly or covertly. Before Palantir, analysts had to search each database separately, manually, and any connections or patterns of activity had to be detected by the individual analyst, usually scratching out his thoughts on a pad of paper - definitely a hit or miss system subject to human error.

Palantir changed all of that by tagging every bit of data separately, so that even if part of a report is classified above an analyst's access, he or she can still see everything else in the report. The system connects all the dots and sorts all the data, even advising an analyst when someone else is working on a similar problem so they can share information and conclusions.

All senior analysts could access the system from their office computers, but only Amy controlled it. Palantir was too powerful and valuable a weapon to risk it by allowing any more people to have administrator privileges.

Amy had used this system to locate Ramsay in Ireland but blocked access to her search from other terminals. At Stoddard's instruction she later destroyed the data. Not even a paper file remained.

The ability to block access to her searches from other users would be vital in the present task.

"Don't look over my shoulder. You make me nervous," said Amy as Strachey hovered behind her.

He bent and kissed the side of her neck and nipped her ear.

"And if you keep that up, I won't get any work done at all."

Strachey eyed the work table with a mischievous gleam. "We could always clear the junk off this table and . . ."

"I thought you said this was a priority job."

"Yeah, another sacrifice for Uncle Sam."

"Stop it. Now let me get to work."

She powered up the cell phone, a Blackberry Bold, typical Government Issue, and connected it with a USB cable to a stand-alone CPU that sat on the work table. "I'll download the data so I can work on it more easily, but no one can find the phone or even tell it's turned on as long as it's inside the vault. The shielding in here blocks any signal."

"Are you sure?"

Amy gave him a look over her shoulder that said he was a nincompoop. "Just because you got a cell signal upstairs in the hallway doesn't mean it would work in here. This vault is impregnable."

"I believe you," he said with exaggerated contrition.

Amy wagged her head from side to side. "Now go upstairs to the cafeteria. Get yourself a nice, hearty breakfast. Then bring me back a giant cup of coffee and a bagel when you're through."

She sat for a few moments after he left and reflected on the strange quirk of fate that had brought two North Carolinians, one black from a poor section of Charlotte and one white from what some considered redneck mountain country, together.   Since the previous December their relationship had evolved from professionally suspicious to one of mutual respect to marital bliss. She was happier than she ever had dreamed she could be, and the quickening she now felt in her belly promised greater happiness to come.   She hadn't told Strachey yet, but she knew he would be pleased.

She turned back to the work table to begin the laborious task of wresting secrets from the dead man's cell phone, but she couldn't keep the smile off her face.

CHAPTER 20

At Arlington Police Headquarters Murphy's irritation had evolved into concern. It was nearing noon now, and her partner, Detective Charlie Cogburn, still had not put in an appearance. She'd tried calling his home, which she imagined must be a dismal bachelor pad way out somewhere in Fairfax County, and his cell, but there hadn't been any response. A check at the motor pool had confirmed that the unmarked Ford they shared had not been returned to the garage or parking lot.

The jerk had gone missing. She checked her watch again and decided it was time to talk to Lieutenant Jefferson.

The lieutenant looked up when she knocked at his open door. "Come on in, Murphy. What's up?" He swept the remains of his daily carryout Chinese lunch aside.

"Cogburn's missing."

Jefferson frowned, "What do you mean, 'missing?'"

"Our shift began at eight this morning, and I can't find him anywhere. I've called his home and his cell, but he doesn't answer, and he never returned the car to the motor pool after he left yesterday."

"When did you see him last?"

"When that Russian policewoman was here. He bolted out the door as soon as she left."

"Maybe he's sleeping one off."

"Maybe, but I'm worried."

"You're worried about Cogburn?" Jefferson was frankly skeptical. The Cogburn-Murphy show was a running joke in the Department.

"Yes, as hard as it might be to believe. He's been acting strangely lately, more so than usual, I mean."

"How so?"

"Since we began investigating the Kondratiev murder. I can't put my finger on it, but something's changed. If there's a word I would never use to describe Cogburn, it's 'mysterious,' but that's how he's been acting. Like he has a big secret or something."

"Maybe he has a new girlfriend."

"Cogburn?" She found the suggestion ridiculous. Cogburn had been married once, but it had ended predictably in divorce years ago, and half his salary still went out in alimony payments. The only women Cogburn might have a relationship with now were the ones who were paid for their services, and not paid very much, or the inflatable plastic variety.

Jefferson grinned. "Yeah, it would be pretty strange, but still it's a possibility."

"And there's the way he handled the Kondratiev case."

Jefferson sighed. "I read his report, Murphy, and I can't disagree with his conclusions. There's no evidence of anything more at play than a mugging gone bad despite what his daughter said. Russians see conspiracies around every corner."

Murphy hid her exasperation. Her instincts had told her that they should dig more deeply into the case; there were political ramifications, after all, but Cogburn had deflected her at every turn. As he was the senior investigating officer, the crime report reflected his conclusions rather than hers.

Frustration did not sit well with Murphy's independent temperament. It "got her Irish up," as her mother used to say. The disappearance of Kondratiev's daughter after their initial interview with her was disturbing – had she been kidnapped, or worse, murdered as well? So Murphy had gone behind Cogburn's back. Without benefit of a warrant, she had used her badge with the doorman to gain entry to the General's condo and discovered that a very careful professional search had been conducted there and his files and computer were missing. Ever since, she had been in a quandary: to reveal what she knew might risk her career, but to remain quiet risked letting an injustice pass.

"May I go look for him?"

"What's your workload look like?"

"The usual car thefts and burglaries.   I'm on them."

"You'll go even if I tell you not to, won't you?"

"'Fraid so."

Jefferson shooed her out of his office.   "Go."

CHAPTER 21

Strachey and Amy arrived at the Winchester safehouse at seven thirty P.M. carrying two buckets of Kentucky Fried Chicken and a host of assorted sides. Ramsay and his wife had not left the place all day. Terry Stoddard had put in a perfunctory appearance at his afternoon staff meeting and then rushed out of Headquarters to return to Winchester where several loose ends required his attention. Cogburn was resting in a private room at the huge Winchester Medical Center complex under a false identity. The detective would pull through, but would be kept out of sight for the foreseeable future.

Ramsay grumbled that he wished the dead Fed had been a better shot. Only Sasha knew if he was serious, and she wasn't telling.

Buchalter occupied a private drawer in the Medical Center's morgue, also under an assumed name.

Strachey was proud of Amy and in awe of her intellect. What she could do with a computer bordered on the magical, in his opinion. When he introduced Amy to the Ramsays, he was curious to see how Ewan, whom he considered an unreconstructed anachronism, would react to his African-American wife. But despite Strachey's misgivings, Ramsay's manner bordered on courtly, and Sasha's greeting likewise was warm and genuine.

They arranged themselves around the dining table with paper plates, plastic utensils, and a six-pack of Pilsner-Urquel that Terry Stoddard produced from the refrigerator.

After casting a dubious look at the fried chicken on his plate, Stoddard said, "OK, Amy. Tell us what you found."

Strachey knew that she was nervous as well as excited about being involved in another 'rogue' operation. Their next step depended on what information she was able to entice out of Buchalter's cell phone, and she had worked on it all day. Strachey already knew that she was about to drop another bombshell on their merry little band.

She began quietly. "The Blackberry had encrypted software, Government Issue, and it took some time to get around, but since we're the Government, too … Well, anyway I found a shortcut. When I got in, there really wasn't much to see. In fact, the phone had been used to call only one number, and I suspect it's a dedicated circuit. That puts the user pretty high up on the totem pole."

"Did you find out who he was calling?" asked Ramsay. He obviously wanted to cut to the chase, and Strachey resented the interruption to his wife's narrative.

Amy nodded at Ramsay. "Yes, I did, but it isn't

going to make figuring out what's happening any easier. The person with whom he was in contact was Brian Tekla, the President's Special Advisor for Terrorism and Homeland Security."

Strachey watched their reaction. Ramsay and his wife looked blank, but Stoddard did a double-take.

"The President's 'Intelligence Czar!" he exclaimed.

Ramsay and his wife looked inquiringly at Stoddard.

The DNCS stood and began pacing as he spoke. "You may not be completely informed about the changes in the Intelligence Community, Har... uh, Ewan. Tekla is another former Agency body with a long pedigree. His father was one of the Agency's founding fathers. Tekla went through the Career Trainee program at the Farm and served a couple of tours abroad, but he wasn't cut out to be a case officer. He came back and re-created himself as an analyst, and from what I know, he was a good one and rose quickly, but he was prickly. His last job at the Agency was Deputy Chief of the Counter-Terrorism Center, and then he jumped to the DNI's office. Despite his personality, his case wasn't like Buchalter's -- someone we would have 'volunteered.' When the new Administration took over, he was drafted to the White House as Special Assistant. He'd won friends and sold himself as a true blue leftie."

Strachey added, "To complete the picture, the

man is an arrogant ass, and he hates the Agency."

"Why would he hate the Agency," asked Ramsay.

"He couldn't cut it as a field operative. His dick lacks the length for it, and he knows it," Strachey answered.

"We need to get to him somehow," said Ramsay.

Strachey was at a loss as to how this might be accomplished, especially if Stoddard wanted to keep the Agency's hand, really his own hand, hidden. This was slippery terrain. A misstep and they would all go down the tubes.

Ramsay said, "We need to shake him up, try to provoke a response that we can use." He looked around the table. "Any ideas?"

"I think I have a way," said Stoddard. His gaze was intent on Sasha.

CHAPTER 22

I've got to stop doing this, Sasha thought ruefully as she walked into the Kennedy Center next evening. Ewan was parked outside in the entrance plaza in a rented Lincoln town car, and she was feeling a little guilty for teasing him mercilessly about his liveried driver's outfit, black cap and all. By contrast, a shopping trip that afternoon to Saks in Chevy Chase had provided the Akris cocktail dress she now wore, black with tulle shoulder insets, and Ewan had not complained about the $4,000 price tag. In fact, he had hardly noticed the dress when she displayed the black La Perla lingerie she bought to go along with it. That had resulted in an impromptu but much welcomed afternoon frolic in their Ritz-Carlton suite. She smiled at the memory.

Ewan was worried about her, she knew, and unhappy that it was she who had run all the risks thus far, but this was the only gambit that would put them in direct contact with Tekla.

The occasion was the opening night performance of the National Symphony's Summer Music Institute Orchestra. Tekla's high school aged daughter, Sandra, was a cellist who had qualified for the prestigious free program. The opening was to be preceded by a cocktail party for parents and invitees, held ironically enough, in the Israeli Lounge just off the Concert Hall. Terry Stoddard's wife was a patron of the Center and a significant contributor to its various programs. Tonight Sasha would use Mrs. Stoddard's get in free pass.

As she approached the entrance to the Israeli Lounge she admired the long Hall of Nations that was decorated with the flags of every country with which the United States maintained diplomatic relations. She and Ewan had waited long enough for a crowd to arrive, and the room was filled with the elegantly dressed glitterati of the nation's capital. It was difficult to see through all the people and she experienced a momentary wave of panic that in Sasha's case amounted only to a slight increase in heart rate, borne of fear that she would be unable to locate Tekla before the bell sounded to signal the attendees to move to the Concert Hall. Cocktails were scheduled to last only a half-hour, and only fifteen minutes remained.

The lounge was a gift from the long suffering people of Israel, donated in an era when there were no doubts about America's dedication to the survival of the small Jewish state. Sasha glanced momentarily at the ceiling, and her eye was drawn to the Weil panel depicting Joshua at the walls of Jericho. She wished she had some of her old Mossad comrades backing her up now. But she and Ewan were alone, and even their small band of CIA "friends" was nearly helpless to assist them.

She wove her way through the crowd to the open bar in the far corner, her eyes probing through the crowd in all directions for her quarry. She and Ewan had found numerous photos of the Special Presidential Assistant on the internet, and Stoddard had provided additional details.

At last, she spotted him chatting with a small group in the corner opposite the bar. He was tall, surely well over six feet, with craggy features and reddish thinning hair. Sasha moved to within earshot and caught fragments of conversation. Tekla was holding forth on how important it was to avoid alienating the adherents of Islam, and Sasha, with another look around the splendid room donated by Israel, thought, *we have met the enemy and he is us.* The man truly must be an ass, as Strachey had said, an ass incapable of recognizing an enemy when he saw one. She began to relish the thought of putting the proper fear of God into him tonight.

A muted chime sounded and people began setting down their drinks and moving toward the doors. Sasha maneuvered herself next to Tekla and matched his pace. As they passed out into the corridor leading to the Concert Hall, she gripped his elbow. "Excuse me, Mr. Tekla?"

Clearly annoyed, he turned his head toward her. He did a double take when he saw her beauty but continued walking. "Yes? What is it?"

"I am Major Fedosova of the Russian Internal Security Service. I'm investigating the death of General Pavel Kondratiev."

Tekla stopped dead in his tracks causing his wife, who was holding onto his other arm, nearly to fall. He turned his full attention to Sasha. "What did you say?" he asked.

Ignoring the question she continued, "We have your man Buchalter, and he's been quite talkative."

"Brian, what's this woman talking about? We're going to be late for the performance." His wife tugged on his sleeve, and he shook her off.

"You go ahead. I'll catch up," he told her.

"That's all right," said Sasha, "don't let me hold you up."

She thrust a slip of paper into his hand. "You can contact us at that number. You should call soon. Buchalter is anxious to hear from you."

She turned quickly and merged into the crowd, letting it carry her away. "Enjoy the concert," she said over her shoulder.

Tekla remained rooted to the spot, mouth agape, as the crowd closed in and he lost sight of her.

She picked up her pace in the direction of the double glass doors and escape. Behind her, Tekla struggled to push through the crowd, but her timing had been perfect.

As he sped away from the curb with Sasha in the back seat, Ewan checked the rear view mirror and saw Tekla charge out the doors only in time to see the tail lights of the black car recede into the distance.

CHAPTER 23

Ewan merged onto Rock Creek Parkway, heading northwest toward Georgetown. In the back, Sasha wriggled out of her dress and began pulling on jeans, a dark cotton pullover, and sneakers as Ewan appreciatively followed the proceedings in the mirror.

"Stop peeking, you pervert."

"It's too good of a show to miss. Why don't we just go straight back to the hotel?" He would never tire of looking at her, he knew.

"You're going to hurt my feelings because I know you don't really mean that last bit. It could be a long time before you see these undies again if this insincerity continues."

"Ha! You can't resist me, and you know it."

"Now you're entering really dangerous territory."

But her reference to what they were actually doing sobered him, and he abandoned the badinage that was a favorite part of their relationship. "At least come on up here to the front seat and keep me company. We can hold hands."

Her transformation complete, Sasha wriggled over the seat back and settled in beside her husband. "How long do you figure we have?" she asked.

"Plenty of time. He's unlikely to leave before the concert is over, and he'll have to take his family home anyway. But I'll bet we've ruined whatever plans he had for the rest of the night. We'll be in place long before they arrive, even if they leave the concert early."

Their plan was simple: stake out Tekla's Foxhall Road house and wait. If Sasha's provocation of the man did not elicit a response they could take advantage of, they would just have to think of something else.

Ewan removed the chauffeur's cap and his tie and tossed them into the back seat then turned his attention to finding their way through Georgetown and up Foxhall Road.

The found a spot on the street where they could observe Tekla's Tudor style house and settled down to wait.

Ewan's cell phone bleated.

"Yes?"

"Glad you've joined the party." It was Strachey's voice.

Ewan was not pleased. "Where are you?"

"About half a block behind you. I thought you could use some help."

"Go home."

"No can do. If you have to follow Tekla tonight, one car isn't enough. He's had enough CIA training to spot a one-car surveillance, and he'll be especially alert now."

Ewan couldn't argue with the logic, but that didn't mean he had to like it. He and Sasha should have come in separate cars, but it was too late now.

"I'm walking up to your car, so try not to shoot me," said Strachey.

A moment later the insufferable man appeared at Ewan's window and drawled, "Evening. Here's something we'll need."

He handed Ewan a small, commercial Motorola walkie-talkie and said, "I paid cash for a set of these at Radio Shack this afternoon. Wholly commercial and untraceable, and they have a twenty-five mile range. Not encrypted, of course, so we'll have to be careful, but we'll toss them after tonight anyway. Keep it set to channel eighteen."

Ewan examined the slim black and gray radio. "You expect me to use this?"

"If we're going to do it right."

"Does Terry know you're here?"

"No."

"Then go home."

"No. You could need help tonight."

"If you get into trouble it'll blow CIA involvement. That's exactly what Terry wants to avoid."

"I won't get into trouble, but you might. If you do, I'll be there."

"That makes me feel all warm and fuzzy inside."

"Good. I was sure you'd see it my way. I'm going back to my car now. I used an alias to rent it. It's a black Sebring. Keep the radio switched on." He walked away into the darkness.

"Damn that man!"

"What he said makes sense," said Sasha.

"I still don't like it. He could blow the whole thing."

"Terry Stoddard seems to have a lot of confidence in him."

"Well, his confidence is obviously misplaced. He's not supposed to be here tonight."

"Have you always followed orders?"

"You're not beginning to like that guy, are you?"

"I didn't say that, but a second car will be useful."

"I should have shot him in Ireland." He wouldn't have, of course, and Sasha knew it, but he had a momentary vision of dumping the CIA man's body into Cleggan Bay and watching it slip out of sight below the surface, and it was not an entirely unpleasant vision. How could Terry Stoddard rely on such an obvious toady? But if the man were nothing more than that, why was he here tonight directly disobeying his boss? Should he attach an unsavory motive to his presence? Ewan mulled over the unpleasant implications as they waited for Tekla.

Sasha read his mood. "You're having evil thoughts, aren't you?"

"I don't know the man. Ergo I don't trust him. And you were ready to shoot him in Ireland, too."

CHAPTER 24

"What in the world is going on?" whined his wife for the twentieth time since leaving the Kennedy Center. "We were supposed to attend the after-concert party.

Brian Tekla drove furiously, his equally furious wife at his side. His distraught daughter sobbed in the backseat. He had ushered them unceremoniously out of the Kennedy Center and bundled them into the car with little more than a few choice curse words, his face contorted with a building rage that was inexplicable to his family.

"It's the job. I've got to go somewhere," he gritted through clenched teeth.

"It's always the damned job, Brian. You have a family, too."

Tekla's knuckles whitened as he twisted his fingers around the steering wheel, imagining it was his wife's neck. Refusing to look at her, he riveted his attention to the road ahead. The daily reproaches were mounting to an unbearable load that only contributed to the pressure now building inside his skull. His daughter's mewling from the back seat added to the growing pile of straws on the camel's back of his distress.

It had seemed so simple. Buchalter was compliant

and competent.   The Russians were more than supportive. So much depended on his success and now something had gone terribly wrong.

Upon arrival at their residence he finally rid himself of the women, backed out of the driveway and sped away. A cell phone call to a special number would trigger a quick response.

*****

Ewan entered the bar at the Mayflower Hotel through the Connecticut Avenue lobby entrance. The brightly lit, cavernous lobby that ran a full block all the way through the hotel to 17th Street was not crowded. He didn't spot Tekla, who had parked on DeSales Street and taken the bar entrance at the corner with Connecticut. The Presidential Advisor might have intended to pass through the bar and exit onto 17th Street as part of a counter-surveillance route, but his absence meant he was still in the bar.

The venerable Washington hotel was familiar to Ewan, even after all the years away from Washington. The bar's lobby entrance was just ahead to his left. With the exception of a coffee stand with a scattering of tables in the lobby, nothing much had changed since he had last been here. The bar was justifiably famous for Sammy the bartender's excellent martinis and its comfortable ambiance had changed not a whit since he had last seen it nearly twenty years earlier. He wondered if Sammy still worked here. Twenty years was a long time and another world away.

He spotted Tekla in a seat at one of the discreet banquette tables in the rear, and Ewan selected a place at the bar that insured a good view. For old times' sake he ordered a martini, Tanqueray Ten with three olives, and waited.

Tekla's reckless driving might have been an attempt at surveillance detection, but his direct route down 'M' Street argued against it. He was a man in a hurry to get somewhere, and now he sat with his eyes shifting back and forth between the two entrances. He was waiting for someone.

Fifteen minutes later the White House advisor sat straight up and focused like a good pointer on the street entrance. He raised his arm a fraction as though he intended to wave but then thought better of it. Definitely not cut out for the Clandestine Service.

A few seconds later he was joined by a well-dressed man with features that to Ewan's practiced eye were obviously Slavic – mid-forties, thinning blond hair combed straight back from a high forehead. He slid onto the banquette next to Tekla who began talking excitedly punctuating his words with short chopping motions with his hands. The Russian, for Ewan had no doubts about his nationality, darted quick glances around the bar and laid a hand on

Tekla's arm to calm him.   How many times had Ewan done the same with nervous sources?

The Russian listened attentively, his expression unreadable, until the American was finished. After a pause, he leaned close to Tekla and said something before rising to leave. The entire conversation had lasted no more than ten minutes.

Ewan slipped his hand into his pocket and keyed the walkie-talkie's transmit button three times to alert Strachey that the target was leaving by the DeSales Street door. The transceiver vibrated in his pocket – Strachey's confirmation. Ewan could not risk tailing the Russian out of the bar in plain view of Tekla. Sasha was already blown, and one of them had to remain incognito. He hoped Strachey was up to the job.

Tekla remained in his seat for only a few moments before hurrying to the exit. Through the window, Ewan saw him head in the direction of his car. There would be nothing more to gain from following him now. He had imparted his information to the Russian and would now return to his residence.

Ewan gave Tekla a minute before rejoining Sasha who had double parked the Lincoln on Connecticut Avenue within sight of the hotel. He keyed the walkie-talkie. "Do you have him?"

"Yes."   Strachey's response was instant.   "But he's a cagey bastard. He's heading toward Adams Morgan. By the way, he's driving the same car you saw the other night at the farm."

Ewan hated transmitting in the clear on a public channel, but there was no helping it. He wondered if the Russians were scanning radio frequencies in this range. "Break it off. He's running a surveillance detection route, and he's a pro. We've got all we're going to get." No sense taking chances, and Ewan had no doubt that the man would wind up at the Russian Embassy on Wisconsin Avenue. Let him drive around in circles for a while.

CHAPTER 25

The three of them rendezvoused in the bar at the Ritz-Carlton, selecting a dimly lit corner table.

"You like to travel first class," said Strachey casting an appreciative eye around the wood-paneled room.

The Israeli Government had rewarded Ewan well for helping them steal billions of Shurgin's ill-gotten dollars nineteen years earlier.

During the course of that operation Ewan had been shot by a former Spetsnaz officer and nursed back to health in an Israeli hospital. It was during his recuperation that romance had blossomed between him and Sasha. He had invested several million of his reward dollars in AOL when it was low, and was one of the smart ones to cash out when the stock hit its zenith. He and Sasha had no money worries.

"I was still in the States when they built this hotel," said Ewan grumpily. "Time was that a man could enjoy a fine cigar in here along with his drink."

Sasha rolled her eyes. He'd cut back drastically on his cigar smoking, but the easy availability of genuine Habanos in Europe was too much of a temptation for him to quit entirely.

"The dictatorship of the proletariat is upon us," remarked Strachey with a wry smile.

"An unexpected convergence of opinion," Sasha observed causing Ewan to grimace.

The waiter brought their drinks, and when he was gone, Ewan addressed the CIA man. "What do you think we accomplished tonight?"

"We poked a stick in their the eye and confirmed that Tekla is cooperating somehow with at least one Russian, most likely the same Russian that was waiting with Buchalter at the farm house, and we both got a good look at him. We can go through the photos we have of Embassy personnel and find out who he is, but I'm betting he's SVR given the fact that he ran a pretty good counter-surveillance route after his meeting with Tekla."

Ewan nodded. "They're bound to be confused. They don't know Buchalter's dead, and they've lost track of Cogburn. If they haven't already done so, it won't take them long to find out that Sasha is not from the FSB. They'll be wondering who it is they're dealing with. The most likely candidate will be the CIA, so Terry may hear from someone soon. We have no more leads to follow, and our resources are limited. Whatever form their reaction takes, let's hope it's something we can take advantage of, something that will put us on the right trail. From what I observed tonight, Tekla's not running the show. I don't think he's going to call the number Sasha gave him. If the man he met was the same as the one at the farm house, he probably knows Buchalter is dead".

Strachey agreed. "If they're confused, then so are we. Does the conspiracy include anyone in the White House above Tekla? Is he an SVR agent, or is he working in some sort of liaison capacity? And most importantly, what is it they're going to such lengths to protect?"

"It could be a high level penetration," offered Sasha.

"Which would mean that Tekla really is an SVR agent, maybe even the penetration they're trying to protect. That would make sense," said Strachey.

"Given his background, General Kondratiev would have had access to highly sensitive information," Sasha chased the idea, but it seemed too easy an answer.

Ewan shook his head. "But his knowledge would have been quite dated by now."

"With a little luck and proper tradecraft such operations can go on for years," offered Strachey.

"Yes," Ewan reluctantly conceded the point, "but for now it's all conjecture. Tekla could well be cooperating with the Russians on a diplomatic level under orders from the White House. There's a lot going on right now in bilateral relations, and the Shurgin visit is coming up.

Sasha knitted her brows. "It would be a very

strange sort of diplomacy that leads to the murder of a former KGB General, the subornation of a police detective, and the attempted kidnapping and probably intended murder of yours truly. Diplomats don't get involved in wet work, and these people are up to their necks in it."

Ewan had to agree. "Yes, they've gone to some extraordinary lengths: Kondratiev's assassination and the cover-up, Russians and Americans acting together. Frankly I can't imagine what information a relic like Kondratiev could have possessed that would justify such risks."

"Whatever it is, it must be enormous for them to go to such lengths," said Sasha. "And there's another loose end we haven't even discussed: Kondratiev's daughter. All we know is that she disappeared, according to Cogburn, immediately following her father's death. She could be on the run, or maybe she's dead, too. If she's alive she could throw some light on all this – whatever it is." She waved her arm vaguely and slumped back in her seat to study her drink with a frown.

A gloomy silence settled over the three as the implications sank in. After a few moments Ewan drew a deep breath and addressed the CIA man. "Are you certain you want to pursue this any farther?"

It was a moment before Strachey answered, and when he did Ewan detected some of the pit bull in the man. "As Terry Stoddard said, if the Russians are mucking about in the White House, I want to know what it's all about. If you two want to bow out, it's OK. You've already done a great deal, and no one would blame you."

Ewan and Sasha exchanged a glance that conveyed instant mutual agreement. "You still need us," said Ewan.

They didn't know it then, but thousands of miles away events were unfolding in Europe that would lay bare the answers to their questions and rock the international order to its foundations. Whether this would happen depended on the determination of an elderly man into whose hands the Holy Grail had fallen.

CHAPTER 26

The news had shattered Viktoria Pavlevna Kondratieva's existence into jagged pieces, like a glass vase smashed by a hurled stone.

They had appeared at her door early in the morning, the two police officers, one an attractive younger woman with sympathy in her eyes and the other an untidy older man whose unshaven face betrayed no emotions other than boredom and cynicism. Her father, they told her, was dead, murdered on the street near his home by an unknown assailant.

Viktoria Pavlevna Kondratieva, known to her friends as Vicky, felt suddenly cold and her eyes lost focus as her knees began to buckle. The female police officer rushed to support her and helped her to a chair while the man simply looked on, his initial indifference now turning to mild curiosity.

With sudden force the realization hit her that she could trust no one, not even the police. In her native country the police were the very last people one could trust, and she wasn't certain it was not the same here.

When they were gone, she remained seated for what seemed like a long time, gathering her strength trying to focus her thoughts, as her father's words reverberated in her mind. *Remember, if they come for me they will come for you, too, so run as far and as fast as you can.*

Though the numbness refused to quit her limbs entirely, her father's words provided the impetus she needed to start moving. She hurriedly began packing. A single bag would have to do. She pulled a large envelope from her desk drawer, but before putting it in the bag, she removed the small stack of brittle pages it held and removed the last one. She recalled the first time she had read the document and how the last page had affected her most. Now she determined that the world should never know its contents. Still she was cognizant of history and her slain father's wishes. She would not destroy the page, but she would hide it where it would not be found.

Later, she repeatedly checked her rear view mirror as she turned west on Route 7 toward Route 66 which would take her to the Dulles Access Road. She knew where she had to go – to the one man her father had told her would understand.

Vicky had not inherited the steel that comprised her father's backbone, nor had she the same sharp intellect. She had accompanied him to the States 15 years ago when she was still in her twenties, a pretty girl, but delicate and with a dependent personality. She was surprised by the ease with which she adapted to her new country and soon found a job at The American University in Washington teaching Russian to the few undergraduates still interested in the language. She eventually discovered romance with a man who took her to California, far from her father, but after ten years the marriage fell apart when her successful husband abandoned her for a younger, prettier woman. Emotionally drained, she returned to Washington to the arms of her father to assist him with his memoirs. She settled into a comfortable, if lonely life.

It was her father's love of his new country and his abiding hatred of the coterie of old KGB hands who now pulled the strings of the Russian Government that had brought about his own death and now drove her into desperate flight toward an unknowable future.

She left her car among thousands of others in the vast, long-term parking lot at Dulles International Airport and rode the shuttle to the main terminal where she bought a ticket on the first flight she could find to Europe. There she would find the one man her father had told her she could trust.

CHAPTER 27

Ewan Ramsay was not the only exile from the Central Intelligence Agency, although the violence that punctuated Ewan's separation and drove him into the arms of the Mossad was unique. There were others, some turncoats and some who viewed their former employer through a prism of sad experience, like a parent helplessly watching as a wayward child piles mistake upon mistake.

Lawrence Nelson had fallen in love with the Gothic and Baroque architecture of Brussels, especially the area around the Grand Place, in the Sixties when he served there as Chief of Station. When he made the decision to resign from the Agency over what he considered irreconcilable differences, he and his wife, Nancy, had remained rather than return to the poisonous atmosphere of Washington where his strong views had enraged enemies and dismayed friends. He and his wife both derived incomes from family inheritances, and they lived comfortably as expatriates. Almost their entire adult lives had been spent outside the United States, first as students in Post-War Europe, and then fifteen years in the field for the Central Intelligence Agency playing a deadly cat and mouse game with the Soviet intelligence services. Since leaving the Agency Nelson had spent most of his time trying to prove the fallibility of his former colleagues.

Their top floor flat was a few minutes' stroll from the Grand Place, and the now elderly couple had many friends, including intelligence officers from various European services, active and retired, who visited him from time to time seeking advice on counterintelligence matters involving the Russians.

But the beautiful city, justly famous for its cosmopolitan hospitality, cuisine, and wonderful variety of beers, became a dangerous place one afternoon in August. The habits and instincts of a lifetime remained keen, and so it was not surprising that he spotted the surveillance almost as soon as it appeared. He was driving his battered VW Beetle, and that was good because spotting vehicular surveillance is many times easier from a car than on foot.

There were two cars, both dark colored sedans, with at least two men in each. His first reaction was amusement. Could this be happening? A circuitous route around the city with stops at various shops, following a meticulous plan laid out long ago for such eventualities, confirmed the pursuit, and amusement was replaced by mild anger mixed incongruously with a new energy born of nostalgia. The experience breathed life into old reactions that had lain dormant for decades.

He had done nothing to provoke such interest, and indeed his enemies cast him as an obsessed and bitter old man with an axe to grind, and did all they could to insure that no one paid him heed.

He was an official non-entity. Yet his profession taught one that pure coincidence rarely, if ever, occurs and should always be viewed with suspicion. Like a ship's captain recognizing the rigging of an enemy sail on the horizon, he instinctively knew the people following him were Russians, as was the visitor that had appeared unexpectedly at his door the previous evening.

They were certainly not local boys. Nelson occasionally advised the Belgians on security matters and knew them well. Whoever was following him was unfamiliar with the city's streets and traffic patterns. But they were persistent and countered his few feints at losing them by becoming bolder in the chase.

Without knowing their intentions he would not lead them out of the city and its protective eyes. Some skills never die, and he managed to maneuver so there were several cars between his pursuers and him and then leave them behind as he scooted through a traffic signal to the consternation of drivers from the cross street who had just begun to edge forward into the intersection when the light turned green.

They must have picked him up when he left home, and he circled back there now. First, to make certain his wife and the visitor were safe and second to put some bricks and mortar between him and these unknown men. If the visitor were to be believed, death already had played a role in this affair, and the sulfurous scent of Moscow was strong. Irrationally, he laughed out loud.

Maybe I'm not so paranoid, after all, he thought. Even paranoiacs have enemies.

He parked illegally outside his building entrance and rushed inside as fast as his arthritic knees would carry him to take the lift to his floor. Inside, he locked the door behind him and headed for a window, shushing his wife as he passed her.

There they were – the two dark cars halted in front of his building. A man stepped out of one of them and stared for a long while up at the flat. Nelson didn't move from the window. They knew he had spotted them, and for the time being it was a stand-off. But for how long?

He watched them deploy two men into the street to take up positions with a view of the building entrance. Nelson did not think their intentions were benign. He wondered if they knew about the alley exit at the rear.

"Then she was right," his wife said behind him.

Turning from the window he saw the concern etched across her face.

"What are you talking about?" He noted for the first time that their visitor was missing and they were alone in the apartment.

"Vicky. She went to that very window and watched the street when you left. She became quite alarmed and told me you were being followed. She was distraught and blamed herself for bringing danger to our door, as she put it. She grabbed her bag and left, saying how sorry she was."

"Where did she go?"

"She didn't say, Lawrence, but I've never seen anyone so frightened."

Nelson turned back to the window. "She was right, Nancy. I was followed, and if they left watchers here when I left, they may have Vicky now. She must have known. She was trying to lead them away from us."

Nancy's voice was strained. "She left something and said you would know what to do with it."

"What?"

"It's on the dining table."

Nancy watched worriedly out the window while he investigated the package. It was wrapped in plain, brown oiled paper, neatly bound with a string. Inside was a green cardboard file folder with no identifying marks that contained several sheets of paper covered with handwriting and some yellowing documents written in Russian with the words '**СОВЕРШЕННО СЕКРЕТНО,**' TOP SECRET in Cyrillic, stamped in faded red at the top of each page. He immediately recognized them as original KGB documents.

He gasped when he saw the subject of the

documents and quickly closed the folder. "Nancy, pack a bag, a small one, and quickly. We have to get out of here right now before they come for us."

There was no room left for doubt in Nelson's mind that the men outside would kill without compunction to retrieve what the folder contained.

CHAPTER 28

While his wife packed, Nelson went to the desk in his study and from the bottom drawer retrieved a heavy object wrapped in a cloth permeated with silicon. It contained a .45 caliber Colt M1911A1 semi-automatic pistol that his father had carried in World War II. Nelson had not looked at the weapon in years but now he inserted a full seven-round magazine and pulled the slide back to rack a round into the chamber.

Viktoria Pavlevna Kondratieva had appeared at their door the evening before, trembling and exhausted, to beg them to take her in for the night. Nelson had first met her father shortly after the former General's hasty departure from Moscow. They were kindred spirits from opposite sides of the Cold War, each in his own way fascinated by the opportunity to exchange reminiscences with a former opponent, both now disgraced by their respective services.

Kondratiev, slightly older than Nelson, served his first tour as a KGB American Targets officer in New York in the early Sixties and then two subsequent tours in the Washington *Rezidentura*, the last as KGB *Rezident*. He rose with uncommon rapidity through the ranks to become the youngest officer ever to make the rank of General in the KGB, a testament more to his operational prowess than his political skills, and was well on his way to becoming chief of the First Chief Directorate, Foreign Intelligence.   But then jealousies and suspicion derailed his career. At the urging of another KGB General who had the ear of KGB leadership, one Vitaliy Mikhailovich Shurgin, he was reassigned from Moscow to Leningrad (now Saint Petersburg) and then relegated to the Second Chief Directorate, Counter-intelligence.   His few remaining friends warned him that a storm was brewing that would culminate in his arrest and trial as a traitor. There was no basis for such an allegation, but KGB internal politics in the new, post-Soviet era cast him as someone infected by Western 'liberal' ideas from his many years in the United States. Only by winning a seat in the Legislature as an ally of Boris Yeltsin that gave him immunity from arrest did he escape incarceration. It was time for him to leave, and when he did he was labeled a turncoat by the authorities.

The General and Nelson spent many an evening discussing old cases and the strategies and tactics of their respective services.   But try as he might Nelson could not wrest from the General information on any but already compromised Soviet espionage cases.   These, especially those involving the most infamous American traitors, were significant, and they eventually formed the basis for Kondratiev's well-received autobiography, published the previous spring in the U.S.

The old KGB, now broken up into the SVR,

foreign intelligence and the FSB, internal security, he told Nelson, was deeply and broadly penetrated by a shadowy group of hard liners led by former KGB General turned politician Vitaliy Mikhailovich Shurgin. When Shurgin attained his ultimate goal, the Presidency of the Russian Federation, several years earlier, he continued his vendetta against Kondratiev by publicly declaring him a traitor.

The previous evening Vicky told them her father had instructed her to turn to Nelson should the need arise, and so here she was. The Nelsons, of course, had read of the General's death, but it was more than common grief that had driven Vicky to Brussels. She told them she was certain her father had been murdered by Russian assassins, and now she feared for her own life.

Her father possessed an ancient but mortal secret, one he kept guarded for decades, but he believed the time had come to reveal it to the world. It was a secret that had changed America from a confident, inspiring nation into a country increasingly afflicted by self-doubt and vulnerable to subversion. The primary beneficiaries were the Soviet Union and its apologists. Today, with the United States, weakened by two wars, a foundering economy, and with its super power crown precariously balanced, his old enemy, now the Russian President, planned to exploit the situation to further degrade the country he hated above all others. General Kondratiev decided the time had come to end the charade.

Kondratiev knew that Nelson had penetrated almost to the core of the secret but was thwarted at the last minute. He respected the American's determination and sense of honor and was gratified by the knowledge that by revealing all he would validate Nelson's longstanding convictions, the convictions that led him to walk out of Langley's doors and accept the opprobrium heaped upon him by former colleagues and the media.

Nelson knew none of this until he saw the documents Vicky had left for him. They were Kondratiev's legacy, and they had become his responsibility. Their mere possession put him and his wife in mortal peril.

CHAPTER 29

At the same moment Lawrence Nelson was weighing the possibilities of escape it was Monday Morning in Washington, and the Director had called Terry Stoddard to his office. The DCI, Frank Capriano, was an amiable man, a former Congressman, and long-time political operative for the party that now occupied the White House. The leaders of that party nurtured an abiding distrust of the Intelligence Community, particularly the Central Intelligence Agency, and so they had installed as Director a man with absolutely no experience in intelligence collection and analysis but with impeccable political credentials. But Capriano was a not unintelligent man, and in short order he recognized the quiet dedication and professionalism with which the people of the CIA performed their esoteric tasks. He was surprised to discover tendrils of loyalty to the ideals of the Agency burrowing into him and establishing sturdy roots. But this is what happens when good men become privy to secrets that reveal the true nature of the world.

Capriano admired Terrence Stoddard as a highly accomplished professional whose polished, almost foppish exterior concealed a core of steel. Stoddard came from a wealthy East Coast family and from the time he entered the Agency in the early Sixties had been a 'dollar a year' man, drawing no salary beyond a single dollar per year from the Government. Men in his position enjoyed an independence denied to most, and there had been several who played key roles in the CIA's early days. The Agency's founders, such as Stoddard's father, had cut their teeth working for the Office of Strategic Services in the war against Fascism and so had imbued the new intelligence service with a liberal spirit that would have surprised most outsiders. Stoddard embodied this tradition, and in him the younger Capriano discovered a kindred spirit.

Their relationship had played a key role in foiling the Iranian attempt to detonate a nuclear device in Spain the previous Christmas. Armed by facts provided by Stoddard, Capriano had prevailed over a dubious White House staff to win the President's agreement to intervene. In doing so he had made enemies, among them Brian Tekla, the President's Special Advisor for Terrorism and Homeland Security, the so-called 'Intelligence Czar.'

Stoddard knocked lightly on the DCI's door and walked into the spacious office to find Capriano already on his feet pulling on his suit jacket.

"Come on, Terry," he said, "We're going to the White House."

"Both of us?"

"Yes. They specifically asked me to bring you along." He put a hand to Stoddard's back as they walked to the DCI's private elevator and gave his Director of National Clandestine Services a sidewise look. "Any idea what this might be about?"

Stoddard mentally ticked off several sensitive operations around the world that might merit White House attention, but it was the Kondratiev affair that worried him. He had not briefed the DCI, and did not intend to do so for the time being, partially to protect Capriano should something blow badly, but mostly because he could not trust the system. Capriano would feel honor bound at least to inform the President, and politicians were an untrustworthy lot. Once a secret was shared with one of them all control was lost. No, best to guarantee deniability for the DCI and protect the operation and the people involved.

"No idea," he replied. "Who called the meeting?"

"Brian Tekla."

Stoddard mentally prepared himself for what he now was certain would be a dangerous, but potentially quite informative confrontation. Sasha had accosted Tekla at the Kennedy Center on Saturday evening, just a little over a day ago. Tekla had not called the telephone number Sasha had given him, probably sensing a trap and was now sniffing around in search of the source of the provocation.

The drive in the DCI's chauffeured limousine to the south entrance to West Executive Avenue between the White House's West Wing and the Eisenhower Executive Office Building was swift. The guards checked their identification and directed them to a parking space from which they walked to a canopied sidewalk leading to deceptively unimposing white double doors that provided access to the seat of power.

Tekla had chosen the Roosevelt Room, a stone's throw away from the Oval Office as the meeting venue, and Capriano and Stoddard were directed to a row of chairs just outside the door to cool their heels.

The DCI snorted and sat down. "He's trying to impress or intimidate us," he said. "He must have forgotten that this is not my first visit to the White House." Capriano had been a senior advisor in a previous Administration and was no stranger to how the White House worked.

The door to the meeting room opened and an unhappy looking Richard Mulvaney, Director of the FBI, came out. Spotting Capriano and Stoddard, he said, "Batten down the hatches. He's in a foul mood."

"When is he not?" sighed Capriano.

They stood and entered the ornate, buff colored room as Mulvaney stomped away. Tekla did not rise when they entered. He was seated at the head of the large conference table that dominated the room, his back to the east wall that formed a half circle with a fireplace in the center.

"Sit down," snarled Tekla. Stoddard was not surprised by his attitude. Tekla did not like either him or Capriano and felt a special antipathy toward Stoddard if for no other reason than the fact that Stoddard was financially independent and beholden to no one. That could make a man fearless, and Tekla wanted people to fear him.

The Italian in Capriano sensed an insult in Tekla's tone. "What's this about, Brian? We have other matters to attend." He remained standing, and Stoddard followed suit.

"You don't have anything more important to do than what the White House wants," Tekla shot back.

Looking around the room in mock search, Capriano waved an arm and said, "I don't see anyone here but you, Brian. Did the President forget to come?"

Stoddard said nothing, relieved not to be the center of attention. The mutual dislike that festered between these two men was becoming the stuff of Washington legend. Tekla believed he should be running intelligence operations, and Capriano ignored him whenever possible.

With an obvious effort, Tekla brought himself under control. To Stoddard's eyes the man was more nervous than angry and suffering under a great strain.

"OK, OK," Tekla raised both arms in mock

surrender.   "Please," he edged the word with sarcasm, "sit down so we can get started."

Apparently satisfied that his honor remained intact, Capriano sat and pulled back the chair beside him for Stoddard.

"I called this meeting to discuss a very important matter, one that could have serious international consequences," Tekla began, and Stoddard marveled at how the man's every word dripped with pomposity.

Neither Capriano nor Stoddard said anything, and after a suitably dramatic pause, Tekla continued, "You know about the death several days ago of former KGB General Pavel Kondratiev."

Stoddard's ears perked up.

"His death," continued Tekla, "has certain political ramifications. He was trying to build interest in some allegedly 'important' information he planned to reveal, undoubtedly a publicity stunt to sell more books. Any information he possessed was dated and useless, but his death prompted immediate speculation from the howling right-wing media that the Russian government must somehow be involved. There is considerable opposition to the new arms control treaty that the President is to sign with President Shurgin, and the naysayers would take advantage of any possibility to stop it.

"This new treaty, gentlemen, is the most important agreement of its kind ever to be proposed." Tekla's voice gained in enthusiasm. "It will continue Russian-American cooperation on nuclear weapons and represent a beginning to general nuclear disarmament by all nations. All we need do is set the example for the rest of the world."

It required some effort for Stoddard not to roll his eyes skyward. The Administration's propaganda on their suicidal arms reduction policies all but physically sickened him. If last year's Spanish episode were not enough, the Clandestine Services daily provided to the policy-makers mounds of intelligence demonstrating that a militarily weakened United States was the very last thing the world needed. But intelligence is only as good as those who must read it and act upon it, and in time-honored tradition Washington's current power elite chose to disregard information that did not agree with their politics. They mistook words for action and saw implacable enemies as potential friends. In fact, the arms reduction agreement with Shurgin would put America's aging nuclear arsenal at a serious disadvantage in the event of a conflict, leaving the world's 'only superpower' helpless to defend its own interests or those of its allies.

Tekla shot them a suspicious look before continuing, "But it's not irresponsible media speculation that prompted me to call you here this morning. Developments over the past few days lead me to believe something much more serious is afoot."

Capriano interjected, "Do you mean to say the Russians actually did murder Kondratiev?"

"Hell, no!" Tekla was emphatic. "Kondratiev's death was the by-product of a common street crime. The police have confirmed this. But someone is stirring the pot, trying to make it look like something else."

"Please get to the point," said Capriano.

Tekla scowled. "Gladly. Late last week a woman claiming she was a Russian police official sent to investigate the Kondratiev murder approached the Arlington Police. The same evening, both the police detective in charge of the case who had been assigned to watch the woman, as well as someone from my office, an experienced operative who was working with the police, disappeared. Saturday evening this same woman approached me with the claim she had 'captured' my security man and invited me to call her. I suspect whoever it is wants a ransom payment."

Stoddard had assumed a 'politely interested' demeanor, one hand folded over the other on the table, leaning slightly forward, eyes on Tekla. He wasn't about to speak unless spoken to.

"This woman," asked Capriano, "is she actually a Russian police official?"

"No."

"You're certain?"

"Yes, the Russians confirmed that they have no record of her."

"Did you make the call?"

"Hell, no."

Stoddard was disappointed that their attempt to draw Tekla out had failed. In retrospect it was unsurprising that such a man would want to keep his distance. How deeply Tekla was involved in the affair was unknowable at this point. But the fact that he had called in the Directors of the FBI and CIA, presumably to enlist their help in resolving the matter of his 'kidnapped operative' supported the idea that he had nothing to hide.

Capriano said, "So, two men are missing, one of them working for you, and you have a phone number and a ransom demand?"

"That's what it looks like."

"I can see why you called in Mulvaney. Kidnapping is FBI turf. But why are we here?"

Tekla scrutinized them for a few seconds before answering. "To find out what you know about it."

A flush rose all the way from the DCI's collar to his hairline measuring precisely the level of his indignation. "The CIA is in no way involved in what you have described."

Tekla ignored Capriano's denial and turned his attention to Stoddard. "And what about you?"

Without altering his posture, Stoddard replied, "As the Director said, the CIA isn't involved."

Tekla's red-rimmed eyes bored into him for a few seconds longer. "Just a few months ago your man Robert Strachey was running around Spain killing people. You authorized that on your own, I believe."

Capriano cut in. "Terry briefed me fully on that operation, and as you will recall, the President supported it, as well."

"Sure, after you presented him with a *fait accompli*," sneered Tekla.

"Tens of thousands of lives were saved," Stoddard said quietly.

"And what's more, it illustrated the threat of unchecked nuclear proliferation, and the President used it to bash the critics of the arms reduction agreement you're so anxious to see signed," added Capriano.

"May I ask a question?" put in Stoddard mildly.

Tekla's by now permanently hostile gaze swiveled back to him. "Go ahead."

"What would anyone have to gain by these actions?"

Tekla snorted. "To spike the arms reduction treaty, of course."

"And exactly how would snooping into the

circumstances of Kondratiev's death and allegedly kidnapping your man achieve such a thing? Why do you think they're related?"

"I ..." Tekla was nonplussed as he found himself struggling to come up with a reasonable answer. The Intelligence Czar suddenly looked like a guilty man caught in a contradiction.

Stoddard pressed his momentary advantage. "What you seem to be saying is that what Kondratiev claimed to know actually had implications that threatened the agreement."

Tekla went white as he realized that he had talked himself into a corner. "That's ridiculous."

"Is it? You've started me really thinking about this now, Brian. Kondratiev's murder on the eve of Shurgin's visit would have been convenient in such a case, wouldn't it? And why so much concern about this allegedly counterfeit Russian policewoman? In fact, what was so interesting about Kondratiev's death that you sent one of your own men to investigate?"

Tekla's lower lip began to tremble. He finally managed to splutter the ultimate Washington cop-out, "That's a White House need-to-know matter. This meeting is over." He stood, somewhat shakily Stoddard thought, and rushed out of the room.

Capriano called, "Nice seeing you, too, Brian," to Tekla's fast disappearing backside then looked at his DNCS and chortled. "That was beautiful, Terry.

You completely turned the tables on the bastard. His fishing expedition landed a shark!"

On the way back to their car Stoddard thought about what Tekla might do next. The man was desperate, and desperate men can be unpredictable. This begged the question of whether he should tell Capriano what was going on. He decided again that it would unfair to the DCI to do so. If things went wrong it was best if Capriano had complete deniability while Stoddard accepted any opprobrium. Capriano was an honorable man with a lot of friends in Washington, and he would protect the Agency. Stoddard would take the fall. And regrettably, he concluded, so would Bob Strachey.

As they were driving away, Stoddard's Blackberry vibrated in his pocket. The caller i.d. was that of a man from Stoddard's and the Agency's distant past, a man who lived in Brussels. He brought the phone to his ear. "Hello?"

The satellite connection clearly carried the tension in Lawrence Nelson's voice over the four thousand miles separating them. "I need help."

Stoddard shot a sidewise glance at the Director who had turned toward him with a quizzical look. "It's my daughter," he managed to smile at Capriano. "What's up, dear?" he said into the phone.

"You're not alone."

"No, but is there a problem?"

"Yes.   A very serious one; Vicky Kondratieva showed up on our doorstep last night, but I think she's been kidnapped and maybe killed. Terry, she left something incredible behind. I'm on the run."

The name sent shockwaves through Stoddard's system.   The Kondratiev affair was growing like Topsy and so was the circle of death that surrounded it.   For Capriano's benefit Stoddard arranged his features into a genial expression. "Where are you?"

"We just crossed the border into France at Valenciennes. I'll be in Paris in about two hours. Getting lost in a big city is the best bet I have at the moment."

I'll call you back in a little while, and we can discuss it."

"Don't wait too long."

Stoddard closed the connection and slipped the Blackberry into his pocket.

"Anything wrong?" inquired Capriano.

"Sounds like boyfriend trouble to me," smiled Stoddard.

"I know all about that."   Capriano had two daughters of his own.

And Pavel Kondratiev had a daughter, Viktoria. The mystery of her disappearance was at least partially resolved. She'd run to Brussels, contacted Lawrence Nelson, and left something 'incredible' with him.   Nelson wasn't the sort of man who ran from nothing or called things incredible that weren't.

As soon as the DCI's car deposited them in Langley's underground garage Stoddard headed for his own car, regretfully turning down the DCI's invitation to lunch in the Executive Dining Room with the excuse that he had to attend to his daughter's crisis.

He confirmed that Ramsay and his wife were in their room at the Ritz-Carlton, and called Strachey to instruct him to meet him there as soon as possible. Thirty minutes later the group assembled in Ramsay's suite.

Stoddard called Nelson and learned that he and his wife had narrowly escaped what was certainly Russian pursuit in Brussels and were still running from it. Their exit from the rear of their building had not been detected, and they were driving a rented car towards Paris.

"We have about an hour and a half before they reach Paris," Stoddard informed the group. "Any ideas about how we can help them? We can't use CIA resources."

"I have a hidey hole in Paris," offered Ramsay. "Send him there."

Stoddard listened to Ramsay's instructions and punched in the number for Nelson's cell phone, which was answered immediately.

"Larry, we have a safe place for you to go to ground."

CHAPTER 30

"Who is Lawrence Nelson?" Strachey had never heard the name.

"Do you remember him?" Stoddard directed the question at Ewan.

"I think I saw him once or twice in the hallways. He left a few years after we joined up, didn't he?"

"Yes. Larry was an early recruit to the Agency, practically one of the founders. My father brought him in, as a matter of fact. I've known him since I was a boy."

Ewan recalled something. "He was Angleton's man."

"He certainly was. He was one of Angleton's most loyal boys to the end."

Strachey perked up. "James Jesus Angleton, the man who almost destroyed the old Soviet Bloc Division because he thought it was infested with Soviet agents?"

Stoddard's head sank beneath the weight of painful memories. "The very same, but that's not the way it really was. The problem was a defector named Yuriy Ivanovich Nosenko."

"Nosenko?   But Angleton wrongfully accused

Nosenko of being a double agent, locked him up, and tortured him. Nosenko was eventually cleared of all of Angleton's accusations and rehabilitated. I heard him speak in the Agency auditorium several years ago."

"What you've heard," said Stoddard, "is the official history of that case concocted to discredit Angleton's position so we could start running ops against the Soviets again. The fact of the matter is that all of the information Nosenko ever provided consisted of outright lies, exaggerations, or information already known to us from other sources and defectors. Angleton had plenty of sound reasons to doubt the man's *bona fides*. Dick Helms, who was Director when Nosenko was brought to the United States, later told Congress that the question of Nosenko's credibility 'hangs like an incubus in the air.' Do you remember when it was that Nosenko defected?"

"Sixty-three or Sixty-four, wasn't it? A few years before my time," answered Strachey.

"January 1964," Stoddard confirmed. "Almost two months to the day after the Kennedy assassination in Dallas. One of the first things he told his handlers was that the KGB had nothing to do with the assassination."

"Do you have a different opinion, Terry?" asked Ewan.

"If Nosenko really was sent over by the KGB to tell that story, it's fair to speculate on their motives.

"You think it's possible that the KGB killed Kennedy?" Strachey was incredulous.

"It would have been an insane risk, a risk that could well have triggered a nuclear war at the time." Stoddard's eyes had a far-away look as he pondered the question that had haunted the Clandestine Services for decades, driven friends apart, and forced Lawrence Nelson to leave the Agency entirely.

"That's not an answer," put in Ramsay.

Stoddard broke out of his reverie. "You're right. It's not an answer. The question of Nosenko's *bona* fides still bedevils us even after all these years, and if his defection was part of a KGB deception operation as Nelson believes, we may soon learn things we'll wish we didn't know."

CHAPTER 31

Had it been possible, Ewan Ramsay would have resettled in Paris. His affinity for the city, its architecture, lifestyle, and amazing people was profound. But after all the years running operations through and out of the country he was too well known to risk all but short sojourns there, despite the benign attitude of the French Intelligence Services. And the memories were bittersweet. He retained good and trusted French friends, but his best friend, counselor, and sometimes protector, the seemingly invincible Volodya Smetanin, had succumbed to old age and a weakened heart several years earlier.

Volodya found himself in the role of a warrior early in life and progressed from killing German soldiers for the British in the deserts of North Africa through years of clandestine battle with the Communist oppressors of his homeland, Russia. It was this magnificent old man who arranged the first contact between Ewan and Sasha, a fateful meeting that took place on a cold winter's evening in a coffee house in Vienna that set them on a path that changed both their lives forever. At that first encounter Ewan did not know that Sasha was in fact a member of the Mossad's kidon unit and could never have imagined that within a year, he too would become part of that elite organization, the only non-Israeli, non-Jew ever to have done so.

Volodya directed his secret networks and ratlines into the Soviet Union from an ancient apartment in Paris's Sixth Arrondissement at No. 13 Rue de Tournon, a quiet, narrow street that began as Rue de Seine leading south from the Boulevard St. Germain toward the Senat building at the foot of the magnificent Luxembourg Gardens. Upon his death he bequeathed the apartment to Ewan, whom he had come to regard as a son. The place had been a refuge for the expatriate American during the most difficult period of his life when he realized that he could never resume his old life in the United States and must remain forever an exile. He maintained it now, unchanged, as a sort of shrine to his deceased friend and mentor.

*****

Before entering the city proper, Lawrence and Nancy Nelson abandoned their rented car at Charles DeGaulle Airport. If the Russians could hack into the rental company files they could pinpoint their location the moment the car was turned in. They rode a taxi to the city center where they switched to the Metro, finally exiting at the Odéon station and walking the short distance to Rue de Tournon where they rang for the concierge and identified themselves as *'amis de Harry,'* in accordance with Stoddard's instructions. Madame Foucault lived in a ground floor apartment inside the small courtyard, just beyond the *porte cochère*, where she had reigned as concierge for over three decades, watching comings and goings and minding her boxes of colorful geraniums. Ewan now paid her to maintain Volodya's apartment and serve as gatekeeper for occasional visitors.

From a car parked across the street a man observed the Nelsons enter the building and placed a long-distance call on his cell phone.

*****

It had been a long time since he had had to convince anyone that he was right, with the exception of his wife, and the unaccustomed debate was beginning to frustrate Ewan. They were in the middle of another strategy session, and he was determined to have his way.

"I don't think it's a good idea for Strachey to go to Paris to extract the Nelsons," he said. "It will directly involve the CIA if things go upside down, and that's what you must avoid, Terry." The action had shifted from Washington to Paris, and Ewan wanted to be where the action was. He suspected that Stoddard's argument had more to do with the difference in ages between him and the younger CIA man. But they were burning time, and the flight to Paris would leave Dulles in a few hours.

"But," said Stoddard, "it's logical, Strachey is unknown in Paris, and no one knows that you and Sasha are here in Washington. That leaves each of you freer to operate. We'll come up with a cover story for Strachey's travel."

"With all due respect, Terry, I know my way around Paris. I'm carrying a French passport, it's my turf, and they're in my goddamned apartment. I'm going. Sasha will remain here to help out."

"Oh, no I won't." Sasha knew the way he thought and had guessed exactly what her husband was thinking. He wanted to be where the action was, and he didn't want her in the way of any of the trouble he normally attracted. Ewan knew she would not be deterred. Where he went, she would go, too.

An exasperated Stoddard threw up his hands. These people were free agents, after all, even if he had recruited them. And Ramsay was right about keeping his hand concealed. "OK, you win." He looked ruefully at Strachey. "Sorry, Bob."

Strachey gave no sign that the decision troubled him in any way. "No problem, boss. But," he furrowed his brow and turned his attention to Ewan and Sasha who already had risen to their feet, "be careful. We've had to rely on insecure commo with the Nelsons."

*****

Later, as the Air France A-340 soared away from Dulles, Sasha turned to her husband with a mischievous grin. "Thought you'd get away for some derring do all by yourself didn't you, old man."

Ewan grimaced at the appellation, considered a few appropriately barbed retorts and immediately discarded them. "I thought I made a logical case." It was great to have a younger wife until she started calling you granddad.

"An excuse to go up against the Russians one more time, you mean," and she was right. After nearly twenty years together, he was like an open book to her.

"If it goes right, we won't see any Russians." He knew he hadn't convinced her.

"Since when have we been able to count on things going right?"

Ewan ordered a single malt scotch from the First Class flight attendant and a steak for dinner, and then stared out the window. Sasha selected something that sounded Middle Eastern. They would eat and try to get enough sleep to see them through the day ahead.

CHAPTER 32

The Russian Embassy in Paris occupies an entire city block on the far western edge of the city in the swank Sixteenth Arrondissement. The gleaming white ultramodern structure houses on its securely guarded uppermost floor a quiet room bathed in the glow of exotic electronics. This is the nest of the Special Communications and Information Service of the FSB, *"Spetsvyaz'"* (Служба специальной связи и информации, Спецсвязь России). The Service both guarantees the security of secret diplomatic and intelligence communications and eavesdrops on the communications of others, and this room in Paris was one of its most important listening posts.

Modern communications intercept systems are omnivorous and their targeting must be prioritized lest the sheer volume of information overwhelm available analytical resources, and thus the Paris operation had a list of priority collection targets. Lawrence Nelson's home and cell phones had been on the list for years, and his recent conversations with Terry Stoddard were snatched from the French microwave towers even before they were bounced off the transatlantic communications satellites.

The transcripts were forwarded to Moscow Center, triggering a high level encrypted telephone call over a heavily armored underground cable to the Senat building which housed the office of President

Shurgin.

Not long thereafter priority orders were dispatched to the Paris, Brussels, and Washington *rezidenturas* of the SVR where hard men received their orders. The reasons for these orders were not shared with them, but such men are trained not to ask questions.

*****

Lawrence and Nancy Nelson settled down to wait in the cozy third floor apartment at 13 Rue de Tournon. It was a veritable museum of pre-revolutionary Russian art with its walls covered with precious Russian Orthodox icons, paintings and antique weapons. The furnishings were quaintly old world with overstuffed chairs and settees, their arms protected by hand knitted antimacassars that likely pre-dated the Bolshevik Revolution. The living room would have been filled with light had they dared to open the shutters that shielded the three tall windows facing the street.

They had very little to unpack, so Nancy headed for the compact, but well-equipped kitchen and was delighted to find it fully stocked. Lawrence discreetly pulled a shutter aside a few inches and scanned the street below where nearly every parking space was occupied. There was a clatter of dishes from the kitchen, and Nancy called, "Come on in here. I'm making coffee and a snack."

There was a small table in the center of the kitchen, and he saw that Nancy had thrown open the windows that overlooked the inner courtyard, filling the room with fresh air as evening approached and the shadows outside lengthened. He settled into a worn wooden chair at the table and placed the leather valise he carried on the floor beside him. While Nancy set out an array of toasted baguette, creamery butter, Camembert, dried sausage, and jams and busied herself with the coffee, he withdrew the file folder from the valise and spread it on the table before him, careful to do as little damage as possible to the yellowing onionskin pages.

The pistol remained in the bottom of the valise.

"You need to eat now, Larry, and get some rest. It was a very long drive, and I know you're exhausted. Put that away until you feel better." Nancy stood behind him and massaged his neck and shoulders that ached from the hours of driving.

He looked around at her with a wan smile. There would be no sleep for him tonight. He was tired and sore, it was true, but the documents might well contain all the answers to a mystery that had destroyed his professional life and dogged him for almost half a century. Rest was out of the question, but coffee, and lots of it, would definitely be needed. He carefully set the file aside as Nancy poured him a steaming frothy mug from the French press and they both tucked into the meal, their first since their hasty departure from Brussels.

*****

As the Nelson's were finishing their impromptu meal Sasha and Ewan were just boarding their Air France flight to Paris. The ocean crossing would take nearly seven hours, putting them into the City of Lights at 5:50 AM the next day, and Ewan hoped the precautions he had taken would suffice until their arrival.

CHAPTER 33

Outside on Rue de Tournon, the watcher waited as the shadows cast by the buildings on his side of the street crawled up the façades opposite until they cloaked them in darkness. Streetlamps flickered on as the lights were extinguished in the cashmere specialty shop next door to No. 13 and the other small shops along the narrow street. In the distance a pharmacy sign glowed greenly at the intersection with Rue Saint Sulpice. Cars pulled out of parking spaces immediately to be replaced by others as the residents of the quartier returned from work and hurried into their buildings for the aperitifs and evening meals of the French middle class. It was Monday, and the nightlife even in the livelier Latin Quarter a short distance away to the east was muted after the week-end. Still the watcher remained alert in his car. His eyes regularly scanned the darkened street in both directions.

Alain de Blottière was an often published expert on international terrorism and criminal gangs. He had first met Ewan Ramsay through the good offices of their mutual friend and comrade in arms Volodya Smetanin. The occasion had been an urgent need for someone reliable to travel to Moscow to meet an untested Russian intelligence source. Under the guise of professor of criminology at the University of Paris, de Blottière was a skilled clandestine operator who worked occasionally with the Dirección de Surveillance de Territoire (DST), France's internal security service.

The professional relationship between the two men grew, thanks in no small part to Volodya, into a personal friendship, and Ewan had no compunctions about calling his friend into service on occasions such as this. So it was that Alain de Blottière, sometime professor, sometime clandestine operative, full-time friend waited in his car across the street from 13 Rue de Tournon armed with a thermos of now lukewarm coffee, several discarded sandwich wrappers, a bottle with a tight lid for bladder relief, and a Glock 20. Even at this hour he could see a single light burning in Volodya's apartment, visible through the slits in the shutters. It was three o'clock in the morning.

They first appeared as indistinct shadows moving on the sidewalk periodically outlined against the dim nightlights of closed shop windows as they passed them. There were three at first and then only two. Within minutes the latter two darkly clad men hunched over the lock at the porte cochère door of No. 13 and forced it open with what looked like a crowbar. De Blottière cursed under his breath as his heretofore quiet, if uncomfortable vigil suddenly became a lot more interesting. Not for the first time he reflected on the prescience of Ewan Ramsay who had called to request his services before boarding his plane in Washington.

De Blottière punched into his cell phone the number of the apartment phone and was answered after several rings by a querulous male voice. "Yes?"

"Mr. Nelson, I am a 'friend of Harry's.' There was a pause, and de Blottière hoped the man recalled the safety protocol.

Then, "Yes? Is there a message?"

"Don't be alarmed, but two possibly armed men have just entered your building and are probably on their way to your door. Are you armed?"

"Yes."

"Take no action unless absolutely necessary. You may have noticed that the apartment door is armored. Please make certain all the deadbolts are in place and retreat to the bedroom. They won't be able to get through that door without explosives. I'll make certain your visitors don't overstay their welcome."

"Understood," Nelson sounded like a pro.

Satisfied, De Blottière broke the connection and immediately punched the numbers 121 on his cell phone, the European equivalent of 911 in the U.S. He reported in a breathless voice that he was a resident of No. 13 Rue de Tournon, and two men had just broken into the building and they appeared to be armed.

The local Commissariat de Police on near-by Rue

Saint Sulpice would be notified, but the French Police de Secours was populated by phlegmatic, unimaginative people, and de Blottière knew they were unlikely to be overly excited by his call. Nevertheless, they would dispatch a squad of five or six gendarmes who carried sidearms to investigate. The question was how long it would take for them to arrive.

De Blottière's Glock 20 was in the glove compartment with a full magazine of fifteen ten-millimeter rounds, plus one in the chamber. These cartridges were more powerful than a .45 ACP or .357 Magnum. If you were hit by one you would go down. But violent actions always were followed by unpleasant consequences and were to be avoided, if at all possible, except in the movies. The occupants of the apartment were secure behind the armored door installed by the ever prudent Volodya decades earlier. The men who had broken into the building would be treated as felons by the police, and their lookout was unlikely to do anything other than warn his comrades when the police arrived. The intruders would have a big problem, de Blottière would be in no way involved, and the apartment's temporary occupants would remain safe. Satisfied that he had all bases covered, the Frenchman sat back to watch the fun.

Five minutes passed before klaxons sounded, softly in the distance at first, but rising in decibels as they drew nearer. The lookout emerged from his niche and looked in the direction of Boulevard Saint

Germain.   Within moments it became clear that the police were barreling up the Rue de Tournon, and the lookout was already speaking into what de Blottière assumed was a walkie-talkie when the blue flashing lights of a police van appeared and the van screeched to a stop in front of No. 13 to disgorge squad of uniformed policemen.   They immediately discovered the broken porte cochère lock and entered the premises with weapons drawn.

Lights came on in the windows of No. 13 and neighboring buildings as residents were awakened by the noise.   Outside, de Blottière watched as the lookout left the area at a brisk walk.   Ten minutes later the police emerged with two men in custody whom they bundled into the back of the van and drove away.   The next days' papers would carry the story of the unexplained break-in by two armed members of the Russian Embassy staff who had been released to the custody of the Ambassador and hurriedly returned to Moscow.

De Blottière phoned Nelson to inform him that the emergency was over.   His watch told him it was 3:30 AM.   The plane carrying Ramsay and his wife would arrive at Charles de Gaulle in another two hours or so, and de Blottière settled down into the car seat in a fruitless effort to ease his aching back. He vowed to sleep straight through the coming day.

CHAPTER 34

It was mid-morning in Washington, and Brian Tekla sat immobile at his desk, lost in thought. Terrence Stoddard had obviously lied to him, and the Russians had been thwarted in Paris. Tekla's confidence was cracking as he sensed disaster rushing pell mell in his direction. As if to punctuate the worst day of his life, before him lay the official missive from the Russian Embassy. Couched in terms of diplomatic nicety was the unwelcome news that the President of the Russian Federation, Vitaliy Mikhailovich Shurgin, must regretfully postpone his visit to Washington due to a temporary indisposition.

This news would throw the White House into confusion and the voracious Washington press corps would set to digging out the backstory. Spin all they liked, the U.S. President's staff could not take advantage of this crisis. The arms reduction and control treaty with the Russians was the cornerstone of the Administration's strategy to reduce weapons of mass destruction worldwide. It was nonsense, of course, because it would serve no purpose but to weaken American military capabilities and anti-missile shield options while strengthening those of her enemies. And this was precisely the aim of Brian Tekla who, like his father before him, served Russian intelligence.

With the rise of Fascism many idealistic young men and women felt morally obligated to fight it, and a left-leaning professor had recruited Tekla's father to the Communist cause in the '30's. Several such ideologically motivated young men had infiltrated British Intelligence, but Adam Tekla was an American, and he joined the O.S.S. during the war and stayed on to help the fledgling Central Intelligence Agency get off the ground. That he had never been discovered was testimony to the assiduousness of Soviet intelligence, well-practiced in the art of deception. The early compromises of CIA operations were laid at the feet of the equally guilty Kim Philby, and the Russians mounted several subsequent deception operations designed to safeguard Adam Tekla's well-being.

Adam Tekla passed his ideology and the ways of deception and betrayal on to his son. When Brian entered the CIA he had never met a Russian intelligence officer because his father even in retirement continued to act as his handler until his death. Brian's CIA career had stalled when he was shunted to the analytical side of the house, and the opportunity to become part of the new DNI was a godsend. He did not have to hide his strong leftist leanings in the prevailing political climate and was a natural to become part of the new administration's staff. For the Russians he ceased to be a counterintelligence source and became their prime agent of influence in Washington.

Everything his father stood for and everything Brian

Tekla hoped to accomplish was wrapped up in the treaty that would once and for all place the feckless Americans in the second rank of world powers. The threat analyses he prepared related to the treaty were well received because their conclusions matched the well-known preconceptions of the White House staff and the President. Once signed and ratified, the treaty would guarantee Russia's ability to forestall any American initiative to install missile defenses in Europe and permit her to stare down the United States in any confrontation, and President Shurgin's goal of a resurgent Russia as the dominant power in Europe would be realized.

Now, all because of the malign intent of a long retired KGB General and the perfidy of Terrence Stoddard and God knew who else, the entire enterprise was in jeopardy.

It had seemed so simple. Kill Kondratiev and find the documents he had somehow stolen from the KGB archives. Like that packrat Vasiliy Mitrokhin nearly twenty years earlier, Kondratiev had secreted a cache of highly classified KGB documents and smuggled them out of Russia. They contained a secret so deadly that history would be changed if it came to light.

Tekla himself had been shocked when told about it, but his loyalties were set in concrete. It was not hard to convince the gullible Buchalter that Kondratiev must die. He had explained to the security man that the old Soviet General had to die 'in the interests of national security.' Buchalter was the sort of mindless patriot who didn't waste a lot of time asking questions, especially when his orders came directly from someone in the White House.

The confidence of his Russian masters in his ability to bring the American side to the table flattered Tekla, and he had performed brilliantly – until now. Shurgin was not about to appear in Washington until the problem was resolved once and for all, and the Russians had told Tekla pointedly that it was his job to hold things together in the meantime. He felt assaulted from all sides, and the culprit was that mendacious CIA bastard Terrence Stoddard.

His Russian Embassy contact, Lev Chertkov, had called early that morning to request a breakfast meeting. Chertkov was a high-ranking SVR officer under cover in the Embassy's political section and could thus meet openly with Tekla. Ostensibly they were discussing arrangements for the arms agreement signing, but in reality the Russian was giving orders to the American.

The meeting took place in the bright, airy breakfast room of the Mayflower Hotel, an easy walk from the White House and one of Tekla's favorite venues, but Chertkov's report on the failed attack on the apartment in Paris and his advance warning that President Shurgin would postpone his visit completely soured Tekla's stomach, as well as his mood. To add insult to injury, Chertkov then informed him of the intercepted phone conversation between Nelson and Stoddard.

"One of your jobs was to control the CIA," Chertkov intoned, and Tekla thought he detected a hint of accusation.

His appetite suddenly gone, Tekla tossed his napkin on top of his half-eaten breakfast and retorted, "I did have it under control. I even talked to Stoddard and Capriano. They denied any CIA involvement."

"What did you expect them to say? You need to get it under control, and quickly. There is too much at stake."

"But what can I do?" Frustration strained his voice into a higher key.

"Don't whine, Brian," said Chertkov. "We don't expect you to shoot anyone. Just be sure you handle the political side, and we'll take care of the rest."

"What do you intend to do?"

"We cannot permit loose ends."

"Stoddard?"

Chertkov nodded. "Stoddard must be dealt with."

"But won't that just arouse more suspicion?"

"The way I have it planned it'll kick up a lot of dust and divert attention in another direction."

CHAPTER 35

Even with a 6:00 AM arrival it still cost Ewan and Sasha nearly an hour and a half to conquer Paris traffic and penetrate to the city center. Alain de Blottière groaned with relief when they stepped out of a taxi in front of No. 13 Rue de Tournon. He painfully unwound himself from his car and stretched to work out the kinks in his back before crossing the street to greet them.

Both saw him coming and smiled a welcome. "My Lord, Alain," said Ewan, "*quelle gueule de bois!* You look like you're coming down from a month-long bender!"

De Blottière rubbed the growth of dark stubble on his cheek with the palm of his hand, severely embarrassed under the gaze of the beautiful Sasha. "I'm not as young as I once was, and sitting in a car all night keeping my eyes open with the help of cold coffee isn't easy or as much fun as it used to be."

Upon hearing the Frenchman's story of the previous evening's break-in Ewan was nonplussed. "That apartment should be the safest place in the world. How did they know where to find them?"

"You have a leak somewhere, my friend," said de Blottière.

Such a conclusion was obvious, and Ewan shot him a pained expression. "Shite! They can't stay here any longer. I'd hoped to keep them off the radar until we could sort things out."

"What's this all about?" asked de Blottière. Ewan had not yet briefed the Frenchman on the Kondratiev affair, only asked him the favor of babysitting the apartment.

"I'm not sure you want to know, Alain. I still don't really have a clue myself, but I hope the people up in the apartment can shed some light."

"Well, you go up and ask them," said de Blottière. "I'm going home to a hot shower and at least twelve hours' sleep."

"You know, Alain, I've always admired your ability to tamp down your curiosity."

The Frenchman flashed him a rueful grin. "It's just that I know you too well, Ramsay. If you need me again, you'll call. By the way, you owe me a fine dinner at a restaurant of my choice." With a tired wave he slumped across the street to his car and drove away.

The two of them passed through the wooden double doors, still sagging open from the broken lock, and climbed the three flights of steps to the apartment, where Ewan rang the bell several times before sliding his keys into the multiple locks. As soon as they were in the entrance hall an older, but apparently quite robust, man emerged from the living room. His robustness was emphasized by a .45 pointed determinedly in their direction. "Who are you?"

Ewan dropped their bags and raised his hands quickly, and Sasha followed suit. "I'm a friend of Harry's," said Ewan. "As a matter of fact, I am Harry, and this is my apartment."

"So you say."

"I believe you spoke with Terry Stoddard, and he in turn gave you directions to this apartment – my apartment. Did I mention that?"

An equally robust older woman came down the hallway from the bedroom. "Oh, for pity's sake, Larry, he gave you the parole."

Ewan liked the fact that she used the old CIA term for a coded recognition phrase.

Nelson lowered his pistol and scrutinized them from under shaggy brows. "Who are you?" he repeated.

"I'm Ewan Ramsay, and this is my wife, Sasha. Terry Stoddard called us in to investigate General Kondratiev's murder."

"I thought you said your name was Harry."

"That's a long, sad story, and we really don't have time for reminiscences now. We have to get you out of here to a safer location."

"Where?"

"I don't know yet."

"That's encouraging, and if last night is any indication of your security measures, we're in deep trouble."

"That's another problem.   You're certain you weren't followed here?"

Nelson bristled and gave him a withering look. "I was running counter-surveillance ops before you were weaned. No one followed us here. We lost them in Brussels."

There were only five people besides the Nelsons and de Blottière who knew the location of the apartment. Ewan trusted the Frenchman absolutely, and besides, de Blottière had no idea who the Nelsons were or that they were in any way involved in the Kondratiev affair. It was inconceivable that Stoddard or his people had betrayed them.

"The phone call," said Sasha suddenly. "It had to be the call for help to Stoddard. We sometimes forget that the Russians have good SIGINT capabilities, too. Strachey warned us about this."

"You may well be right," said Ewan. "Whatever it was, we have to get out of here now. They could come back."

He cursed himself for not having rented a car at the airport, and after a few moments' thought he said, "Sasha, look after things here. I'm going to rent a car, but not in this neighborhood. I'll hoof it to the *Place de la Concorde* and use the agency at the Crillon. Get everything packed and ready. We'll leave as soon as I return."

He hurried down the spiral wooden staircase and after informing Madame Foucault that the apartment would soon be vacant again, set off at a brisk walk toward the *Place de la Concorde*. He calculated that it would take him fifteen minutes to reach the Crillon hotel and another twenty to make arrangements for the car using his alias French documents. He should be back to Rue de Tournon inside an hour, and he had until then to come up with an escape and evasion plan. The Russians had killed once, maybe twice, and tried to kill again for whatever it was that Lawrence Nelson now possessed. He did not doubt that they would try again.

CHAPTER 36

After Ewan's departure Sasha went into the apartment's central hallway and removed a painting from the wall, revealing a safe from which she retrieved several items. Nancy Nelson gasped when she saw what they were.

First came a pair of Glock 38's that, despite the appellation carried an eight-round magazine of .45 G.A.P. bullets. Ewan and Sasha had long used the nine millimeter Glock 17, but the heavier punch of the .45 appealed to them despite the smaller magazine capacity. An enemy might still be able to fight after a nine mil hit, but a .45 would knock him on his ass, and he'd stay down. Along with the guns were two custom made leather shoulder holsters, extra magazines and several boxes of ammunition. Next came two Ruger LCP's, small .380 caliber "pocket" pistols fitted with laser sights, and matching ankle holsters that also contained sheaths for knives, one of which Sasha immediately strapped to her leg. She placed everything else but one of the Glocks into a leather shoulder pack and returned to the living room, where she opened the shutters on one of the windows and stood watching the street.

Over her shoulder she said to the Nelsons, "You'd best pack your belongings now and stand by to leave. We have about an hour before Ewan returns with a car.   And Mr. Nelson, please give me your cell phone."

She immediately removed battery and SIM card and broke the SIM card in two.

Like her husband, Sasha was chagrined by the unforeseen Paris developments. Their information-gathering mission now had gained the added dimension of a rescue operation against unknown odds. She didn't expect their adversaries to give up without a fight and quite probably they had the apartment under surveillance, which meant that she and Ewan also had been exposed.

They should be enjoying long walks across the moors and cozy evenings in Irish pubs instead of putting their lives on the line in a desperate struggle triggered by the murder of a KGB General on the far away streets of Arlington, Virginia. Under her breath she roundly cursed the CIA for pulling Ewan out of retirement for this fool's errand.

She could hear the Nelsons talking in the back bedroom as they packed their belongings and wondered if they really possessed the key to unlocking the mystery of Kondratiev's death.

Forty-five minutes later and three stories below in the street an electric blue car pulled to the curb. Ewan stepped out and looked up at the window. Time to go.

Transferring the Nelsons out of the building and into the car could be dangerous, and Ewan had pulled as close to the entrance as possible. Nancy Nelson looked nervous while her husband had a determined expression and a hand in his coat pocket where Sasha knew he gripped his pistol. The old boy had grit!

Sasha preceded them down the stairs and out into the *porte cochère* where the wooden door still sagged open from the broken lock. Ewan had both doors on the passenger side of the car open. When he nodded, the three of them scurried the few steps across the sidewalk into the car, and they surged away from the curb.

"Interesting choice of vehicle," she said, commenting on the color. The car immediately told Sasha that her husband had a plan. Electric blue was not the ideal color to elude surveillance, and upon seeing it she guessed that Ewan was not thinking about escape. Her husband was not a man to avoid confrontation but rather one who sought it because it offered the most efficient means to resolve conflict. If you can see your enemy, you can eliminate him. For Ewan, confrontation was not a tactic, it was the whole game to win or lose. She had fought at his side many times, had saved his life and had hers saved by him, but time was an implacable enemy that was slowly eating away at his abilities. She loved him deeply and had learned to trust his instincts, but at 66 he was neither as fast as he used to be nor as he imagined he still was. Men, she had discovered, in their mind's eye were always 25 years old in spite of abundant external evidence to the contrary. Now she sensed that Ewan, far from avoiding danger, relished the idea of seeking it out one more time. He was still strong, still ran three miles every other day, and she felt guilty that she could even for a moment doubt him. Nevertheless, she was worried.

His lean, handsome profile creased into a familiar grin. "It's an Audi S6," he told her with a hint of boyish exuberance. "The Crillon offers an excellent selection of luxury cars. This one has a V-10 engine, handles like a sports car, and is actually quite comfortable."

"What do you have in mind?"

"We'll take a little spin in the country to see if they had the apartment staked out, as I expect they would, and whether they put a tail on us."

Ewan drove them north out of the city and onto the Autoroute du Nord in the direction of Picardie. Sasha guessed their destination. "Compiègne?"

"You're quick, darling. Good guess." He checked the rear view mirror. "And by the way, we have two cars following us."

CHAPTER 37

Ewan's plan was not to evade surveillance but rather to lure it into a trap. If a pack of wolves is on your trail, best to stand and fight before your resources are exhausted and you are run to ground. For this reason he had chosen a brightly colored car that his pursuers would have no trouble keeping in sight, but a car nimble and powerful enough to outrun them if necessary and control the chase. Their pursuers were driving Mercedes E Classes, nice transportation but no match for the sleek Audi sports sedan. The extra power and better handling would come into play when he sprang his trap. The only uncertainty was how many opponents they would face when the time came.

Another advantage was the fact that the battleground would be of his choosing. The Forêt de Compiegne, Compiegne Forest, was intimately familiar both to him and Sasha from numerous week-ends spent picnicking there and wandering its many paths. The forest covered nearly 35,000 acres that spread like an emerald fan north, east, and south of the historic town of Compiegne and was crisscrossed with narrow lanes, forestry and hiking trails.

The Autoroute du Nord leading out of Paris was a toll road with few exits, which would allow the surveillants to feel confident during the first stage.

The fun would begin when Ewan turned off toward the forest and they had to narrow the gap.

He turned off the Autoroute and stopped at the toll booth noting in the rearview mirror the two Mercedes pulling to a stop in the toll plaza some distance behind them. With several kilometers to cover before entering the forest proper he had several choices of route; it was important to remain in populated areas as long as possible for the time being, so he headed toward Lacroix-Saint-Quen after which he would switch to the D85, the two-lane main east-west road through the forest. He needed to be where the trees grew thickest for his plan to work.

At this point surveillance would realize that they were exposed, and they might decide to take advantage of the secluded area to run them off the road. That was where the Audi's superiority would come into play and permit Ewan to keep the upper hand.

He explained what was going to happen to his passengers as Sasha checked the weapons, her face set in grim lines.

In the rear seat Nancy Nelson said, "Oh, my God, Larry! What have we gotten ourselves into?"

In the mirror Nelson's face betrayed no fear, only the calm façade of a trained field officer. "It'll be ok, honey," he said. "Just do as Ewan said. Get to cover and stay out of sight."

The forest began to close in on both sides after they cleared the outskirts of Lacroix-Saint-Quen, scrubby at first but then becoming denser with trees and undergrowth still laden with summer foliage. The two Mercedes began to close the gap between them as Ewan had known they would. He depressed the Audi's gas pedal and the car accelerated smoothly, quickly reaching 120 kilometers per hour, and the Russians did likewise. Everything now depended on his ability to outpace the two Mercedes and beat them to the 'S' curve that lay some five kilometers ahead. Even if the Mercedes could match his speed on the straightaway they could not match the Audi's acceleration. The Audi effortlessly swept them to 170 kilometers per hour, and Ewan was gratified to see the gap widen to a useable distance as the oaks, beeches, and birches became blurs on both sides of the road.

As soon as they cleared the curve and the two Mercedes were out of sight, Ewan downshifted dramatically, throwing everyone against the seatbelts, and drifted the rear of the car hard to the left so they faced the forest on the right side of the road; he then gunned the engine to shoot them at high speed into a narrow dirt lane that led deep into the forest. After two hundred meters they came to a clearing where Ewan slid the Audi to a halt near the tree line on the right.

Following Ewan's instructions, the Nelson's tumbled out and scrambled behind some large rocks just inside the tree line before Ewan swung the car to the other side of the clearing where Sasha leapt out and took cover. Through the trees Ewan saw the Mercedes speed past the entrance to the lane. It wouldn't take them long to figure out what had happened. He pulled the car to the back of the clearing and got out.

Keeping low, he made his way through the trees in the direction of the main road. Already he could hear the two surveillance cars returning to the entrance to the lane. Lying prone behind the trunk of a large fallen tree, he watched and waited.

The two cars stopped and sat for a moment with their motors idling. Ewan had purposely parked the Audi in line of sight to the main road where its bright blue hue would show through the trees, like a light attracting a moth. Now he expected the Russians to fan out and move toward the clearing, perhaps sending someone to flank their quarry. As anticipated, there were two men in each car, and the four stood together in the road to confer shortly before moving into the woods. All had weapons drawn. They weren't looking for a polite chat.

It was hard to guess what the Russians anticipated, but they must know the Nelsons were well into their seventies and would not expect them to possess a great deal of mobility or put up much of a fight. Also, they had not yet encountered armed resistance and so, while proceeding cautiously, would feel confident that they had the upper hand in numbers and firepower. Had they known more about the man and woman escorting the Nelsons, they might have hesitated.

One of the men, short with a bull neck, circled farther out – the flanker Ewan had expected. He lay behind the trunk and waited until the man was five paces beyond. Ewan had drawn his knife from its ankle sheath and now moved silently forward and in an almost balletic motion rose and wrapped his arm around the Russian's neck while simultaneously plunging the six-inch blade into his kidney. The blow caused instantaneous shock, and the Russian collapsed to the ground without a sound. He would be dead within minutes. Ewan retraced his steps to circle behind the remaining three pursuers.

They were by now too far ahead for Ewan to repeat the knife attack, so he drew the Glock 38 as he matched their speed. They moved forward in a single echelon, about ten yards separating them, and now the two flankers spread further to the right and left as they neared the clearing. Ewan crept ahead toward the one on the right who would soon be on top of the Nelsons' hiding place. If he got too close to them Ewan would fire, but he didn't want to start the shooting before Sasha because if she fired first it would draw all three toward her, away from the Nelsons, and they would have the Russians in a crossfire.

But it was not to be. The sharp crack of a large caliber pistol sounded from in front to the right, and a bullet slammed into a tree about ten feet from where Ewan was crouching. This was startling because all the Russians had their backs to Ewan, and it took a second for him to realize that Nelson must have been the shooter. The old boy had fired his antique .45 when he saw the Russian approaching, but instead of protecting himself and his wife, he had attracted the undivided attention of the three pursuers who now directed their fire at the rocks behind which they lay. Chips flew in every direction as bullets pulverized the rocks.

The man directly in front of Ewan began to creep to his right, and it would be only a few seconds before he was behind the Nelsons. Ewan had no choice, and he fired at the man's head, killing him instantly and causing his companions to redirect their attention and their fire in Ewan's direction. He dropped prone to the forest floor and squeezed off two rounds in the air to keep their attention on him.

There were two reports in quick succession, and then silence, followed a few seconds later by two more that were spaced farther apart. Ewan recognized the cough of his wife's Glock and stood. She was in the clearing standing over the remaining two Russians, to whose heads she had just administered coups de grace. Sasha and Ewan had learned long ago that the 'use the least amount of force necessary' approach was an unsatisfactory method of dealing with enemies who were trying to kill you. Let them live and they could come back at you another day. Eliminate an enemy for good, and the world became a safer place.

Ewan checked the man he had shot. The back of his skull was blown away, and he needed no further assistance into the hereafter.

"You can come out now," he called to the Nelsons. "It's all clear."

The two septuagenarians rose slowly from behind their rock pile, Lawrence Nelson still with his .45 at the ready. They surveyed the carnage, then turned to stare at Ewan and Sasha and asked, "Who in hell are you people, anyway?"

Ignoring the question, Ewan said, "Why don't you put that gun away and help your wife back into the car while Sasha and I attend to business?"

Nelson took another look around the clearing and shook his head before leading Nancy towards the Audi.

"We have some tidying up to do." Ewan already had grasped the feet of the man he had shot and was dragging the body into the clearing to deposit it next to the others.

"There's another one up there not far from the main road," he said. "I'll get him while you bring their cars into the clearing." The Russians had driven both cars into the lane, blocking the way out.

A few minutes later, as he dragged the body of

the stocky Russian through the woods an excited babble erupted from the clearing. A beaming Sasha met him at the tree line. "Guess what I found in one of the cars," she said.

Ewan looked over her shoulder to see Vicky Kondratieva sobbing in the embrace of Lawrence Nelson.

"She says they brought her from Brussels last night. They needed her to confirm that none of her father's documents were missing after they'd taken them from Nelson."

Forty-five minutes later they drove away leaving the two Mercedes in the clearing, each containing two corpses. They would most likely not be discovered until autumn denuded the trees and the clearing became fully visible from the main road. Ewan did not envy those who would make the grisly discovery.

Ewan's immediate purpose was to get as far away from Compiègne as possible so he reversed their course of the morning and headed south.

"We have several problems," he said to the other three.

Lawrence Nelson's voice had a sarcastic edge. "You mean besides the four bodies we left back there in the woods?"

"I seem to remember you shooting first, but to answer your question, yes. That matter is past and settled.   They tried to kill us, so we killed them. Now we have to think ahead."

"You're not going to call in the authorities now?"

"Why would I do that?"

"Wouldn't it be best?"

"No, I have no intention of subjecting myself or Sasha to a police interrogation.   Besides, if you think the French cops can protect you from the Russians, think again."

"So you actually believe they intended to kill us?"

"They had guns, and they were after us, correction, they were after *you,* for the second time.   Don't forget what happened to General Kondratiev. Those guys weren't looking for polite conversation."   He scowled at Nelson in the rear view mirror.   "And we don't have time to dwell on it. You called Stoddard and asked for help. We're it."

Nelson slumped back in his seat, still perplexed. Ewan remembered times when there had been a sort of gentlemen's agreement between the CIA and the KGB. Things had changed. Right now he needed to get everyone onto the same page.

"As I was saying, we have problems. I agree with Sasha's deduction that they intercepted your phone conversations with Stoddard.   Other than betrayal by one of the tiny group that knows what's going on, it's the most likely way they could have known about the Paris apartment."   He glanced over his shoulder at Nelson. "You didn't tell anyone else, did you?"

"Of course not!" Nelson was indignant.

"Did you communicate in any way with anyone other than Stoddard after you left Brussels?"

"No."

"OK, that's a point for the other side, then. I salute their communications intercept capabilities. Now, we must assume that those goons back there reported this car's license number to the Center. It's what we would have done. That means they can trace the rental info and, bingo, they have the identities Sasha and I are currently using. They're fairly well backstopped, of course, but we'll have to ditch them."

"Awww," said Sasha, "I really liked the DuPonts. They were fun people."

"Yeah, me too." The alias documents were the work of the Mossad's highly capable documentation bureau, and the technicians would be unhappy to see their handiwork tossed in the waste can. "But now we need another set of docs and another car, not to mention a bolt hole for you two. I hate logistics."

"Aren't we going to the States," asked Nancy from the rear.

"I don't think that's a good idea just yet," replied Ewan. He had thought this aspect of their predicament through and decided against putting the Nelsons on a plane, and now there was the unexpected appearance of Vicky Kondratieva. Getting them all to the States was ultimately a decision for Terry Stoddard, but for the time being the logistics were too risky. Acquiring commercial passenger manifests was child's play for any modern intelligence service, and even if he and Sasha travelled under different aliases, Vicky and the Nelsons had no false documents and would have to fly under their true names. That would raise a red flag at Moscow Center.

The best way to protect their charges for the time being was to get them off the Russian radar. They could request assistance from the Mossad, but he wouldn't do so without Terry Stoddard's approval, and Ewan judged the Mossad's appetite for becoming involved in this particular affair as questionable, at best. Besides, no one yet knew what had triggered this chain of events, except perhaps Lawrence Nelson and Vicky Kondratieva. For the near future they needed time to talk and a safe place in which to do it.

"We stashed our rental car at Charles DeGaulle," offered Nelson.

The airport was just a short distance ahead off the Autoroute.

"Did you keep the keys or leave them in the car?" asked Sasha.

"I left them under the driver's side sun visor," replied Nelson. "Do you want to switch cars?"

"No," replied Ewan, "we need a clean car with no connection to you or the 'DuPonts.' But you've given me an idea."

He dropped them all at the main terminal at Charles DeGaulle with instructions to make themselves visible to all the security cameras they could find and then wait for him at the airport train terminal. He returned the car to the rental agency where he mentioned that he was due to board a flight for the States and then joined the others to ride the RER city train to the Gare du Nord.

They walked to a café on the Boulevard de Denain across from the station's neo-Corinthian façade with its nine statues and took an inside table. "Time to dump the DuPonts," said Ewan. Sasha took the documents he handed over and dropped them into her bag from which she extracted a large manila envelope she had taken from the apartment safe and tore it open. Inside were complete sets of new French documentation for her and Ewan. The old documents would be destroyed at the first opportunity.

"You stay here and have a nice, long lunch until I return. I'm going to rent another car." He stood and left the restaurant wishing he had time for a meal himself.

A half-hour later he returned behind the wheel of

an Alfa Romeo 159 to collect them. "Have you ever visited the Loire Valley?" he asked?

CHAPTER 38

Vitaliy Mikhailovich Shurgin, President of the Russian Federation, crumpled the report in his hand and seethed over the incompetence of the SVR. How could four seasoned operatives simply vanish? Their disappearance left him hanging on the horns of a dilemma that had international repercussions. He was on the brink of achieving one of his major foreign policy goals but now risked an embarrassment that could bring everything crashing down around him.

The office he occupied in the Kremlin's Senat building that also housed the Presidential living quarters was sumptuously decorated with a crystal chandelier, priceless antiques and paintings depicting his country's past glories. Taking stock of his surroundings he recalled the first time he had entered the office years ago for a meeting with President Boris Yeltsin. He had been uncharacteristically nervous because then, too, his career hung by a thread.

But the ruddy faced Yeltsin had offered him vodka and promoted him to a position of prominence. The price had been the life of his closest friend and collaborator, but he had not hesitated because his dream of a resurgent and powerful Russia was more important than any friendship.

Just a few years before the meeting with Yeltsin Shurgin had been a KGB General. Communism did not rule his life, but he was a patriot, and he savored the power afforded by his position. As the old Soviet Union crumbled and disintegrated around them a desperate KGB leadership entrusted to his keeping all the foreign reserves of Russia, nearly thirty billion dollars in gold and securities as well as the cash and gold reserves of the Central Committee of the Communist Party, another twenty billion dollars.

The plan was to keep the funds safe until the KGB could restore order, but Shurgin realized this was a pipedream when the coup against Mikhail Gorbachev failed. The unexpected opportunity was irresistible. In a just world, the funds might have been used to help stabilize the chaotic economic situation of the newborn Russian democracy, but Shurgin had other plans, and helping the deluded partisans of 'Western' thinking who then controlled the government was not among them.

Instead he created a clandestine revanchist organization, known as 'Russian Rebirth,' that today stretched its tentacles from Moscow to Zürich and around the world, buying up the country's raw materials assets and industries at fire sale prices through myriad front companies and using the strength of allies in criminal organizations for muscle. There had been setbacks, some serious, but he had forged ahead never losing sight of his perceived destiny and never slackening in his implacable hatred of the United States of America, until he finally achieved the pinnacle of political, as well as financial power.

He worked to distract and weaken America by secretly assisting her enemies, such as Iraq and Iran. This would give him time to rebuild the military and political might of his own country. In his view Russia must once again be feared and respected in international circles.

America might still be a super power, but it was a super power with a limp wrist. Adventures in Iraq and Afghanistan consumed her military and the rise of Iran was a problem with which they had proven incapable or unwilling to cope.

America, as Shurgin saw her, was declining, her spirit sapped by financial excesses and her population easily distracted by whatever inane story that dominated its frenetic news cycle. The Americans had placed their destiny in the hands of the inward looking, self-flagellating Left at a time when the country's attention should be focused on external dangers. America was now a country divided against itself, ripe for the next step in Shurgin's plans.

He had negotiated an arms control and reduction agreement that would weaken America's ability to play a major role on the world stage while preserving and improving Russia's nuclear capabilities. Projection of power was the key to America's international status, but now they had agreed to reduce the number of launch platforms to such a level that their options would be severely limited. And there would be no 'missile shield' for the Europeans. The Americans would be unable to promise unlimited support to the allies who had relied on U.S. protection for decades but who now would drift inevitably under the sway of Russia.

But without warning the entire construct had been jeopardized by one man's failure of fidelity to his homeland: Pavel Kondratiev. Yes, the old General was dead, but the threat survived.

Violence had served Shurgin well, and he had ample means at his disposal to mete it out anywhere across the globe, but a bullet was useless if the target were not in sight. Not all the targets were invisible, however, and for now he would have to be satisfied with a piecemeal approach that he hoped would provoke his enemies to make a mistake that would put the Kondratiev papers within his grasp.

CHAPTER 39

From its source in West Virginia the Potomac River flows toward the Chesapeake Bay, at one point crashing down in a frenzy over the jagged rocks of Great Falls, some fourteen miles above Washington, DC. Where it passes Arlington Bluff, separating the District of Columbia from Virginia, the river is traversed by the historic Chain Bridge. The bridge connects the affluent Palisades/MacArthur Boulevard sections of the District with similarly well-to-do communities in Arlington and Fairfax counties on the Virginia side where such luminaries as Bandar Prince Sultan of Saudi Arabia and the Kennedy's have their splendid compounds.

Despite the picturesque setting, Chain Bridge provides passage for over 20,000 cars per day, contributing to the nightmare of snarled traffic during Washington's infamous rush hours. Nevertheless, it is convenient and a preferred short-cut, especially for those hardy souls who live in the District and work at CIA Headquarters because after crossing into Virginia one can turn immediately right onto Route 123, known as Chain Bridge Road, and continue directly to the entrance of the Langley campus. Even with the traffic it's a pleasant drive that affords a breathtaking view of the Potomac and tantalizing glimpses through the trees of the estates of the wealthy and famous.

Had Terry Stoddard been living abroad on assignment, he would have taken a different route to work each morning and been ever vigilant for surveillance and ambushes. But he lived in a fine old house in Georgetown and the drive along Canal Road and across Chain Bridge had become habit. Though he might have varied his routine occasionally by taking Key Bridge to the George Washington Parkway, he favored the drive along the river for its familiarity and beauty.

In the Loire Valley Ewan Ramsay and his charges were sleeping, but the sun had first appeared only an hour earlier in Washington as Stoddard finally inched onto the bridge in the slowly moving morning traffic. He drove his Saab 9-3 convertible with the top down despite the acrid fumes from the other cars. The morning was brilliant, and he would enjoy it now because his plans called for a long day within the confines of Headquarters. A CD of Flamenco guitar by Manos de Plata, one of his favorites, added to his enjoyment.

Once across the bridge a high stone retaining wall bounded by a sidewalk descended toward the traffic signal at the intersection with Chain Bridge Road. Stoddard edged the Saab into the right turn lane without noticing the cardboard box on the sidewalk next to the retaining wall.

He didn't hear the roar of the explosion as the improvised explosive device detonated beside his car, its force reflected and projected violently outward by the retaining wall. The Saab and other cars near it were rendered into twisted, jagged shards of metal and hurled through the air, leaving dirty flaming debris and black smoke to fill the air along with the coppery smell of blood and the cries of the injured.

Ahead, at a vantage point just beyond the GW Parkway overpass, Lev Chertkov pocketed the cell phone he had used to trigger the IED and surveyed the carnage. Satisfied that the device had achieved the planned result, he walked to his car and headed out of the area via North Glebe Road.

The IED was identical to the ones used by the Iraqi and Afghani *mujahedeen* with the exception of the type of explosive used. He would have preferred to use an EFP, an explosively formed projectile that would have shot a tube of sun-hot molten metal into Stoddard's car. It was a more selective weapon and would have limited the collateral damage. EFP's were manufactured in Iran for use by the *mujahedeen* in Afghanistan and Iraq against armor with deadly effect, and he'd hoped that Shurgin could prise one from his Iranian friends. But the Russian President thought it too dangerous to implicate the Iranians, preferring instead to use the ubiquitous IED.

Tomorrow's headlines would be full of speculation about an attack and the indiscriminate murder of innocent civilians that would be attributed to Jihadist terrorists. In the present climate, no one would suspect Russian Intelligence, and no one would suspect that the bomb had been intended specifically to kill Terry Stoddard.

As he drove away Chertkov considered his next target. The American public was largely unaware of Stoddard's mysterious executive officer, Robert Strachey, but Brian Tekla's White House access meant he knew all about Strachey's heroics in Spain the previous year, as well as his appointment to a post with suspiciously vague responsibilities. He had identified Strachey to Chertkov as the DNCS's most likely ally in stirring up the Kondratiev affair.

Another IED was a definite possibility, but Chertkov had not yet decided. A more targeted approach also would serve and would leave much less of a mess.

CHAPTER 40

Amy clung tightly to Strachey's arm as they emerged from the Headquarters auditorium into the bright sunlight. Rather than return to their offices via the tunnel that led from the dome shaped auditorium, commonly known as the "bubble," back into the main building they chose to walk across the forecourt in hopes that the open air would provide some surcease from the sadness that had permeated the memorial ceremony they had just attended. The CIA's well-kept grounds could well have been a tranquil college campus with its shade trees and winding walks. The grounds had been designed to inspire peaceful contemplation, but now their minds were filled only with jarring thoughts of the violent death of the Head of the Clandestine Services. Director Capriano's moving eulogy to Terrence Stoddard, as well as the two other Agency employees who had perished in the blast, had moved the audience of Agency employees to tears.

The investigation into the tragic attack was ongoing by a hastily created inter-agency task force led by the FBI, but the initial forensic analysis showed that the perpetrators had used an improvised explosive device identical to those used by the *mujahedeen* in Afghanistan, and that fact had inevitably leaked to the media. Washington and the entire country were in an uproar of indignation and anxiety. The experts had long anticipated that such attacks inside the United States would soon be added to the terrorists' repertoire.

The death of the Director of National Clandestine Services, the universally respected Terrence Stoddard, in the attack led to speculation that he had been targeted specifically, but this was still debatable according to the experts. Nineteen people, including Stoddard, had died that day on Chain Bridge and another twenty injured.

Strachey and Amy paused at the familiar statue of Nathan Hale that stood beside the Headquarters entrance. The resolute Hale was posed heroically, hands bound behind his back, awaiting execution, the first American executed for spying on behalf of his country and the first of many to die in such service. Now Terry Stoddard's name would be added to the list, and another gold star would be added to the marble Wall of Honor just inside the main entrance.

"Do you think it was terrorists, Bob?" Amy's eyes overflowed with tears. She had not known Stoddard personally for long, but she had come to respect the man's quiet resolution and fearlessness, and she knew that her husband revered him.

Strachey had known Stoddard for years and more recently, as the DNCS's executive officer, had grown close to him. The sadness of the loss would come to him later, but right now he was angry, profoundly angry, and he desperately needed to identify a target upon which to vent his rage. Strachey had definite plans for the perpetrators of the Chain Bridge atrocity.

"I can't accept for a second that his death was random. It's just too much to believe that he was not specifically targeted. The bomb exploded right next to his car, and it was remotely triggered by someone who waited until that second to detonate it. No, the purpose of the attack undoubtedly was to kill Terry. There could be a lot of different reasons someone would want to do that, but the smart thing to do is look for proximate causes. What's he been doing lately that could drive an enemy to such an extreme?"

Amy had come to the same conclusion. "So you think it's connected to Kondratiev?"

"If we're looking at proximate causes, yes. We already knew that whoever's behind the Kondratiev affair doesn't mind killing people. There's the General himself, the attempt on Cogburn's life, the kidnapping of Kondratiev's daughter, and Ramsay's just experienced another bloodbath in France. The problem we have is that no one outside of Terry, you, me, and the Ramsay's knew anything about what we were doing."

"But why go after Terry? As you say, no one knows that he or anyone else at the Agency is involved."

"I'm not so sure of that anymore. Ramsay's convinced that Nelson's calls to Terry were intercepted."

"That implicates the Russians. They have the means and, apparently, the motive." Amy's tears were forgotten as her agile mind shifted to analytical mode to sift through the facts and collate them in logical sequence. "So when Ramsay and Nelson eluded them, you think, they went after Terry because he was the only other target they could identify?"

"That's my guess. And they'll be coming after anyone else they think is involved."

Amy had concentrated so much on Stoddard's death that this had not occurred to her, and she was suddenly frightened. She put her arms around her husband and held him close. "Bob, if anything happens to you…"

Amy had another reason, a new one, for her anxiety: she was newly pregnant, and she had not yet told her husband.

Strachey stroked her hair. "Don't worry about me, sweetheart. You know I can take care of myself, and forewarned is forearmed." He didn't tell her that he was more concerned for her safety than for his own. She was his greatest vulnerability, and anyone coming after him would know it.

She took a step back and shook herself to regain her composure. "Do you think they'd try another

IED?"

"They're crude devices and almost impossible to trace. And Islamist terrorism gives them the perfect cover."

"Jesus, that's an act of desperation, some would say an act of war. What are they trying to protect?"

"Once we have that figured out we may be able to identify who's behind it all with a little more precision than just 'the Russians.'"

"Do you think the documents Nelson has contain the answer?"

"Ramsay thinks so. He says he read them, but he didn't want to discuss particulars on the phone."

They had to be careful. Ramsay had briefly reported events in France to Strachey on an untraceable pre-paid phone Strachey had given him prior to the Ramsays' departure. Even so, their conversation had been cryptic.

"What are we going to do?"

"The Ramsays fly in this evening, and we'll have to huddle and go over the documents. From now on we'll have to be extremely careful and alert."

"Are you sure the Nelsons will be safe?"

"Ramsay says they and Vicky Kondratieva are under the protection of some French buddy of his." Ewan had arranged for de Blottière to look over the group in a chateau hotel in the Loire Valley, where they would remain incommunicado until it was safe to come out of hiding.

"Shouldn't they all come to the States?"

"Too dangerous until proper arrangements can be made." Strachey shuddered at the thought of an airliner being blown out of the sky.

"I don't know how we're going to do this without Terry."

She had a point. In his position Stoddard could pull strings and give orders that would not be questioned. Strachey could not. In fact, that morning Capriano had announced that the Assistant DNCS, John Hewling, would temporarily be acting until a replacement for Terry Stoddard was named. Hewling was a good man, but although he hid it well he resented Strachey's position as Stoddard's closest confidant. He would probably be named to replace Stoddard permanently, and Strachey would most certainly be re-assigned. They had very little time and several loose ends, not the least of which was Detective Cogburn who was now recovering under a different name at the Winchester Medical Center.

"If we want to continue this, and I do, we'll have to do it on our own," said Strachey. If he had to, he would carry on alone, but Ewan and Sasha Ramsay were on their way back to Washington, and he hoped he could continue to count on their help. The loss of Terry Stoddard, above all the manner of his death, had encased Strachey's heart in a block of ice, and there it would remain until he had avenged his friend and mentor.

CHAPTER 41

The six of them, Ramsay, Sasha, de Blottière, Vicky Kondratieva, and the Nelsons were ensconced in a luxurious suite in a chateau hotel not far from Chinon in the Loire Valley.   Ramsay had once again enlisted the service of his French friend, telling him to make sure he brought his Glock along.   De Blottière would act as bodyguard until arrangements could be made for the Nelsons and Vicky to travel to the States.   The Frenchman had demanded his recompense for the job in Paris, and Strachey had treated them all to a wonderful meal at La Licorne, a one-star restaurant in near-by Fontevraud L'Abbaye.

"Tell us about Nosenko," said Ramsay.   He had just finished reading the document Vicky had brought to Nelson.

"He was a braggart, a drunk, and a liar, not to put too fine a line on it," replied Nelson.   He had told this story many times before and was pleased at last to have an audience with good reason to believe him.   "We were excited at first but then we started finding things out.   He did not hold the rank he claimed, and he had not held the positions he claimed.   When the information he provided was vetted it looked like chaff to us.   We had another KGB defector at the time, one we trusted, and when Nosenko's information was discussed with him, he told us it made no sense.

"The Russians have a long and successful history of running elaborate deception operations against their enemies, and we became convinced that this was the case with Nosenko. What Kondratiev's document reveals is that it was actually one deception operation inside another. At first we thought his mission was to throw sand in our eyes to protect a high level penetration of the Agency. It was the most logical explanation we could come up with, and to be frank, I still think that was part of it. But as the document shows, the bigger deception was that the KGB, under orders from Khrushchev, and with the active assistance of the Cubans, engineered the assassination of President Kennedy. We considered this, of course, and concluded that if Nosenko was lying about everything else, he could be lying about the assassination, as well. Besides, even had he occupied the position he falsely claimed in the KGB, it's unlikely he would have been able to state conclusively that the Russians had nothing to do with the assassination. That's what Dick Helms meant when he testified to the House Select Committee on Assassination that the doubts we had about Nosenko hung 'like an incubus' over the Agency.

"We isolated Nosenko and interrogated him for months on end, but he clung to his claim to be a *bona fide* defector. All of that crap about how we tortured and mistreated him was bogus. We did isolate him, with proper authority to do so, but he was never physically mistreated.

"The problem was that Nosenko put us on full counterintelligence alert and the atmosphere at Langley became poisonous. The Soviet Bloc Division was paralyzed by suspicion. Innocent people were suffering, and careers were ruined. It was a situation that could not be permitted to endure. For better or worse, the Office of Security was assigned to review the case, and they produced a shoddy piece of work that exonerated Nosenko by ignoring hard evidence. Then the witch hunt against the anti-Nosenko faction went into full gear, and the rest is history. I resigned after that."

"The document leaves a lot of questions unanswered," said Ramsay. "The descriptions of Oswald's training, his meeting with the KGB in Mexico City, and Khrushchev's orders are clear enough, but a lot of things happened after the assassination itself that beg the question of exactly how the Russians could have accomplished it all. I wish we had the last page of the document." He looked pointedly at Vicky. "Your father was somehow involved, wasn't he?"

She hung her head, refusing to meet his eyes, and it was obvious to everyone in the room that Ramsay's question was on the mark. Vicky was still in a fragile state following her abduction and rescue.

Sasha's rebuke was sharp and immediate. "Back off there, *Connolly*, she's been through a lot."

Sasha only used his true name when she was unhappy with something he'd done, and he was immediately contrite. They needed Vicky's cooperation, and he didn't want to drive her into a corner.

Sasha moved to sit next to Vicky, took her hand and spoke to her softly in Russian. "I know this is difficult for you," she said, "but it's vitally important. Your father was going to make all of this public, wasn't he?"

Vicky nodded mutely.

"This was something that bothered him so much that he was determined to make it public regardless of the consequences, something he felt he had to do to make peace with his own conscience. Don't you think that his wish, perhaps the most important thing he had left to do in his life, should be respected? I know you want to protect your father, but is it something he would want you to do?"

Fat tears rolled down Vicky's cheeks. "I don't know," she stammered.

"Listen, Vicky," Sasha continued, "you've seen what your father's enemies have done. The General was murdered to prevent him from making this information public. They've chased you, kidnapped you, and tried to kill us all. Until we carry out your father's wishes completely, they'll keep on trying and you'll never feel safe. The only way to put a stop to it is to make everything public. This was your father's last wish."

Sasha knew it would be comforting for Vicky to hear this in her native tongue. She felt a kinship for this exile, having been born in the Soviet Union herself before her family emigrated to Israel. Her own father had died a hero's death as an Israeli soldier in the Egyptian desert in the Six Day War in 1967. Though she had been just a child at the time, she still felt his loss. It was what had motivated her to defend Israel from its enemies, first in the IDF and then the Mossad.

Vicky held her head in her hands for several long moments before looking up at the others. With an effort, she composed herself and said, "Yes. You are right. It is what my father would have wanted. I begged him not to do it, but he was adamant. In the end, I think it was my own shame that caused me to remove the page. It was a mistake that I now regret. I intended to destroy it, but in the end I couldn't. I'll take you to it."

CHAPTER 42

Under new aliases, Ewan and Sasha took a suite at the Four Seasons in Georgetown. They rented a Mustang at the airport and on the way into town called Strachey to ask for a meeting that evening. News of the Chain Bridge massacre had reached them in Europe before their departure.

When he arrived, the CIA man was grim. Amy accompanied him, looking anxious. The men exchanged condolences with a handshake, and Sasha took Amy into her arms.

Ewan invited everyone to sit and poured drinks from a bottle of Lagavulin he had purchased at Eagle Liquors on 'M' Street. Fatigue, tension, and grief hung in equal parts in the room, and the strong whiskey might at least ease some of the tension. There was a lot of thinking and planning to be done.

Ewan raised his glass in salute. "To Terry Stoddard. May whatever we do now be worthy of him."

The men downed their drinks, and the women sipped theirs with Amy nearly choking as the potent liquid burned her throat. She set her glass back on the table as it struck her that in her newly discovered condition she should avoid alcohol entirely.

Ewan chose to be frank. "You realize they'll come after you next."

"Ewan," Sasha scolded, "that was unnecessarily brutal."

"Just the truth and they need to know it."

Strachey replied, "The thought had occurred to us."

"OK, we'll have to think up some counter-measures," Ewan said after a moment. "Let me put it to you straight. I think we've gotten to the bottom of this business, and it's all the more reason for you to be careful. It's dynamite, old dynamite, to be sure, but still plenty potent with more to come, enough so that the Russians feel justified in killing to keep the lid on it." He paused for a second. "The KGB had a hand in the Kennedy assassination."

Amy gasped and Strachey looked hard at Ewan. "Can we back that up?"

Ewan rose and walked to the luggage stand where he took a large envelope from his carry-on bag. "This," he said, "will explain it. It's an old KGB document that General Kondratiev evidently smuggled out of their archives."

"Let's have a look." Strachey held out his hand.

"It's in Russian."

"I'll struggle through it," said Strachey drily.

The yellowing document, dated 1967, was not a file *per se*, but rather a memorandum to the then newly appointed Head of the KGB, Yuriy Andropov. Judging from the first few paragraphs it appeared that the ever judicious Andropov had demanded briefings on matters involving the spy agency that might negatively affect the international position and standing of the Soviet Union, not to mention his own well-being. In other words, if there were skeletons lying about in closets, he wanted to know where the doors were and whether they could be kept shut.

Ramsay sat back and struck a wooden match with which he caressed the tip of a cigar, ignoring Sasha's disapproval while he studied Strachey's reaction to the document's contents. Amy was reading it over her husband's shoulder. Impressive. They both understood Russian. Ramsay had feared it was a dying art at the CIA.

At length Strachey looked up. "There's something missing. The last page ends in mid-sentence."

Ramsay blew a perfect smoke ring before answering. "You're right. The last page isn't there. We'll be able to get our hands on it as soon as Vicky Kondratieva returns to the States." He remembered Vicky Kondratieva's face when she had agreed. There had been shame there, but determination, as well. "But there's plenty of explosive content before it gets to that point," he finished.

"Had this come to light in 1963 it would have

meant war."

Ramsay frowned. "Maybe, maybe not. Remember, just a year earlier the world stepped back at the last moment from the brink of an all-out nuclear war during the Cuban Missile Crisis. Everyone was scared that it had come to that. No one had any stomach to ratchet things up again, least of all Washington."

"But the Russians apparently weren't so cautious following the crisis."

"Caution was a word Nikita Khrushchev didn't understand, and reading between the lines of that document it's clear that between him and Fidel Castro there was a surfeit of ambition and ideological heat. Khrushchev was a hero to many because he unmasked Stalin's sins, but he was a fervent Communist and a tough guy who had served as commissar on the front lines at Stalingrad during the height of battle. And Castro must have been pretty pissed off over CIA attempts to assassinate him."

For a moment Ramsay could see the feisty Russian Premier's bald head, gapped teeth, and sly, swinish eyes. "He meant it when he threatened to bury the West. Remember he approved the repression of the Hungarian uprising in '56, as well as the erection of the Berlin Wall in '61. You're too young to remember, but I'm not. Putting nuclear tipped missiles in Cuba was an act of monumental rashness and miscalculation. The

Bay of Pigs fiasco had convinced Castro he could stand up to the Americans because he read as cowardice when Kennedy abandoned the invasion force on the beach. Khrushchev was convinced he had the measure of Kennedy, as well, especially after their first meeting in Vienna where Kennedy's weak performance failed to impress, but when the Russians were forced to back down during the Missile Crisis he was profoundly embarrassed. Castro harangued him, and his position as General Secretary was undermined. Khrushchev was a nasty piece of work, and he wanted revenge. He ordered the KGB to come up with a plan to kill Kennedy."

Amy shook her head. "It's still hard to believe, and I'm not sure anyone would believe it now, even if this document were made public."

"Did you know," Ramsay asked, "that in 1978 a very high ranking Romanian intelligence officer defected to the CIA and told us that the KGB had 'programmed' Lee Harvey Oswald to kill Kennedy? Nobody wanted to believe it then. I also recall that in 1991 the head of the KGB, Bakatin, ordered a complete review of the KGB records relating to Oswald. He intended to make them public and clear away any lingering doubts about the KGB's role in the conspiracy, but all the files were sent to the Byelorussian KGB in Minsk, where Oswald had lived, and they vanished. Evidently someone decided their revelation would be a bad idea.

"Then in 1999 Yeltsin finally gave President Clinton a file that contained copies of allegedly official high level Soviet correspondence concerning Oswald. Judging from what we have in our hands now, the purpose of the Yeltsin documents was only to further the deception that the Russians had nothing to do with the Kennedy assassination, and the 'file' contained no KGB documents. It was clearly intended to debunk previous suspicions that the Soviet Union and Cuba were involved. Nevertheless, the Yeltsin documents revealed that there had been unusually high level interest when Oswald popped up in the Soviet Union in 1959.

"Somehow the Andropov memo must have escaped exile to Belarus, and Kondratiev found it in the Moscow archives. According to it Oswald was considered a valuable defector because what he told the Russians about American high altitude radar eventually enabled them to shoot down Gary Powers' U2 spy plane. Oswald was resettled in Minsk where he continued to be monitored by the KGB. He was a restless, pugnacious guy, and a rabid commie, so the KGB thought he could be useful as a sleeper inside the U.S. Evidently the KGB's Directorate 'S' gave him extensive training to operate as an illegal before he returned to the U.S. in the summer of 1962. By that time the Soviets were preparing to install the missiles in Cuba."

Amy asked, "Do you think his mission was somehow connected to the missiles?"

Ramsay had had a lot of time to think about the Andropov memo on the flight from France. "I don't think so, at least not his original mission," he replied, "He was a contingency asset with no access to information of importance and with no influence. His greatest value to the Russians was that he was actually an American. They might have planned eventually to use him as a cut-out or to retrieve dead drops. But according to the Andropov memo, after Kennedy faced down Khrushchev and Castro in October 1962, the Soviets started planning the assassination, and Oswald's name came up. They wanted an American assassin, and he was their best bet, despite his imperfections. In September 1963 Oswald was called to Mexico City where he received his orders from a high ranking KGB American Targets officer. The rest is history."

Amy had followed the conversation carefully. "But how did they know in September that Kennedy would be in Dallas in November? It wasn't announced publicly until much later."

The girl has brains, thought Ramsay. "Ah, but that's the question, isn't it? And there's more: was Oswald's killing part of their plan? It was terribly convenient for the Russians, wasn't it? The American assassin killed in turn by another American before he could implicate the KGB. It's too much to believe that the Russians simply got lucky."

Amy grew thoughtful and turned to Strachey.

"Let's get back to Headquarters. I have some research to do."

"Whoa," said Ramsay, "we still have a lot to talk about. There are a lot of loose ends, including how we're going to protect you."

"What do you say we get together for dinner tonight after we've all had time to think? We'll both be at Headquarters until then." said Strachey.

Sasha instantly agreed. "That's a good idea. We need some time to rest. We've crossed the Atlantic three times over the past several days."

Again she was acting like she thought he was an old man. Or maybe he was getting too sensitive. Was that a sign of advancing age? He sure as hell didn't FEEL old.

"OK," he relented. They agreed on a discreet restaurant in Winchester, and the Strachey's left.

Succumbing to a 'youthful' urge, Ramsay turned to his wife and ogled her from head to foot. "Well, now," he said in a low voice. "Just what sort of 'rest' did you have in mind?"

His bodacious wife smiled invitingly and headed for the bedroom leaving a trail of discarded clothing in her wake.

CHAPTER 43

"President Shurgin has rescheduled his visit. He'll be here in three days for the treaty signing. You are the first to know, and you will deliver the message to the President."   Lev Chertkov's voice was intense.   "Are you certain you have seen nothing that would cause him to change his plans?"

Chertkov and Tekla were again breakfasting at the Mayflower.   Anyone caring to study the two men would have surmised from their posture and demeanor that the subject of their conversation was unpleasant. The Russian was clearly in control as he leaned over the table toward Tekla whose habitual arrogance had been replaced by manifest unease.

Outside the hotel Washington sweated through the warmest August in memory as the bureaucrats, politicians, and pundits speculated on the Russian President's reasons for postponing his visit.

"I would have told you if I heard anything," snapped Tekla, irked by Chertkov's assumption of superiority.   The Russian did not seem to appreciate to whom he was speaking. Since the murder of General Kondtratiev, everything the SVR officer touched had turned to shit, and Tekla was suspicious that Chertkov was now planning to foist some of the blame on him.

The Russian's stony visage did not change, and it was impossible to read his thoughts. Without taking his eyes from Tekla's face he said, "I should hope so."

Tekla thought he detected a hint of suspicion in Chertkov's voice. "Are you trying to imply something, Lev? I would hate to think so. My family was serving the cause before you were born."

"I meant nothing more than what I said, and the 'cause,' as you so quaintly put it died long ago. No one is a Communist these days. But there has been more bad news."

Still angry, Tekla demanded, "What now?"

"Things appear to have gone awry in France. We've lost contact with the team we sent there after the debacle in Paris."

Brian Tekla was stunned. He had always viewed the KGB and its successor, the SVR, as supreme when it came to field work. Unlike the American intelligence services, they were unfettered by laws and regulations that constrained their activities. If someone needed killing, they were killed; if a country like Georgia had to be invaded, it was invaded. The incompetence in the present instance surprised and frightened him. "What do you mean 'lost contact'?"

"They followed the Nelsons and the people accompanying them, apparently a French businessman and his wife, out of Paris with orders to kill them and retrieve the document. The team still had Kondratiev's daughter with them so they could authenticate what they found. Since then there has been no contact."

"You mean they lost the Nelsons' trail?" Tekla was hopeful he had heard wrong the first time.

"No, our team disappeared."

Tekla gaped at the Russian. "That's impossible."

"Nevertheless ..."

"What are you going to do? The longer that document remains in the Nelsons' hands the more likely it becomes that they'll make it public. And, frankly, Lev, there is more at stake here than just the treaty." First the crooked cop Cogburn had dropped out of sight along with Buchalter, and now an entire SVR operational team!

"I know that. But there is one small bit of intriguing new information."

"I'd like to hear some good news for a change," said Tekla petulantly.

Chertkov said, "It concerns the wife of the French businessman. The team described her as tall, with ash blond hair, and extremely beautiful. Does that description suggest anything to you, Brian?"

"You think she's the same woman I saw at the Kennedy Center?" A woman matching this description had cropped up on three separate occasions related to the Kondratiev affair, once at the Arlington police station where she claimed to be a Russian police officer, once at the Kennedy Center where she made the same claim and now again in Paris. After a thoughtful pause Tekla was dubious, "There are a lot of good-looking blondes in the world."

Chertkov stared at him for a moment. "I think it's time to change our plan and for you to try to contact her using the telephone number she gave you."

Tekla had from the first believed the woman's demand that he call her about Buchalter was an entrapment ploy, and he remained leery of the idea. "But you think she's in France," he objected.

"Maybe, but right now that telephone number is the only connection we have to the people who were working with Stoddard. The woman can't be the only one. It's worth a try."

"But it would implicate me directly. I can't risk that. Look at what these animals have done already!"

Chertkov's slightly slanted Slavic eyes remained expressionless as they pinned the American to his chair. "You can, and you will," he said, "Orders from the Center."

A pang of desperation squeezed Tekla's heart and filled his chest with ice. What he was being asked to do would put the work of two generations of his family in jeopardy.

Chertkov couldn't miss his hesitation. "There is no choice. There is no other way. You will do as ordered."

Tekla wondered what his father would have done.

CHAPTER 44

The four of them gathered over burgers and beer (Amy ordered iced tea) in the dark corner of a Winchester bar. The Strachey's had driven directly from CIA Headquarters, and he had just spelled out how Stoddard's absence severely limited their operational possibilities. "No more safehouses, no more clandestine medical care without Terry's intervention. We're on our own now."

"It won't be the first time for us," said Ramsay.

"Nor for us," said Strachey, "but we need to do more than just protect the Nelsons and the Andropov Memorandum. This has turned into more than a murder investigation. The Andropov Memorandum carries political implications far beyond that; at least the Russians think so. But logically they shouldn't. The culpability lies with the old Soviet Union, not the new Russian Federation. Shurgin could easily distance himself from a decision made by Khrushchev half a century ago."

"It's because of the effect the revelation would have on American public opinion," ventured Amy. "Camelot was an iconic period, and Kennedy's death left a deep scar on the American psyche. The wave of indignation that would sweep this country would put the arms reduction agreement on the skids. The Left would be wounded, and no one would feel they could trust the Russians, post-communists or not, especially given the fact that former KGB officers now control the Russian Government. Even Yeltsin tried to cover it all up."

"So it's murder and high-stakes politics," said Ramsay, "not uncommon bedfellows.

Sasha was unconvinced.   "There have been numerous theories about Soviet involvement in the assassination, some of them quite convincing. A new allegation would just stir the conspiracy theory pot again, and you can bet there would be high level official denials, both from the Russians and the U.S."

"But this time there's documentary evidence," said Ramsay.

"Even so," replied Sasha, "they'll claim it was fabricated. To make the allegation stick we'll need unquestionable confirmation that the Memorandum is the real deal."

Strachey frowned. "There might be a way," he said, "but it'll take some work."

Ramsay took a contemplative sip of his beer. "Nelson told me that his primary suspicion, and that of the other members of Angleton's team, had always been that Nosenko's real mission was to protect a high-level penetration of the Agency. That's what led to the so-called 'witch hunts' at Langley and eventually to Angleton's removal and disgrace."

"There have always been claims by conspiracy nuts that the Agency itself was somehow involved in Kennedy's death. Could there be a connection?" asked Sasha.

"Oh, shit!" The unusual exclamation from shy Amy caused all eyes to turn toward her.

Strachey lifted his eyebrows at his newly tea totaling wife. "Well?"

"Well," replied Amy, "you remember we wondered about how Oswald or the Russians could have known about the Dallas trip so far in advance of the official announcement?"

"Yeah."

"I did some research this afternoon, and it wasn't hard to discover that the Dallas trip had been in the planning stages since June 1963 when Kennedy, John Connolly, and Johnson met in El Paso, five months before the assassination. Details were kept secret, but key government security agencies, including the CIA, received periodic updates."

"So a penetration of any one of those agencies could have tipped off the Soviets far enough in advance to prepare for the assassination," said Strachey.

Amy nodded and gulped down some iced tea as the implications coalesced in her head. "It makes you wonder what's on that missing page."

Sasha gave her a Sphinx-like look. "We have

some news.   Vicky Kondratieva concealed the missing page, and she's going to let us have it as soon as we can transport her here."

Surprised, Amy took a moment to consider this, her brows knitted. "She must have had a reason for not wanting anyone to see that page, and I'll bet it was because her father was somehow implicated in the assassination. If I'm right, he planned his press conference as a sort of confession – the first time anyone admitted to personal involvement in the assassination, and he was a KGB officer assigned to Washington at the time."

"That's strong stuff. A picture is emerging from the jigsaw," said Ramsay.   "The Russians killed Kondratiev and then went after his daughter in order to get their hands on the Andropov memo. They didn't count on her making her way to someone like Nelson, and they certainly didn't expect us to join the festivities. We've resolved the question of who killed Kondratiev and why, and now we have to decide how and when to make the memo public, including the final page."

Strachey interjected, "We have to do something about Terry Stoddard's murder, too. We all know the Russians did it. That fact, as well as the memo should be made public. Otherwise everything that's happened would be for nothing."

"That would mean revealing Terry's direct involvement and compromising our operational security," said Ramsay. "That could blow back on you, Strachey."

"I know," replied Strachey resolutely, "but I won't allow Terry's murderers to get away with it."

Ramsay studied the CIA man across the table. Revenge was something he understood well. Sometimes the taste was sweet, but it also could be bitter. One thing he knew for certain was that it was best when administered personally. "That may be something we'll have to take care of by ourselves."

"One way or the other," nodded Strachey, "they're going to pay."

Ramsay was gaining new respect for the CIA man. "Agreed," he said. "But I'd like to get the final pieces of the puzzle in place so we have a complete picture before making a decision. When the Andropov Memorandum hits the streets we don't want there to be a lot of unanswered questions. That's what's bedeviled all the assassination conspiracy theories to date."

Sasha spoke up, "I have an idea. Let's go back to the beginning – to Brian Tekla."

Before she could say more she was interrupted by the distinctive ringtone of a cell phone. Her eyes widened in disbelief. "Speak of the devil," she said as she retrieved a throwaway phone from the depths of her handbag. "It has to be Tekla calling. He's the only one with this number."

The others were as startled as she. Tekla had failed to call them after Sasha accosted him at the Kennedy Center. Why had he waited so long?

Signing to the others to stay where they were, Sasha rushed outside the bar to the street to escape the noise and music inside. She pushed the receive button. "Yes?"

It was Tekla's voice, all right. "Ms. Fedosova?"

"Mr. Tekla. You waited a long time."

"We need to meet."

*****

Sasha returned to the group displaying a smug smile. "He wants a meeting."

Amy's eyes went wide. "What did you tell him?"

"That a long time has passed since we made the offer and things have changed. I told him we'd get back to him. He didn't sound happy."

"Perfect," said Strachey. "Any meeting Tekla wants is a trap for sure."

"I agree," said Ramsay. "But the ball is in our court, and we need a new plan."

Strachey addressed Sasha, "Just before he called you had an idea about Tekla. Care to elaborate?"

"Well, I think the correct phrase is to 'put the cat among the pigeons.'"

CHAPTER 45

Next morning Brian Tekla followed the pleasant aroma of freshly brewed coffee from the upstairs bedroom down into the kitchen, where his wife was setting out the breakfast dishes.

"Brian," she called out, "did you send for a car to pick you up this morning?"

"No, I'm driving myself today." He had spent a restless night, finally falling asleep well past midnight. Tekla felt caught in a vise, his notorious arrogance replaced by a generalized presentiment of disaster that he couldn't shake. He was a major mover and shaker in Washington, sought after by the news networks, his face well known to the public, but now he had begun to feel like a mere pawn in a game he no longer controlled.

"That's odd, then," said his wife. "One of the White House SUV's is in the driveway."

Tekla walked to the front of the house and looked out a window. Yes, there was a large, black SUV waiting with the motor running, the driver behind the wheel. The damned motor pool must have screwed up again.

From the kitchen his wife said, "I'm sending Sandra out with a cup of coffee for the driver."

He headed back to the kitchen. "Ask Sandra to tell the driver he can go."

The kitchen was connected to the garage via a mud room, and he heard the door close behind his daughter and the automatic garage door rise as she went out to the waiting SUV. He had just poured himself a cup of steaming coffee when a scream pierced the air.

Tekla's wife started in alarm. "That was Sandra!"

Tekla froze for a second before setting his cup on the counter and rushing through the mud room and out the open garage door to find his daughter still shrieking as she stared in horror through the open door of the SUV. A sickly odor penetrated his nostrils as he reached her side.

"Sandra, what is it?"

The teenager could only point wordlessly at the vehicle before she turned and vomited onto the ground.

Tekla approached carefully and looked inside; the odor grew stronger the closer he got.

He started backwards in horror and revulsion. A very obviously dead Leon Bucholter was behind the wheel of the SUV, strapped tightly upright by the seat belt.

After so many days, even in cold storage in the morgue of the Winchester Medical Center, Buchalter didn't look good. The body was fully dressed in the clothing he had been wearing when he was shot, and the front of his shirt and jacket was black with congealed blood. Mercifully, Buchalter's eyes were closed, but his green-tinged face was slack in death, and his mouth yawned wide.

Tekla's mind locked as he stood there engulfed by the miasma of death that spilled over him from the open car door, and he didn't notice the piece of white paper peeking from the breast pocket of Buchalter's jacket.

Belatedly he became aware that his frightened wife had come outside and had her arms around their daughter, shielding her from the sight and leading her back to the house as she stared reproachfully over her shoulder at Tekla.

He stumbled back from the car, swatting the air with his hands to dispel the ripe odor. His first coherent thought was to call Chertkov. He would know what to do.

His wife and daughter, calmer now, were seated at the kitchen table when he returned. "I've already called White House Security," announced his wife. "They're sending someone, and they'll notify the DC Police."

Tekla's mind was now a swirl of calculation. White House Security meant the Secret Service, the 'sneaks,' as Secret Service personnel were known. They would in turn notify the FBI. It was already too late to notify Chertkov. He silently cursed his wife.

As his mind began to function clearly again he flashed on the white paper in the corpse's pocket. It had obviously been placed there to be noticed. As the realization hit him brakes squealed outside and by the time he was out again through the garage doors a DC Police black and white was parked at the end of his driveway and two policemen were standing beside the SUV. He overcame the panic that again clutched at his gut and walked slowly out to meet them.

Within twenty minutes two unmarked cars, one from the Secret Service and the other from the FBI, and two more black and whites had joined the first, along with a truck from the Bomb Squad. The area around the SUV was marked off with yellow crime scene tape, and no one was allowed to approach until the vehicle had been checked thoroughly for explosives. The houses in the immediate vicinity were evacuated.

CHAPTER 46

Cogburn's disappearance was nearly forgotten in the wake of the Chain Bridge massacre. Every cop in the Washington region was on high alert. Washington bureaucrats and the chattering classes, accustomed to being insulated from the events in which they claimed expertise, were walking on tippy toes. In this climate, Murphy feared the Kondratiev case might be buried forever and she felt she could no longer avoid sharing her thoughts with Jefferson. Early on a Monday morning in late August, nearly a week since her last conversation with him about Cogburn's disappearance, she knocked on the frame of the lieutenant's open door.

The habitually cool Jefferson looked a bit wilted around the edges today. His suit coat hung over the back of his chair and his tie was loose at the collar. He had been concentrating on his computer screen when she knocked. He looked up and saw her. "Come on in."

She decided to get right to the point.

"Marty, I'm more than convinced that Charlie's disappearance is somehow connected to the Kondratiev case." The words tumbled out in a rush, like water through a broken dam.

"Hold on, Krystal. Slow down. Now, why don't you take a chair and tell me what's on your mind?"

Embarrassed, she sat stiffly facing Jefferson across the desk. "I'm sure that Charlie's disappearance is connected with the Kondratiev murder."

Jefferson waited silently. She couldn't read his face, so she plunged on.

"I told you he'd been acting weird ever since the murder, right? Well, the day of the murder we notify the daughter, and she disappears immediately after. Never even claims her father's body. Charlie ignores the daughter's claim that the Russians were somehow involved and writes the murder off as a mugging gone bad. No matter how hard I try, he won't budge from that position."

She kept her eyes on Jefferson's face. Fatigue had carved lines where none had been before. Like every senior police official in the region he was dealing with the fallout from the Chain Bridge bombing. But despite the fatigue she could read nothing in his eyes.

"It's just all too damned suspicious," she charged ahead. "Then that female Russian cop comes snooping around to find out what we knew. She leaves and Charlie shoots out of the station like a rocket. I think he must have followed her. But he never came back. That makes two people who've vanished, and I know it's linked to Kondratiev, and that Russian cop is up to her sweet ass in it."

Jefferson sat there for a moment looking at her as though he were trying to make up his mind about something. Finally, he rested his elbows on the desk and leaned forward. "You may be right, Krystal, at least about some of it."

She was surprised. The last thing she'd expected was agreement.

Jefferson continued, "We checked on Major Fedosova, the Russian policewoman. It's a matter of protocol. The Russian Embassy liaison knew nothing about the visit and checked with Moscow. There is no one matching Fedosova's description in the FSB. She was a phony."

This was completely unexpected and somewhat insulting. The investigating officers should have been advised already. She didn't like being kept in the dark. "A phony cop?"

"Yes, a phony Russian cop interested in Kondratiev."

"Wow."

"Uh huh. And there was another development this morning in DC that might be connected. I'm going to put you in touch with a friend of mine at the FBI. I'm sure he'll want to talk to you about this. I'll tell him to call you."

An hour later Murphy's cell phone warbled. The caller identified himself as Executive Assistant Director Enoch Whitehall of the FBI. That sounded like a pretty high rank to Murphy.

When he told her he wanted to discuss the

Kondratiev case, she didn't answer directly. "Why is the FBI interested in Kondratiev?" There was more than curiosity in her voice. She had become suspicious of everything and everyone.

"His name came up this morning in connection with another matter."

"What 'other matter?'" she asked sharply.

"I can't say over the phone, Detective Murphy. Would it be possible for us to meet?" Whitehall's voice remained tranquil.

"You name the time and place." She didn't intend to stonewall him. She wanted to discuss the case. He wouldn't be the only one asking questions.

"Can you meet for lunch today at the Capitol Grill? Say 12:30? Just ask for my table."

"I'll see you there."

The Capital Grill was a short walk from the J. Edgar Hoover Building, and Whitehall arrived before Murphy, who had to deal with parking. When she entered and asked for him, the maitre d' escorted her to a table in a corner where a tall, almost cadaverous man in a charcoal gray suit sat waiting. His dark eyes were deep set on either side of a long, aquiline nose, a classic hatchet face. He rose and pulled out a chair for her.

"Thank you for coming, Detective Murphy."

Murphy had decided that her normal cop attire of

jeans and a polo shirt would be inappropriate for the DC landmark restaurant and there had been just enough time to run past her apartment and change into a forest green dress. She's loosed her auburn hair to let it fall to her shoulders. Several pairs of male eyes followed her as she walked to Whitehall's table.

They placed their orders, and when the waiter left, he said, "There are some developments that may interest you." His voice was soft, almost without intonation.

Murphy's green eyes shone with interest. "Please enlighten me."

"I'll be happy to as long as you agree to be frank with me in return."

She wondered how frank the FBI man would be with her. "OK."

"Do you know who Brian Tekla is?"

"I've seen him on the news. He's some kind of White House advisor, one of the 'Czars.'"

"Correct. He's the so-called Intelligence Czar. A DNI security officer named Buchalter showed up this morning at Tekla's home – dead. He'd been dead for a long time. It wasn't a pretty sight. The man hasn't been seen since the day your Charlie Cogburn disappeared. There was a note on the body linking Buchalter to the Kondratiev murder. The note was written in Russian."

"That's fascinating," she said, "but why did you want to see me?"

"Tekla told FBI Director Mulvaney that Buchalter was working with your partner, Cogburn, on the case of a woman who claimed, apparently falsely, to be a representative of the FSB. Both Buchalter and Cogburn disappeared at about the same time. Your lieutenant informs me there have been no developments concerning Cogburn?"

"So it's really Cogburn you want to talk to me about? He's completely off the map. He literally ran out of the office as soon as that Russian cop left Headquarters, and no one has seen him since."

"Tell me what you think about the Kondratiev murder."

"So, you really see a connection?"

"Uh huh."

Her face brightened as if she had met a long lost friend. "Me too."

Whitehall's lips twitched in what might have been a smile. "What do you know about Buchalter's connection with Cogburn?"

"Absolutely nothing, but contact with a high level guy from the White House would explain his recent behavior. Cogburn never mentioned it to any of us, and it's really strange that he wouldn't, knowing him. Working with the White House would be a big deal, and it's not the kind of secret he would be able to keep unless he had a very good reason. Do you think Cogburn's dead, too?"

The question didn't reflect so much an abiding concern for her partner's welfare as professional curiosity. And there was something else. She was holding something back, waiting for him to pry it out of her.

"Tell me about the Kondratiev murder investigation."

"What investigation? Cogburn was convinced it was a common street crime - a mugging and robbery - and without a lot of luck we weren't going to identify the perp." The way she said it made it plain that she didn't agree.

"But you weren't convinced?"

She frowned and hesitated a beat or two, trying to make up her mind whether she could trust him. "No," she finally answered.

"Why not?"

"There were too many atmospherics to disregard – all that stuff in the news about his book and the press conference he'd scheduled. Cogburn just brushed it all aside as if it didn't matter."

Murphy had done her homework. General Kondratiev's book provided accounts of most of the major Soviet penetrations of the US Government from the early sixties to the time Kondratiev left the KGB in '89. According to the experts there was little reason to doubt what he wrote. He, himself, had handled many of these cases over the course of three tours in the United States, the first beginning in 1963. A stir was created by the end of the book where he claimed to have in his possession proof of a major KGB operation that had not yet been uncovered, one that would astound the American public and cause America to seriously re-evaluate its relationship with Russia. That stirred some excitement in the media and a lot more public interest in the book. The General scheduled a press conference at which he promised a major revelation.

She stopped abruptly, considering what to say next.

"What else?" he asked.

The waiter arrived with their orders, and they sat in silence until he left. Murphy picked up a fork and stared at her plate.

"Go on," Whitehall urged. "I think you have more to tell me."

She still didn't know whether she could trust him.

"Off the record?" she asked.

It was his turn to frown. "If you like."

She looked back down at her plate and pushed some lettuce around with her fork. "I searched Kondratiev's apartment without Cogburn's knowledge."

"Why did you do that?"

"Because that ass insisted it wasn't necessary."

"So, you didn't have a warrant?"

"No."

"OK. Did you find anything?"

She breathed a bit more easily. The FBI man didn't appear concerned that she had broken the law.

"Someone had ransacked Kondratiev's study. His computer and all of his files were missing."

"Did you tell Cogburn?"

"Hell, no! And this was just before the phony Russian policewoman showed up."

"And what did you conclude from what you found, Detective?"

"That it was a lot more than a common mugging. Whoever killed him wanted something Kondratiev had. I think it was the Russians. When that woman showed up at HQS I didn't know what to think. She asked all the right questions, but if the Russians killed Kondratiev, why was she really there? I thought maybe it was to make certain things stayed covered up."

This was a logical conclusion, one she thought Whitehall could accept.

"Do you think Cogburn was involved in a cover-up?"

"What do you think, Agent Whitehall?"

He ignored her question. So much for candor from the FBI.

"Do you think Cogburn could have killed Buchalter as part of a cover-up?" he asked in a voice that might just as well have been used to ask the time of day.

She speared a slice of tomato on her fork and held it suspended between the plate and her mouth. "Wow," she said, "wouldn't that be something? But from what I know of Cogburn, he didn't have it in him."

She realized she was thinking of Cogburn in the past tense.

Whitehall persisted, "You've as much as said that Cogburn covered something up in the Kondratiev case, that maybe he was part of a conspiracy. If he killed Buchalter, it would explain why he disappeared, wouldn't it?"

Murphy carefully replaced her fork on her plate and chewed the tomato for a moment. She swallowed and said, "I hadn't exactly pictured things that way. This guy's body turning up now after a week is weird, but a note written in Russian looks more like the work of that phony FSB cop than Charlie Cogburn who had a hard enough time with English. She might even have killed him, too. But what I don't understand is where Tekla fits in."

Whitehall apparently wasn't ready to share his impressions of the President's Intelligence Czar. "So, there are two viable suspects: your Charlie Cogburn and the mysterious 'Russian woman.'"

"Russia, Russia," she said, letting her exasperation show. "There's way too much Russia in this case. If you think Cogburn killed Buchalter, could he have been working for the Russians as a kind of agent?"

"Or paid assassin."

"Same thing. Believe me, the thought of Charlie Cogburn as a paid assassin stretches credulity. He was a putz, a misogynistic and not very smart putz. He definitely was not secret agent material."

She was still talking about Cogburn in the past tense.

"But you agree it's a logical theory that he killed Buchalter, given what we know?"

"It's a possibility, sure, but I just don't see it. My money's still on that Russian woman."

"Ah, the mystery woman."

She found the phrase annoying.

Whitehall continued, "She accosted Brian Tekla at the Kennedy Center last Saturday evening?"

"No! What did she want?"

"She offered to ransom Buchalter."

"That doesn't make any sense if Buchalter was already dead."

The corners of Whitehall's mouth curled up into a tight smile that told her he thought she was onto something. "I agree. It makes me wonder what she was really after."

"So, who do you think is behind it all?" She'd concluded, as had he, that there was a conspiracy.

It was Whitehall's turn to pause. She didn't think he'd worked it all out yet and was using her as a sounding board.

"You could be right about the Russians," he said slowly. "It's a logical conclusion if one assumes that Kondratiev was holding something valuable, perhaps threatening to them."

"Such as?"

"Ah, but that's the question, isn't it, the elusive McGuffin? If we knew the motive we could solve the mystery. To tell you the truth, Detective, I haven't the foggiest idea of how to get to the bottom of it all. What is certain is that whatever Kondratiev had is the key."

CHAPTER 47

Charlie Cogburn was a lucky man, but he didn't feel so lucky at the moment. The bullet had taken him high and broken his clavicle. It was healing nicely, though not without pain. The hospital staff treated him humanely, if a bit impersonally, except for the fact that his foot was chained to the bed, and he didn't have the slightest idea where he was.

How could that bastard, Buchalter, have shot him and why? He'd done everything the White House guy had asked "in the name of national security." The money was a nice bonus, but he hadn't bargained on being tortured, kidnapped, and then shot. His world had turned upside down in a hurry, and he wasn't sure whom to blame.

'The Price is Right' had just begun on the TV in his room when the door opened to admit a tall athletically built man he didn't recognize.

"How are you feeling today, Detective Cogburn?"

Cogburn didn't answer, certain that whatever he said would be wrong.

"I have a proposition for you," the man continued, "How would you like to get out of here? The doctor says you're well enough."

The question surprised him and put Cogburn in a

quandary: hell, yes, he wanted out. Hell, no, he didn't want them to kill him. But if they had gone to all the trouble to patch him up, why would they kill him. "Huh?" was his reply.

"I asked if you would like to get out of here."

"Why?"

The tall man smiled amiably. "Why? Well, we thought you might like to go home. You know, suck down a few beers with the guys. Tell them about your week."

"How do I know you won't kill me?"

"You don't. But if you do as I say, you should be fine. You might even turn out to be a hero. What do you say?"

"What do you want me to do?"

"Nothing very difficult. Go to the authorities and tell them everything you know about the Kondratiev murder."

"You mean about Buchalter?"

"Absolutely. We especially want you to be sure and tell them everything you know about him."

"And all the other stuff that happened that night?"

"Whatever."

This was crazy. Cogburn tried to figure out if the man was serious, but his thought process petered out rather quickly. This sort of stuff was way outside his experience.

"You'll really let me go?"

"I promise. But you have to do what we say. It'll be easy; all you have to do is tell the truth."

"The truth?"

"You know, how Buchalter approached you, paid you off to bury the Kondratiev investigation, and then tried to kill you. He DID try to kill you, you know."

"What about the other people, the man and that Russian woman?"

"Tell them whatever you know, which is very little apart from the fact that they saved your life."

"That guy was going to cut my ear off!"

"Buchalter was going to KILL you. You need to get straight who are your friends and who are your enemies, Detective." The man grabbed Cogburn by the ears and turned his head from side to side. "And it seems you still have both of your ears, after all."

He jerked his head out of the man's grasp. "What happens if I refuse?"

The tall man shook his head. "Do you like fish, Cogburn?"

"Fish?"

"The alternative is a long nap with the fishes." The man bared his teeth and suddenly looked very feral.

Why was this happening to him? He wished he'd become a plumber like his father.

"Yeah, OK, I'll do it," he said weakly.

"Excellent." The tall man's smile returned to amiable. "There's just one more thing ..."

CHAPTER 48

Murphy groped in the dark for the jangling cell phone and managed to knock it off her bedside table. "Damn it!"

A glance at the glowing hands of her clock told her it was two in the morning. She turned on the light and found the phone about a foot under the bed. The caller i.d. showed it was Lieutenant Jefferson calling.

"Lieutenant," she said, "what's up?"

Jefferson's answer jerked her fully awake. "We found Cogburn."

"What? You found his body?" She'd come to think of Cogburn as deceased.

"In a manner of speaking. We found him parked in his own unmarked police cruiser in front of Headquarters a quarter of an hour ago. I'm on my way there now. You want to come, too?"

That was the way Buchalter had shown up, but he had been dead. "You mean he's alive?"

"He's alive."

Murphy wondered if perhaps aliens would land on the White House lawn next. "I wouldn't miss it. I'll be there in a few minutes."

Charlie Cogburn was alive! There were a lot of questions he'd have to answer, and she wouldn't miss it for the world.

She scrambled out of bed and threw off the Indianapolis Colts jersey she habitually slept in, stepped into the bathroom and splashed some water on her face and brushed her teeth before pulling on a pair of jeans, sneakers and a tee shirt. She grabbed a light jacket from a peg beside the door in case it rained.

They had Cogburn in one of the interrogation rooms when she got there. Jefferson had arrived just before her. Someone had brought in a plate of Dunkin Donuts and a carafe of fresh coffee. She eyed Cogburn as she poured herself a cup. He looked thoroughly confused and frightened, although his eyes fixated on the front of her tee shirt when she walked in, and she realized she'd not taken the time to put on a bra. The man just couldn't help himself, no matter what. His left arm was in a sling. She could almost feel sorry for the schmuck -- almost.

"I didn't want to start until you arrived, Krystal," said Jefferson.

"Thanks." She turned her attention to Cogburn. "So, you gonna tell us what happened, Charlie?"

Cogburn didn't say anything for a full minute as he struggled to organize his thoughts. This was unusual because Charlie Cogburn hardly ever thought before he spoke.

"I was kidnapped and held against my will," he began.

"What happened to your shoulder," Jefferson asked.

"I got shot."

"Who shot you?"

"A guy named Buchalter."

Murphy almost dropped her coffee. "Leon Buchalter?" Jefferson raised an eyebrow at her but remained silent, looking on.

"Yeah, I think his name was Leon. He worked at the White House."

She needed to inform Whitehall as soon as possible. This would really stir the pot. "Uh, Lieutenant, can we step outside for second?" she said to Jefferson.

When the door to the interrogation room had closed behind them she said, "I don't think we should question him any further until we inform the FBI."

"What's this about the FBI?"

"Enoch Whitehall thinks Cogburn is involved with the kidnapping and murder of a White House security man named Leon Buchalter. They both disappeared at the same time, and they allegedly were working together. Buchalter's body turned up early yesterday morning, and now Charlie shows up on our doorstep."

"Whitehall thinks Charlie might have killed Buchalter?" Jefferson was incredulous.

"He's not certain, of course, but now we have Charlie claiming that the other guy shot him. It might have been self-defense."

"We need to look after our own, Krystal. I won't have the FBI questioning one of our people before we have all the facts ourselves."

"Lieutenant, this thing goes deeper than you might think, and it's somehow related to the Kondratiev murder, maybe even the White House. The way Whitehall was talking we could be dealing with international espionage here. The Bureau will be into this, like it or not."

Jefferson was not happy. She'd just dropped a stink bomb on him. She braced herself for a dressing down.

"Jeez, Krystal, why didn't you tell me the FBI was interested in Cogburn?"

"I didn't know for sure until yesterday, and you were out when I got back. I was going to fill you in today."

"Yesterday." He let the word hang for a moment like an accusation. "What about this fellow, Buchalter?"

"Whitehall claims he was working with Cogburn, but Charlie never mentioned it to me. Did you know?"

"Of course not. What's the jerk gotten into? The entire Department could be damaged by something like this."

"All the better reason to let the FBI in on the ground floor, Marty. Like it or not, we're in the middle of a Federal investigation."

She endured Jefferson's frustrated scowl for a beat before he said. "We're still going to question him here tonight. You can call Whitehall first thing in the morning. No need to ruin his night, too." He gave her a look that brooked no rebuttal. "With some luck Charlie might tell us something useful."

*****

Enoch Whitehall arrived at Arlington Police Headquarters just before eight AM to find a bleary-eyed Murphy sitting on the steps outside waiting for him. She held two large Styrofoam cups of coffee and handed one to him.

"You should have called me last night," he said.

"Jefferson wouldn't permit it, and you shouldn't blame him. He was just trying to protect the Department."

"Has Cogburn said anything?"

"Oh, lots. You'll be amazed. He talked all night. You'll want to hear it for yourself, but I recommend you wait awhile and let him rest. He's near collapse, and he's recovering from a GSW," a gunshot wound.

For Whitehall that was not necessarily a bad thing. "I'm taking him into FBI custody."

"Is that really necessary?"

"I received the autopsy results on Buchalter late yesterday. The bullets that killed him came from Cogburn's 9MM Beretta." All law enforcement weapons' forensic data were on file with the FBI.

Despite their previous conjectures, Murphy was still surprised. "Are you going to charge him with murder?"

"A preliminary charge of kidnapping and murder will suffice for us to take him into custody."

"I still say it's not Charlie's style."

"Maybe he had help."

"Oh, he had help all right. Wait 'til you hear. By the way, he says Buchalter shot him. And he says that it was that Russian woman who shot Buchalter – with Charlie's pistol, of course."

Murphy could see that this news did not sit well with Whitehall. She seemed to be pissing everybody off. This case was rife with unexpected twists and complications. What was missing was motive.

"Mind if I tag along?" she asked. What she really wanted at this moment was a hot shower and change of clothes, but she wanted to remain in the middle of this thing, whatever it was.

"I'd welcome it. I want you to sit in when I question him. It might make him feel more comfortable, and you could catch any contradictions in his story."

CHAPTER 49

As Whitehall and Murphy were meeting, Strachey, Ramsay, and Sasha were sipping coffee around a table in a suite at Georgetown's Four Seasons Hotel. Amy was dozing on the sofa. She'd spent the night there because Strachey refused to allow her to go home alone.

The previous night had been a busy one, especially for Strachey. He's placed a hood over Cogburn's head and left it there until he had driven the wounded cop around the entire Beltway several times before leaving him in the car in front of Arlington Police Headquarters and slipping away. Strachey used the time to impress upon Cogburn the consequences he would face if he did not do exactly as instructed.

Leaving Buchalter's body in Tekla's driveway in the pre-dawn hours of the previous morning had been even more taxing.

Now they waited.

"I think we've stirred the pot sufficiently to steer the authorities in the right direction, don't you?" Sasha asked.

"Dropping Buchalter's body in front of Tekla's house with that note was a stroke of genius, if a bit macabre," said Strachey. "If there were any alcohol here, I'd toast you, Sasha, despite the early hour."

In fact, the entire plan had been Sasha's while the execution was left to the boys.

"You could have been big in the Mob," Strachey concluded, and saluted her with his coffee cup.

"She is big in the Mob," was Ramsay's wry comment. "It's just an Israeli mob rather than the Italian one. And you did a good job convincing Cogburn, Strachey. The miserable bastard must have sung them an entire opera by now."

Praise from Ramsay was a rare thing, and in spite of himself Strachey smiled. "Even a one-eyed pig would begin to focus on Tekla now. But the fat lady has yet to sing."

Ramsay grimaced at the mixed metaphor and said, "I've set things in motion." While the CIA man was driving Cogburn in circles Ramsay had been on the phone with de Blottière. He'd instructed the Frenchman to charter a private jet to ferry the Nelsons and Vicky Kondratieva from Paris to a small airport outside of Washington. Ramsay hoped the Israelis wouldn't mind his using a Mossad-backed black American Express Centurion card for the charter. He would pay them back later.

"They'll land in three or four hours," said Ramsay. "Sasha will take the Mustang to fetch them."

Sasha was the only one of the four who had gotten a decent night's sleep. She would make the three hour drive west to Shenandoah Regional Airport to make the pick-up and bring the travelers back to the Four Seasons.

"There's not a lot of time left," said Strachey. Shurgin arrives tomorrow, and the agreement is to be signed the day after."

"Timing is everything," sighed Ramsay, "but I'm glad we've stopped playing defense and gone on the offense."

CHAPTER 50

Chertkov examined Tekla through slitted eyes. The man was falling apart. How could this gutless wretch have become the SVR's most powerful penetration of the American Government? In the beginning dealing with the man's arrogance and overweening pride had tested Chertkov's patience as an agent handler. But now, in the face of adversity Tekla was like a child pleading with his parents for protection from a bully.

"They're getting too close, Chertkov. Buchalter worked directly for me, and now they'll tie him to Kondratiev thanks to that note they found in his pocket. I didn't like the way that FBI agent was looking at me."

"Buchalter is dead. He's not going to say anything to incriminate you. All you have to do is keep quiet. They can't prove a thing."

"And I say you're wrong. The whole Kondratiev thing is being resurrected."

"We're handling the Kondratiev matter," Chertkov insisted.

"Not very well, so far."

Chertkov was barely able to control his exasperation. "Your place is NOT to question,

Tekla," he snarled, "Just play your role and say the words we give you. The rest is no longer your concern."

"Not my concern, you say? Whose neck is at risk here, yours? No, mine! I'm thinking about coming in."

Now he had Chertkov's full attention. "Coming in? You mean running away to Moscow? Now? That's completely out of the question."

They would never allow Tekla to defect. A defection would lead inevitably to the very questions Moscow did not want to have asked. No, they would kill Tekla before letting the world know he worked for Moscow. Chertkov was genuinely surprised that Tekla did not realize this. His father would have. Adam Tekla had been of the old school.

Tekla gave him a look like a man whose dog had just bitten him.

Chertkov adopted a soothing tone. Maybe he could reason with the coward. "You needn't worry. There are problems, yes, but we will do absolutely nothing that could bring suspicion on you. The worst is over, my friend." *But we will kill you if you step too far out of line*.

"What about Bob Strachey?" asked Tekla. "Wouldn't it be better to concentrate on him? He could lead you to the others."

"I'm working on it, but Strachey is keeping a low

profile. It's possible he suspects we'll go after him next. Right now we need to follow every lead, and you will make that phone call."

CHAPTER 51

"Detective Murphy?"

The voice was resonant, authoritative, and dripping with testosterone. Murphy was sitting in traffic on her way home, desperate for a hot shower, a nosh, and some much needed sleep. A late afternoon thunderstorm had broken the oppressive heat, but slowed skittish Washington drivers to a snail's pace as they peered fearfully through their windshields as though they had never seen rain before.

The day had seemed to drag on forever as the hapless Cogburn was interrogated in a small, airless room at the J. Edgar Hoover Building, and Murphy was grateful when Whitehall finally had called it a day. She actually felt sorry for Cogburn, who would spend the night under guard in an FBI safehouse on Capitol Hill where they would finally permit him to rest. His story was preposterous, especially the bit about being tortured in General Kondratiev's apartment by the Russian woman and some man who looked like Clint Eastwood, but it was consistent with the facts as they knew them. Although the reason for all the mayhem still eluded them, her suspicions still centered on the Russians. And she knew that Whitehall was thinking along the same lines.

"Yes," she answered, unable to keep the weariness out of her voice.

"My name is Robert Strachey. I'm with the Central Intelligence Agency. We need to talk."

First the FBI and now the CIA? Murphy's weariness was washed away by a sudden rush of adrenaline. "What do you want to talk about?"

She'd wager a large amount that she already knew the answer.

Strachey didn't disappoint her. "General Pavel Kondratiev."

Bingo! They agreed to meet at a small bar near her apartment.

A half-hour later he walked straight to her table without hesitation after a quick scan of the bar's denizens. She was the only woman there.

Strachey was a good looking man, moderately tall, with brown hair parted on the left, blue eyes, and an easy way of moving that suggested he might once have been an athlete. She placed his age at somewhere in his early to mid-forties. He wore tan Dockers and a dark green polo shirt under a light windbreaker damp from the rain.

Most importantly he matched the description Cogburn had given of the man who had dropped him at Arlington Police Headquarters in the wee hours of the morning.

"Detective Murphy, thank you for meeting me on such short notice."

She shook his extended hand and invited him to sit. They ordered beer from a tired looking waitress. "What does the CIA have to do with Pavel Kondratiev?"

"You like to get straight to the point, don't you," he replied, unruffled. "I'm here to give you information."

"That's not the way the CIA usually works."

His lips curved into a wry smile revealing straight white teeth, but his eyes remained serious. When the beer was delivered to their table and the waitress had retreated behind the bar, he took a sip from the frosted mug before continuing, choosing his words, she guessed.

"You're right. The Agency is normally preoccupied with protecting secrets rather than divulging them. But this is a special case, and it doesn't really involve the Agency."

"You're here on your own then?"

"More or less. Until very recently I worked directly for DNCS Terry Stoddard. Terry was running an unsanctioned investigation into the murder of General Kondratiev."

She recognized Stoddard's name. "Your boss was killed in the Chain Bridge bombing." *How many more shoes were going to drop before this was over?*

"Yes."

"Why was he interested in Kondratiev?"

"For the same reason he was killed."

"Kondratiev or your boss?"

"Both."

"But Chain Bridge had nothing to do with Kondratiev. Several people were killed besides your boss."

"That's what it was meant to look like. Terry Stoddard was killed because the Russians discovered he was investigating Kondratiev's murder."

"You're saying the Russians were responsible for the Chain Bridge bomb as well as Kondratiev?" They were entering Neverland, and the phrase 'wilderness of mirrors' came unbidden into her mind.

"There is no doubt whatsoever that the Russians did it or paid someone else to do it."

Her expression must have betrayed her astonishment, and while she was still processing the possibility that the Russians had detonated a bomb in the capital of the United States Strachey pressed on. "I know that what I'm telling you might seem preposterous, but that's only because you don't yet have all the facts. That's why I had to meet you."

Murphy began to regret her easy agreement to meet this man. She should have called Whitehall first. "And you're going to give me 'all the facts?'"

"As best I'm able."

Belatedly, she asked, "May I see your identification."

The wry smile returned, and he reached for his wallet. Murphy wrapped her hand around the grip of her service pistol, the action concealed by the table top, but his hand when it reappeared held only a thin wallet, from which he extracted a plastic coated i.d. card with a photograph. It identified him as Robert Strachey, Special Executive Assistant to the Director of National Clandestine Services. He was the real deal.

"May I continue now?" he asked when she handed back the card. "And you can take your hand off your gun."

Unchastened, Murphy brought her hand out from under the table. "You're saying this is not an official CIA matter and that you're acting essentially as a private citizen?"

"You could say that, but I'm not a private citizen. I'm a highly trained intelligence officer, and I want to help you."

"Why me?"

"You were one of the original investigating officers."

"Go on," but she was unconvinced

"The murder of General Kondratiev on the eve of his press conference rang alarm bells at the CIA, especially among the older hands, but there was nothing the Agency could do about it, not officially, at least. Terry decided to mount his own operation, what we call a hip pocket operation, to get to the bottom of it when it appeared that the police investigation was at a dead end." He raised an eyebrow at her.

Murphy didn't rise to the bait. "You said you had information, Mr. Strachey. I'm not here to answer your questions about an ONGOING police investigation." She wondered what he would say if he knew the FBI was now on the case.

He shrugged and continued. "Do you know who Yuriy Nosenko was?"

The name was vaguely familiar, but she couldn't place it. "No."

"There's no reason you should know about him, I suppose. He was a KGB officer who defected to us in 1964."

Murphy had been born in 1979. "I think I might have seen a movie about it once."

"His defection ignited a war inside the Intelligence Community - was he a genuine defector, or did the Soviets dispatch him on a deception mission to conceal an important secret? In the end he was exonerated and the doubters banished. I now know that Kondratiev possessed information showing that Nosenko was indeed on a mission for the KGB, an important mission with two objectives: one to protect the identity of a high-level penetration of the CIA, and the other to conceal the Soviet hand in the assassination of President Kennedy."

Strachey stopped talking as he waited for the import of his words to sink in.

"You're serious?" she asked in disbelief. "This is all about another crank conspiracy theory?"

"I didn't expect you to accept it without proof. But let's leave that part for later and return to Kondratiev. I assume you've thoroughly debriefed Cogburn?"

"You're the one who dropped him, aren't you?"

"Yes," he replied without hesitation.

"You realize this implicates you in the murder of a federal officer?"

"I had nothing to do with that. Terry Stoddard did, however, arrange some excellent medical treatment for your partner, who was shot by the federal officer. When he was fit, I returned him to you."

"Who killed Buchalter?"

"I'm sure Cogburn told you."

"Does the alleged 'Russian woman' work for the

CIA?"

"No."

"Who is she?"

"A friend. The CIA's only involvement was confined to providing medical assistance to Cogburn and keeping him out of sight and safe until he was well enough to be released from the hospital. And even that was unofficially arranged by Terry Stoddard personally. Cogburn was treated at a hospital far from Washington under a different name. As I said, there was NO official CIA involvement. The Agency does not run domestic operations. I can give you one piece of information that will be new to you, though."

She waited.

"Cogburn's life is still in danger. Buchalter had company at the farmhouse where he was shot, Russian company. A car with diplomatic plates was seen leaving the site. Those plates correspond to a car registered to First Secretary Lev Chertkov of the Russian Embassy. Chertkov is a high ranking SVR officer. In my opinion Kondratiev was killed by Chertkov, Buchalter, or Cogburn."

Cogburn had said nothing about seeing anyone from the Russian Embassy at the farmhouse to which he claimed to have been taken by the Russian woman and her male companion. All he had said about Strachey was that he had brought him from the hospital. So how did Strachey know there was a Russian diplomat involved? There was more to this, a lot more, but she didn't think she would learn everything tonight.

She would realize later how wrong she was.

"And there's something else you should know about Chertkov. He's Brian Tekla's primary contact at the Russian Embassy."

"What's your point?"

"I don't think you're obtuse, Detective."

She needed to call Whitehall. The waters had risen way above her comfort level.

As if he read her thoughts Strachey said, "Before you do anything else, would you be willing to come with me to meet someone?"

"Now?" She groaned inwardly as fatigue again dragged against her muscles.

"Right now." He made it sound like a challenge.

"Who?"

"Vicky Kondratieva. She's waiting outside in my car."

CHAPTER 52

A light breeze was blowing and the rain had tapered off by the time they left the bar revealing early evening stars through breaks in ragged, scudding clouds. The oppressive heat of the day was gone, and the ozone-traced air felt cool on Murphy's skin. Strachey's car, a late model BMW 330 CI, was parked halfway up the block. Vicky Kondratieva sat in the back seat, her sharp featured face etched with apprehension. She started when Strachey opened the car door, but then recognized Murphy at his side.

"You are the detective who visited my house."

Murphy leaned into the car through the open door and took Vicky's hand over the seatback. "Yes, Ms. Kondratieva. I was sorry to bring you such sad news. Where have you been? We've been anxious to speak with you again."

Strachey slid behind the wheel and interrupted before Vicky could answer. "We'll get to that later. Right now, we have someplace to be."

This was against procedure, but Murphy wasn't going to stop now. She was getting answers to the questions that had nagged at her since the Kondratiev murder. The re-appearance of the General's daughter was another unexpected development, and Strachey's words about

Russian spies and the Kennedy assassination still reverberated in her skull. She wasn't sure she could believe it all, but she wouldn't back out now. She got into the car beside Strachey and closed the door.

Strachey drove toward Rosslyn before turning onto Route 50 in the direction of Falls Church. Without the benefit of the driver's rear view mirror, she didn't see the Mustang that pulled into traffic behind them, but she guessed where they were going. Murphy's cell phone rested in the pocket of her jeans, and she resisted the strong temptation to call Whitehall. She wondered if the CIA man would object.

"Could you reach into the glove compartment and hand me the pistol you'll find there?" Strachey asked.

She shot him an 'are you kidding' look.

"Don't worry, Detective Murphy. This is Virginia and I have a lawful concealed weapons permit. I was also a Boy Scout and they taught me to always be prepared."

She opened the glove compartment and found a vintage Walther PP in a worn leather holster. Without a word she handed it to him, and he clipped the holster onto his belt.

Twenty minutes later, they pulled up in front of the familiar small townhouse that Vicky Kondratieva rented a few blocks from the center of Falls Church,

Virginia.

Vicky grew increasingly nervous as they approached the door. They entered and switched on the lights to reveal a chaotic scene of overturned furniture, broken glass, and unrecognizable bits and pieces strewn carelessly about. Murphy recalled the neat Scandinavian décor from her earlier visit. The scene was repeated in every room of the house. Spines were ripped from books, pictures removed from the walls, cushions slashed, and glass crunched beneath their feet everywhere they walked. Someone had done a very thorough search, and they had not bothered to be neat about it.

In the kitchen, the contents of the refrigerator had been dumped on the tiled floor, and Strachey knelt to examine the mess. The items from the freezer were still partially frozen.

"This was done today," he said, "and not many hours ago, at that."

*****

Across the street behind a darkened upper story window of a vacant house with a yellow foreclosure notice pasted to the door a man snapped several pictures with a camera equipped with a night vision lens and called to his two companions. "The lights are on. I recognized the Kondratieva woman, and there is another woman and a man with her."

He spoke in Russian.

One of the men to whom he spoke had entered the country via Canada; the other had crossed the border into Arizona from Mexico with the help of a highly paid 'coyote.' Both carried documentation identifying them as Jordanian nationals. But in reality they were Russian, members of the elite Banner Unit, *Vympel* in Russian, controlled by Department "S" of the *Sluzhba Vneshney Razvedki*, or SVR, the Russian foreign intelligence service. Created by the KGB near the end of the Cold War, Banner was dedicated to assassination, terror, and subversion on enemy territory.

The man with the camera was a subordinate of Lev Chertkov from the SVR *Rezidentura* at the Russian Embassy. Another three-man team was in Arlington watching the late General Kondriatiev's condo. They had been looking for Vicky Kondratieva for a long time.

Chertkov's man was under strict orders to remain far away from any action in which the special operations team might engage. His task was to observe only, report back to Chertkov, and relay his orders to the team. He now punched in Chertkov's secure cell phone number and waited for his chief to answer.

Chertkov's response to the news of Vicky

Kondratieva's return came in two words. "Take them."

The SVR team would have preferred to wait for their targets to exit the house and then take them out one by one from a distance, but their orders were to capture the Kondratieva woman alive. They had no such orders for her two companions, however, and they would rely on silenced pistols and the advantage of surprise to complete their mission.

The two exited the abandoned house via a rear door and slipped into the alley in back where they split up and headed in opposite directions. They would enter the block from either end, converging on Vicky Kondratieva's townhouse from the front and rear. The *Rezidentura* officer would keep watch and warn them should their targets try to leave.

*****

Several minutes later inside Vicky's house Strachey's Blackberry buzzed with the receipt of a text message that consisted of one word: "Red."

His reaction was immediate. "Everyone take cover!" He wrapped an arm around Vicky and pulled her down into a corner by his side even as he drew his Walther.

Murphy was nonplussed and remained standing.

"What the hell are you doing?"

The sound of the splintering front door and a matching crash from the kitchen at the back of the house brought her immediately into the picture. A man dressed in dark clothing stepped into the living room with the elongated barrel of a large pistol aimed directly at her. She was still drawing her service weapon when a shot split the air, and the intruder crumpled to the floor, bright red blood geysering several feet from a hole in his forehead.

Vicky Kondratieva screamed, and Murphy turned to see Strachey motioning her to the floor as he brought his pistol around to bear towards the rear of the house. It took a split second for Murphy to realize that Strachey had shot the attacker and in all likelihood saved her life. But now, someone was approaching in a hurry from the rear of the house, alerted by the sound of Strachey's shot.

Murphy had her pistol drawn by this time, and she and Strachey had the passage covered when the second intruder skidded to a halt at the sight of his companion's body. He raised his pistol searching for a target only to discover two weapons trained on him.

The intruder was surprised to encounter armed resistance, but *Vympel* operatives do not surrender, and their reflexes are lightning fast. The man immediately leapt behind an upholstered chair, managing to squeeze off two rounds as he went down that would have taken off Murphy's head had she not dove to the floor an instant earlier. His pistol emitted only muffled coughs. Being in the open made her the assailant's easiest and therefore primary target, and she scrambled desperately for cover. Strachey no longer had an angle that would permit him to cover her, and she realized she could not make it in time. She fired blindly in the direction of the assailant, but the shots went high, and she saw the man rise to bring his gun to bear on her again. Things started to move in slow motion, and she knew she was about to die.

A surprised expression appeared suddenly on the assailant's face, and something appeared to protrude from the side of his neck as his shoulder was washed in crimson. He managed to fire once more as he toppled to his side, but the round buried itself in the floor. Murphy looked up toward the shattered front door and thought for a wild instant that she saw Clint Eastwood standing on the threshold before he disappeared into the darkness outside.

Except for his legs, the man on the floor was hidden by the chair behind which he had taken cover. His legs twitched grotesquely for several seconds before going still. Keeping her pistol at the ready, she cautiously approached, signaling Strachey to remain where he was with Vicky until she was sure they were clear.

The man was dead, eyes still wide and bulging in the same surprise Murphy had glimpsed as he fell. A large knife was buried deeply in his neck, its point visible on the other side. She looked again in the direction of the open front door. SOMEONE had been there and thrown the knife.

"Who was that?" Murphy still stared at the door.

"What do you mean?" asked Strachey blandly over his shoulder as he led a trembling Vicky Kondratieva toward the back of the house away from the sight of the dead men.

"The guy who threw the knife?"

"Sorry. I didn't see anyone. The dead guy must have fallen on his own knife."

Murphy stomped angrily after them. *Goddamned CIA games!* "Look," she said, "I have to call this in. We have two dead people in there." She jerked a thumb over her shoulder. "There WILL be questions, and you're not fading away into the night this time."

"I know. But we have things to do first," he said, leading Vicky to a kitchen chair. He put an arm gently around her shoulder and said, "We must get it now, Vicky, before anyone arrives. We're going to put a stop to this once and for all."

The General's daughter squeezed her eyes tightly shut and nodded. She rose to walk to the smashed kitchen door. The back yard was overgrown with neglect, but had clearly been landscaped with a variety of decorative bushes and flowers. Vicky

Kondratieva stooped over a bed of brightly flowering mums and pulled one of the plants from the earth. Beneath it nestled a glass jar containing a folded sheet of paper that she handed with obvious reluctance to Strachey. Her shoulders shook with silent sobs.

"Thank you, Vicky. It's what your father would have wanted."

What now, buried treasure? Murphy asked herself as she called the Falls Church Police on her cell phone. "They'll be here within five minutes, Strachey. If there's anything you want to tell me before this place is swarming with cops, you'd best do it now."

Strachey removed the paper from the jar and unfolded it. After a cursory glance, he placed it in his pocket.

"What's that?" asked Murphy.

"Something we need."

She held out her hand. "You'll have to hand it over."

"Why?"

"It's material evidence."

"Evidence of what?"

Murphy was momentarily confused as the adrenaline from the unexpected violence drained from her system.

"Look," Strachey began, and she knew he was going to ask her to ignore evidence. "This is just a piece of paper as far as you're concerned. The 'material evidence' is those two bodies inside the house. We did nothing illegal in coming here, and we did nothing illegal in defending ourselves. It is Vicky's house, after all. What I saw was a home invasion by armed men intent on killing whomever they found inside. That was the crime. We're all witnesses. You don't know that this piece of paper had anything to do with it."

Murphy's mind clicked back into gear. "Motive."

"Who knows what their motive was? They broke in. They tried to kill us all. That's all that needs be said for now. Perhaps when you identify the intruders there'll be more to say."

"You didn't know them?"

"Never saw them before in my life, Scout's honor." Strachey held up his right hand with three fingers raised.

"You brought me here for a purpose," said Murphy. "I'm assuming it wasn't so I could get shot at."

"Correct. First, I wanted to put you back in touch with Vicky, and second I wanted to give you something. May I assume you're working with the FBI on the death of Leon Buchalter?"

"Yes." So he'd figured that out, too. This guy was always a step ahead of her. The FBI she could understand – they were cops just like her, but the CIA was an animal of a different stripe.

"Excellent." He pulled a folded plastic document folder from his inside jacket pocket and handed it to her. "Vicky was going to explain this to you, but we don't have time now. I'm sure your Bureau friends will figure it out soon enough. I wouldn't show it to the police if I were you because it would just waste time. You should take it to the Bureau. Right now it's important for her safety that I take Vicky as far away from here as possible. But she's not going to disappear again."

Sirens sounded in the distance.

CHAPTER 53

Across the street Chertkov's watcher remained at his post snapping pictures. The gunshots that had shattered the evening's silence signaled that something had gone terribly wrong. The Vympel operatives were carrying suppressed weapons, so the loud reports meant they had encountered unexpected resistance. A moment later the figure of a tall, lanky man in dark clothing materialized seemingly from nowhere at the open door of Kondratieva's house. He made a motion with his arm and stood there for only a few seconds before slipping away.

It became very quiet then, and when the operatives did not reappear he feared the worst. Still he waited. And then approaching sirens sounded. Within moments the street below was flooded with police cars and uniformed figures.

Every instinct told him to bolt, but he forced his breathing back to normal and continued to watch. He would not leave unless the police turned their attention to the abandoned house where he was hiding. The night dragged on, but after an hour he was rewarded when the Kondratiev woman and her two friends emerged from the house accompanied by several police officers. As soon as he was able to capture clear images of the unidentified man and woman he called Chertkov to report.

Chertkov's voice was angry but controlled. He asked for verbal descriptions of the two people with Kondratieva. "Is the woman tall and blond?"

"No, she has dark hair and is not particularly tall. She seems to be leading the discussion with the police."

When he described the man, Chertkov exclaimed, "It must be Strachey from the CIA. I want you to follow him, and I want him dead. It's worth your life if you lose him. The other team will link up with you as soon as possible." Chertkov instructed him to synchronize his walkie-talkie to the frequency used by the other team.

He gathered his equipment and left by the rear door, using a near-by alley to cross over to the next block where he had left his car. He drove around the block, found a dark area where he could park and still keep the Kondratiev house in view Then he waited, binoculars glued to his eyes as he kept watch on Strachey's BMW.

The conversation with the police which was clearly not entirely amicable lasted a long time, long enough for the second team to cover the distance from Arlington to Falls Church and take up position.

*****

There are a limited number of observation points

that offer optimal lines of sight for any surveillance operation. This means that a professional, no matter who he's working for, nine times out of ten, will choose one of these same points to get the job done, such as the vacant house across the street from Vicky's home. The same was true of the position on the street now chosen by Chertkov's watcher.

Ramsay, slumped behind the wheel of his rented Mustang with the seat pushed back the maximum distance from the wheel, took a keen interest in the new arrival who might have been a resident returning home for the evening, had it not been for the diplomatic tags on his car. The binoculars left no room for doubt.

*****

All things considered, the Falls Church cops were more than reasonable, aided no doubt by the fact that Murphy was a fellow officer. She'd decided to go with Strachey's idea until she could talk to Whitehall. The facts of the incident with a single exception were pretty straightforward, the exception being the origin of the commando knife in the neck of the second intruder.

Strachey reluctantly handed over his Walther PP to be checked for ballistics. The officers promised it would be returned to him in due course, which probably meant months from now. He said he was going to the Four Seasons Hotel in Georgetown where he had arranged for a suite. Murphy wrote her cell number on the back of her business card and handed it to him. "Keep in touch," she said before turning back to her Falls Church brethren.

She had to get in touch with Whitehall pronto.

She watched Strachey's BMW pull away from the curb and was surprised a few seconds later to see two cars follow after him, one a late model Chevrolet Malibu with diplomatic plates and the other a Mustang. "More damned CIA fun and games," she thought.

CHAPTER 54

Strachey helped Vicky into his BMW and got behind the wheel. Before he could start the engine his Blackberry vibrated. It was Ramsay.

"You've picked up a watcher," he said, "and he probably has company. They'll follow you out of here. Do you still have your weapon?"

Strachey swore under his breath. "No, the cops took it. How about you?"

"The only weapon I had is still in that guy's neck."

"We're practically surrounded by cops right here, and they all have guns," said Strachey.

"It's tempting, but that's a last resort. If you ask them for protection now, they'll ask too many questions that you'll have to answer, and that would endanger our plan."

"If I leave and these guys catch up it'll endanger our plan, too, probably fatally. We can't just drive around aimlessly and hope we can outrun them. From what we've seen tonight, these guys are desperate and they're ready to kill to get their hands on what we have."

"You do have the last page, then?"

"Yeah, and I gave the originals of the others to

Murphy like we planned. She'll take them to the FBI." Strachey's mind was racing in search of an idea that would guarantee Vicky's safety without upsetting the timing of the events they needed for their plan to work. The first step was getting the Andropov Memorandum, minus the final page, into the hands of the FBI. They would translate it and they had the resources to authenticate it. The next step was to make the memo's contents public and force the Bureau to admit they possessed the original and that it was real. Vicky's part in the final step was vital. But if everything spiraled out of control tonight and they lost possession of the page in his pocket, either to their pursuers or the FBI, their leverage would be gone. The FBI could not be counted on to share their goal of exposing the KGB hand in the Kennedy assassination. This was high-level politics, and politicians sometimes preferred to let sleeping dogs lie.

Vicky had listened to his end of the conversation, and it was enough for her to surmise that the danger had not passed. She was looking at him wide-eyed. After all she had been through he couldn't and wouldn't force her to take another mortal risk without her agreement.

"Vicky, we've still got a problem. There are more of them out there waiting for us to leave. We have a choice: we can remain here with the police and ask for their protection, which means we would have to explain everything that has happened and very likely surrender the last page of the memo, or we can take our chances. If we do the former we'll lose control of the only thing that will prove that what we're saying is true. If we run, I can't guarantee the outcome. What we do now is your decision to make."

Vicky knew their plan. To place her safety in the hands of the authorities now risked failure. "We have to continue," she said, "for my father."

Strachey spoke into his Blackberry, "Ramsay, we're going to make a run for it. Let's hope this BMW can justify what it cost me. Stay with us so we can see how many cars and people we have to deal with and hope we can figure something out on the fly." As the one most familiar with the turf, Strachey knew that the choice of a route would be his decision.

"How well can you drive that thing?" asked Ramsay.

"I took the defensive driving course at the Farm, and I've had a couple of occasions to use the skill since then."

"Let's hope so. I'm ready whenever you are, so you'd better get out of there before the cops begin to wonder why you're waiting around."

"I'll keep the phone turned on and switch to hands free mode. Stay in touch."

Strachey engaged the gear and pulled away from the curb. He had to decide whether to turn back in the direction of Washington or strike out for the suburbs. It was late, nearly midnight, and the streets were empty. If he chose Washington he would face innumerable traffic lights and limited distances that would restrict use the BMW's acceleration and handling, meaning pursuit could easily keep pace or even catch up to him. He pulled the shift lever back to manual mode so he could control the gears with the paddles mounted on the steering wheel and headed for the suburbs. Lee Highway would take him west toward Merrifield and had fewer traffic lights than Route 7 that would take him north into the tangle of construction around Tyson's Corner.

Ramsay's voice came over the speaker. "We have an advantage, Strachey. Russians are lousy drivers."

CHAPTER 55

As expected, Lee Highway was practically deserted at this late hour and Strachey caught the light still green at the intersection with Route 7. He accelerated smoothly through the gears and was nearly at the crest of a gentle hill before the headlights appeared behind them, disappearing as he headed down the other side.

"You have two cars behind you, and they both just boomed through the stoplight at Route 7." Ramsay again. The second car had been waiting on a side street and pulled immediately behind the Malibu. It was another Chevy, an Impala, and it carried three men. Ramsay had pulled out behind the Impala. "I'm a block behind them keeping pace. What are you planning?"

"I don't know yet, but I'm sure something will crop up." Strachey pushed the BMW to seventy and concentrated on trying to time the lights ahead while his mind worked furiously to think of a way out of the predicament.

"Ramsay, I've got an idea, assuming you are a helluva driver."

"Go on."

Strachey outlined his plan. He knew there was a long stretch of straightaway not far ahead on which the pursuing Russians could be counted upon to pick up speed. A deep concrete storm drain ran along the right side of the roadway.

"We're coming to the straightaway now, Ramsay. Are you ready?"

"I've got it."

*****

Ramsay stomped on the accelerator to bring the Mustang up fast behind the second Chevy, gauging his speed carefully first to match its speed and then to move in close. It happened fast when he made contact with the left rear corner of the Russians' car and the physics took over. The nudge he'd provided propelled the Chevy's rear at an angle and at a speed that exceeded that of the front wheels. This caused the Chevy to skew sideways as the driver vainly fought to regain control, but the road surface was still slick from the rain earlier in the evening, and again the laws of physics won. As the car neared the point where it was heading sideways down the roadway it flipped and rolled side over side before plunging into the storm drain where it came to rest on its roof.

Ramsay slowed the Mustang as the Russians careened out of control ahead of him and watched the violent results of the maneuver he had just performed. Ramsay had taken a big chance. The so-called 'pit maneuver' was usually performed only at speeds under 35 miles-per-hour because to attempt it at high speed risked wrecking both cars and causing collateral damage to people and property.

He pulled to the side of the road and watched for a moment before stepping out of his car and opening the trunk. Having found what he was looking for he slid down the side of the concrete storm drain and approached the wreck. The two passengers had been thrown clear and lay not far apart a few yards distant. Through the sagging driver's side door he could see the driver immobilized by twisted metal and still restrained by his seat belt.

A groan from one of the passengers caught his attention and he approached carefully, aware that the Russians most certainly were armed. A look at the man who was trying feebly to move confirmed he was in no condition to use a pistol. Both of his legs were bent at unnatural angles and sharp ends of bone protruded from one torn trouser leg. The second passenger lay unmoving not far away. They were large men, well-muscled, with closely cropped hair, probably *Vympel* or *Spetsnaz*, he thought.

Ramsay knelt over the first man and brought the tire iron he carried from the Mustang's trunk down across the side of his head. He arm swept through the vicious motion twice, and the sound the tire iron made when it hit the bone was like that of a melon breaking open. Ramsay walked to the second Russian and repeated the action. These were enemies he would not have to fight again another day.

The driver, he discovered, was still alive and relatively unharmed. He had seen what Ramsay had done to his comrades, unable to extricate himself from the wreckage, and he cringed as the tall man approached.

There wasn't much time. They were not far from a residential neighborhood, and the banshee shriek of tires and rending metal may have attracted attention at this quiet time of night.

Ramsay grabbed a bloody handful of the driver's hair and brought his face close. "Who are you?"

When he didn't get an immediate response he brandished the tire iron, and the driver stammered his name. "Rumyantsev. Igor Rumyantsev."

"You're from the Russian Embassy?"

"Yes. Third Secretary."

"You're SVR. Who sent you?"

The driver hesitated only a second before replying, "Chertkov. It was Lev Chertkov." In his eyes appeared a faint glimmer of hope that this confession would save him.

Ramsay had all the confirmation he needed. He

judged the angle insufficient to administer the same *coup de grace*, and so he reversed the tire iron in his hand and shoved the sharp end through the driver's eye and into his brain. He returned to the Mustang and drove away at high speed.

The first man Ewan had killed in cold blood, close up and personal, had been a close friend and fellow CIA officer who had betrayed him and wished him dead. That killing had sent a pain profoundly into his soul, and it was weeks before he was able to square it with his conscience. Nearly two decades had passed since then and he no longer tortured himself with remorse at the death he administered to enemies. He had seen these same enemies kill innocents and, worse, rape, torture and maim his wife, and he no longer bothered to analyze whether he was meting out justice or revenge, or whether he had become a full-blown sociopath. He lived with the certainty that men such as those he had killed tonight were better dead than left alive to do more harm.

"Strachey, are you still there?" Ramsay spoke into his Blackberry.

"Yes."

"I'll try to catch up and take care of the other one."

"No need. He turned off right after you flipped his buddies. I think it scared him off."

Ramsay took a quick look in his rear view mirror

thinking it was possible the other car had doubled back to come after him, but the road behind was clear. "Let's drive around a while longer to make sure we're clean. Then we'll head back to the Four Seasons. And, Strachey, that was a good idea. I told you Russians were lousy drivers."

*****

At the Four Seasons Sasha put down her cell phone and said, "They'll be here in about an hour. They had a few problems, but it's OK now." Ramsay had not provided any details.

Amy sat at the desk working on her laptop putting the finishing touches on an English translation of the Andropov Memorandum. She and Sasha had worked on the document most of the afternoon and evening and were now ready to assemble an electronic document package containing photos of the originals together with the translation. By the time the men returned with Vicky they would be ready to send the package to the list of e-mail addresses Amy had compiled.

CHAPTER 56

Oblivious to the events in Falls Church of the preceding evening, Vitaliy Mikhailovich Shurgin tapped his foot nervously on the marble tiled deck of the extravagantly fitted out Ilyushin 96-300, the wide-body Presidential aircraft of the Russian Federation.   Already descending along a gentle glide path into Andrews Air Force Base, just outside Washington, DC, the big gilded jet seemed to float across the Maryland landscape. Preoccupied, Shurgin stared at the interior wall next to him. It was covered in white Russian silk decorated with religious scenes.   Ahead in the cabin a bible and prayer books lay nestled in a gold box. The Orthodox faith was so elementally Russian. The opiate of the masses. Marx's iconic characterization of religion sprang to mind. What better way to distinguish himself in the minds of the Russian public from the decrepit leaders of the Soviet era than to take advantage of Marx's astute observation and embrace religion? It had worked for the Tsars; why not for him?

In the old days the KGB had exerted iron control over the Russian Orthodox Church.   Many of its priests, and even its highest prelates had been KGB agents and informers.   Someone once observed that when Russia adopted Christianity in the Tenth Century the people had not so much submitted to

God as brought him into their homes as a pet in the form of the ubiquitous Russian icon. The KGB had made of Him a submissive pet. Now the Church was a symbol of a resurgent Russian nationalism. Shurgin could support that.

Under his inspired leadership Mother Russia would rise from the ashes of Communism and the disastrous post-Soviet capitalist experiment to become the dominant world power. She possessed vast natural resources and people with strong backs. The capitalist experiment had brought with it foreign ideas of 'democracy' and 'freedom,' but these had infected mostly the urban literate, the intellectuals, and university students – the traditional 'enemies of the state.' But Shurgin knew that Russians were not made for democracy. They needed a strong leader, someone to show them the way, to inspire them because only by uniting them in purpose could the strength of the nation be wielded properly against her enemies.

The land rushing up beneath him now to receive the Ilyushin's wheels was sharply defined by the slanting rays of the rising sun. This was enemy territory. The Americans were still powerful though weakened by years of war abroad and a growing lack of faith in their institutions. Now was the perfect moment to bring them finally to their knees, when they would not even recognize the fact that they had been stripped of their military advantage. Russia would be America's military equal at last, even more than an equal. Russia would be superior because she had a leader who was dedicated to her greatness and not afraid to use his power.

With the Andropov Memorandum still missing Shurgin's mission was not without risk.   He should have had Kondratiev shot when he had the chance in Russia, but the old fool had somehow gotten himself elected to Parliament and was thus immune to arrest under Russian law.   Shurgin was still building his strength at the time and had not dared touch Kondratiev, and then the bastard had escaped to America.   It had been the General himself who revealed in a letter to Shurgin that he possessed the Andropov document.   If Shurgin did not turn from his current path, if he did not institute real 'democracy,' Kondratiev threatened to make it public.   Even with their political disagreements, how could the former KGB General, a son of Russia, turn his back on his native land so completely?   As he had with other enemies -- journalists, television news reporters, and arrogant 'oligarchs' -- Shurgin ordered the General's death and the retrieval or destruction of the document.

The death of the General had afforded some small measure of satisfaction, but the missing document still threatened Shurgin's mission to America.   For the time being those who possessed it had been driven to ground and were afraid to come out of hiding.   He decided to take the risk of going to Washington while the document was still in limbo.   Normally, he would have preferred to hold all the cards, but the arms reduction agreement, an agreement that in fact required only the Americans to weaken their arsenal, was too important to his strategy to postpone any longer. With a little luck either his people might still seize the document or he would find a way to neutralize it. The Kennedy assassination remained a vivid scar on the American consciousness, but it had happened half a century earlier at the height of the Cold War. Neither he nor the new Russian Federation could be held accountable for the sins of Khrushchev. But there was other damaging information that pointed to a contemporary sin.

The Ilyushin's wheels touched down, the pilot's skill preventing even the slightest bump, and through his window Shurgin could see the motorcade waiting on the tarmac, American and Russian flags flying side by side, the American President waiting to shake his hand when he deplaned.

CHAPTER 57

"It's incomplete."

It was nine in the morning and Murphy sat in a conference room at FBI Headquarters with Whitehall and a Russian language translator. The latter had joined them a few minutes earlier to report on the document Strachey had given Murphy at Vicky Kondratieva's house.

Murphy was feeling the effects of a second straight night without sleep. Outside a beautiful day was getting underway, unusually cool for late August in Washington, a benefit from the lingering effects of yesterday's storm.

Murphy thought immediately of the piece of paper Strachey had stuffed into his pocket and swore to herself that when this was over she would never have anything to do with the CIA again.

Just before the police arrived at Vicky's house, Strachey had given her a plasticine bag containing four sheets of yellowing paper. They were the originals, he said, of a top secret KGB memorandum prepared in 1967 for Yuriy Andropov, whoever that was. Strachey suggested that the FBI would be quite interested in the contents because they contained the information General Pavel Kondratiev had intended to make public and for which he had been murdered. These papers, he said, were at the root of everything that had happened – Whitehall's long sought after motive.

The Falls Church police had questioned them all thoroughly before letting them go. The fact that she was a fellow officer lent credibility to their statements. Honoring Strachey's wishes, Murphy did not mention the buried glass jar partly because she was sure neither Strachey nor Vicky Kondratieva would confirm it, and partly because the CIA man had saved her life. And technically Strachey was correct in describing the incident as a violent home invasion. Neither of the intruders had said a word during the confrontation, least of all about looking for a piece of paper, but until they were identified no other motive fit the situation as Murphy saw it.

She called Whitehall shortly after midnight and arranged to meet him at the Hoover Building. She would have to report the incident to the Arlington Police as soon as possible and turn in her badge and gun, the badge because she would be on temporary leave while the incident was investigated and the gun because it would be subjected to forensics analysis. The fact that she had killed no one made no difference. They would find the two bullets she had fired buried in the wall, but that didn't change the fact that people were dead. Strachey had already surrendered his pistol to the Falls Church investigating officers.

Lieutenant Jefferson would again be unhappy that she went to the FBI before reporting to Arlington, but she was convinced there was more at stake here than the pride of the Arlington constabulary. If half of what Strachey had told her was true, what she held was way above the pay grade of anyone in Arlington.

*****

"What do you mean, 'incomplete'?" Whitehall's sharp question to the translator brought her back to the present.

"The fourth page ends in mid-sentence," replied the translator, a short, balding fellow with an unkempt fringe of graying hair. He had worked on the faded single-spaced Cyrillic document since being called in by Whitehall several hours earlier. He pulled off his glasses with one hand and rubbed his aching eyes with the other. "It's obvious that one or more additional pages are missing," he finished.

Whitehall turned his attention to Murphy. "This is everything Strachey gave you?"

Mentally hurling imprecations at Strachey, she replied, "Yes. There was another piece of paper, but he didn't give it to me."

"Another piece of paper?" Whitehall gave her a sharp look.

She told him about the glass jar Vicky Kondratieva had retrieved from her garden, and Whitehall slapped the palm of his hand on the conference table, startling Murphy. "Damn the CIA! What are they playing at here?"

"Who knows? What does the document say?" ventured Murphy.

Still fuming, Whitehall looked expectantly at the translator.

"Well," the translator's voice was hushed, almost reverential, "for the most part it deals with Lee Harvey Oswald. This memorandum may have been one of a series on past operations prepared for Andropov when he became head of the KGB. It says that Oswald was trained in the Soviet Union as an agent and dispatched to the U.S. to await contact and orders. Later, Nikita Khrushchev was so outraged by the Cuban Missile Crisis that he ordered Kennedy's assassination. The Cubans were involved, too. Oswald was called to a meeting in Mexico City where he received his orders." He licked his lips. "It also says that Yuriy Nosenko was sent to the CIA as part of a deception operation designed to conceal the KGB's role in the assassination and to divert attention from a high-level penetration of the CIA."

Whitehall shook his head in disbelief. "Do you think it's genuine?"

The translator licked his lips again. This was

the key question, and he knew it, so he answered carefully. "I can't say for sure, but the document is similar to other originals I've seen from the KGB archives. The age of the paper seems about right, but this should all be confirmed by the forensics experts."

Whitehall turned again to Murphy. "Do you know what this means? President Shurgin's plane touched down at Andrews about three hours ago. This very afternoon he and the President will sign the new strategic arms reduction agreement at the White House." His voice trailed off as another thought struck him. "Do you think the CIA has hatched a plot to wreck the agreement? Could they have killed Kondratiev, as well as Buchalter?"

"You're not really asking me that, are you?" returned Murphy in a tired voice. The same idea had occurred to her, but she'd discarded it as improbable. She figured Whitehall would do the same. Besides Strachey's claims there was just too much evidence militating against such a theory. "I'd bet anything that the guys who tried to kill us last night were after this document, and probably whatever it was that Vicky Kondratieva pulled out of that mason jar. Strachey's CIA, and they tried to kill him, too. And remember what he said about that Stoddard guy and Chain Bridge. I think this document is the motive you've been looking for, and I think the Russians are after it. Strachey claimed that a Russian diplomat was present when Buchalter was killed and that he's pals with Brian

Tekla. What do you think that's all about? There are a lot of loose ends, but the Russian thread runs through it all."

Whitehall dismissed the translator with orders to deliver the document to the FBI lab for authentication. When they were alone Murphy waited as he mulled it all over. At last he said, "You're in this very deep, Detective, too deep to climb out now. In fact, you're the only person who pulls together all the aspects, from Kondratiev's murder until today."

He scrutinized her for several more beats before continuing. "You and I are going to see Director Mulvaney right now. I'm going to ask him to call your Chief and have you seconded to the FBI for the duration of this case."

Murphy was too tired to protest. She wondered if they might eventually ask her to push the button that would send nuclear tipped missiles speeding toward Moscow.

CHAPTER 58

The National Mall began filling early with tourists eager to take advantage of the picture perfect weather. At the Tidal Basin the dome of the Jefferson Memorial gleamed in the sunlight, and all over the city white marble and Indiana limestone dazzled against a cloudless sky. The brewing storm remained invisible for the moment as bureaucrats, politicians, and visitors enjoyed a welcome respite from the summer heat.

Shortly before noon President Shurgin emerged from Blair House and inhaled deeply of the freshened air. Across the cordoned off portion of Pennsylvania Avenue, directly opposite, stood the White House framed by its manicured lawns and gardens. Shurgin descended to the sidewalk where his escort of Secret Service and Russian security men waited. In a few moments he would partake of a formal luncheon to be followed by the treaty signing ceremony in the East Room. American and Russian flags were festooned everywhere along the street, and the usual crowd of protesters in Lafayette Park had been replaced by enthusiastic partisans of the treaty waving signs and flags. Shurgin smiled and waved at the crowd, all the while recalling the years and funds the KGB had spent subverting American 'peace' movements.

The signing ceremony would be followed by a brief

press conference on the South Lawn after which a motorcade would escort him back to Andrews Air Force Base in Maryland for his flight home. He did not want to remain in Washington any longer than necessary.

The Russian President's wiry figure was draped in a finely cut light wool summer suit that had been made by a Saville Row tailor. His Egyptian cotton shirt was hand-made and his red tie was from Hermés. Nearly seventy, Shurgin was proud of his trim waist and well-known athleticism. He was an expert rifle shot and held a black belt in Jiu-Jitsu, facts that were played up frequently in the Russian press to enhance his image as a vigorous leader. His people liked a strong, virile leader, and Shurgin played the role well. Critics said his bravado was a compensation for his small stature. But that, too, was an exaggeration. At five feet seven inches, he was taller than many Hollywood idols. His reddish blond hair had begun to thin, and he kept it trimmed short these days, but both friend and enemy alike referred to him as 'the fox.'

The thought of his nickname evoked unbidden memories of the late General Yuriy Ivanovich Morozov, his closest and most trusted friend of many years. A man of imposing bulk, Morozov had been the Russian bear to Shurgin's fox. Morozov had been capable of extreme violence and cruelty, but was also a font of common sense and restraint that counter-balanced Shurgin's sometimes dangerous impetuosity. The partnership had worked well during the turbulent years immediately following the end of Soviet Communism, with Shurgin on the outside handling money and strategy and Morozov still a General in charge of Directorate 'S,' the SVR's illegals department where he wielded the power that kept Shurgin's enemies in check both at home and abroad.   Shurgin wished his wise friend and counselor were still at his side, but Morozov had died years ago with a garrote around his neck in a basement cell at Lubyanka.

Morozov had not lived to see his friend achieve the apotheosis of Russian political power because it would not have come to pass at all had Shurgin not betrayed him to his death.   The Russian President felt little remorse for his act of treachery.   One had to do what was necessary, after all, and Morozov would have understood completely.

He wondered what his friend would have advised regarding the Kondratiev matter.   Would he have urged more caution?   Would Shurgin have heeded his advice?   Kondratiev's perfidy was longstanding, and Shurgin would have had him killed long ago had it been possible.   Whatever happened now, the traitor was dead.

CHAPTER 59

The East Room is the largest room in the White House and occupies most of the first floor of the east wing. Compared to the ancient splendors of the Kremlin, it left Shurgin unimpressed. The Americans, after all, had little history compared with Mother Russia, and it showed.

The signing ceremony was brief, to be followed by a short press conference. A temporary stage had been erected on the South Lawn with two podiums and crossed Russian and American flags as a backdrop. The two smiling presidents mounted the stage side by side and the U.S. President gave his opening remarks, laudatory both of the treaty and his Russian counterpart.

After this the press was given the opportunity to ask questions, and the first came from a representative of the Russian media. It was a softball question for Shurgin, one of a list of such questions his staff had prepared and distributed to the tame Russian press corps days before. The next was to come from an American reporter, and Shurgin thought he detected an expectant stir among the Americans.

Vance Morgan, the Fox News representative, had won the draw for the first question, and as he rose, Shurgin again noted a ripple of anticipation. "My question is for President Shurgin," said Morgan, "Mr. President, as a former high-ranking officer of the KGB did you possess direct knowledge that the Soviet Government orchestrated the assassination of President John Fitzgerald Kennedy?"

There were cries of surprise and outrage from the White House staff that had gathered around the edges of the press conference, and the U.S. President grimaced in consternation. "That's a highly inappropriate and preposterous question," he said into his microphone. Turning to Shurgin, he said, "I apologize, Mr. President, you don't have to answer that."

Shurgin remained unruffled and nodded his thanks to the U.S. President with a tight smile.

Morgan persisted, holding up a sheaf of papers. "In my hand are copies of a memorandum, dated 1967, to then KGB Chairman Yuriy Andropov that contains the details of the alleged Soviet plot. We understand that at this moment the FBI is authenticating the originals." Nearly every American reporter present waved their own copies in the air.

This was a nightmare for Shurgin. He realized he had rolled the dice and lost. Exerting enormous self-control to maintain a calm demeanor, he raised his hand to silence the crowd. The pool television camera zoomed in on his face. "This ridiculous question should not have been asked on a day in which our two countries signed a pact that promotes the cause of world peace and stability. I believe there are hundreds of so-called conspiracy theories concerning the assassination of your President. Some of them accuse the Central Intelligence Agency. But whatever you choose to believe, the fact remains that the Soviet Union no longer exists. The Soviet Communist government and its apparatus no longer exist. Russia emerged from those dark times as a new, free, and democratic nation devoted to peaceful progress, as our action in signing the treaty here today clearly demonstrates."

At his side a clearly unhappy U.S. President said, "President Shurgin is entirely correct. This is a day for celebration, not provocation. I think we should end the press conference now."

A wail of protest arose from the American reporters, all of them shouting for a specific response to the accusation. Copies of the Andropov Memorandum, as it would come to be called, along with an English translation had been received via an anonymous e-mail explaining its origins at their respective editorial offices early that same morning. Most of the reporters were glad that Morgan had drawn the straw to go first because few of them actually relished asking such a question. But now that it was in the open, pursuit of an answer was fair game for all. The CBS reporter shouted, "This document was allegedly in the possession of General Pavel Kondratiev. Did your government sanction his murder to keep him quiet?"

"That's enough," shouted the by now clearly irate U.S. President. "This is over." The two heads of state marched down the steps from the stage stony-faced. Everything had been carried live on television throughout the country and the world. It was one of those infamous moments captured forever by the camera and would not soon be forgotten.

After Shurgin had been seen off with profuse apologies, the U.S. President turned in fury to his staff that had failed to warn him of the impending public relations nightmare. Was it true that the FBI had the original documents for authentication? If so, why had the President not been informed?

The Chief of Staff determined that in accordance with the new protocols established by the Administration regarding contacts within the reorganized Intelligence Community, Director Mulvaney had informed the President's 'Intelligence Czar' by phone that morning and couriered a provisional English translation directly to Tekla's office where the trail ended. The White House logbook showed that the 'Intelligence Czar' left shortly thereafter. His present whereabouts were unknown.

To complicate matters further the networks were reporting that General Kondratiev's daughter, Viktoria, would hold a press conference later that same afternoon. The arms reduction agreement had been signed but was now completely overshadowed by a nightmare that had become part of American mythology.

CHAPTER 60

Lev Chertkov stared at the televised press conference debacle with the sort of fixed attention a condemned man might reserve for the gallows. As his Embassy colleagues gasped, only the SVR man was aware of the sordid background. Despite his best efforts, the Kondratiev affair had at last spiraled completely out of control, and Chertkov was at the center of the maelstrom.

Any fool could see that worse was on the way. He had known it since the early hours of the morning when the man he'd assigned to coordinate the Vympel operation reported to him everything that had transpired during the car chase, and the Fairfax County Police already had notified the embassy of the crash of one of the official Embassy cars involving three deaths, one a minor Russian diplomat, in reality one of Chertkov's SVR subordinates, and two others who carried Jordanian documents. Chertkov should have handled the assignment himself, should have seen to it that vehicles that could not be traced to the Embassy were used, but there had been no time given Shurgin's imminent arrival, and after his heroic success against Terrence Stoddard his proper place was to remain in the background where he could provide guidance to both teams.

His man confessed he had witnessed the crash and instead of returning to the scene to clean things up ran back to the Embassy with his tail between his legs to report to Chertkov. The only accomplishment of the evening was the positive identification of Robert Strachey, something he had already divined. He wondered how long it would take the Americans to identify the *Vympel* operatives as Russians and put together the two dead at Kondratieva's house and the two in the car. With luck their true origins might remain unknown, but Chertkov was no longer a believer in luck, especially with the FBI and its array of technology and investigative power now on the case.

Chertkov's luck had run out, and he knew it. The biggest problem he now faced was what to do next.

This was all President Shurgin's fault. He had driven Chertkov mercilessly and there had been no time to mount a real covert operation. It had seemed a clever idea to have Tekla order Buchalter to kill the old man. It should have been clean, with no trace of the SVR hand, especially with the help of the bribed police detective. Tekla's assurances that Buchalter was an experienced and trustworthy operative had proven untrue. Yes, he had searched the General's condo and recovered the computer and files, but even these early successes turned in the end to ashes.

When it had started, working directly under sealed orders from the President of the Russian Federation had seemed like a marvelous opportunity. He had had visions of meeting Shurgin personally to receive his gratitude -- perhaps a promotion, perhaps moving into the ranks of the President's personal coterie. Killing an old man on the street and retrieving documents was a no-brainer, even for that fool, Buchalter, so easily convinced to do his 'patriotic duty' by Tekla.

But this morning coming face to face with the Russian President was the last thing Lev Chertkov wanted to do. Shurgin had been publicly humiliated. There were stories about the Russian President, dark stories. If the life of even his best friend was unsafe in his hands, how then could 'the fox' be expected to behave toward a man who had failed him so spectacularly? First there would be a message from Moscow Center calling him back home for 'consultations.' After that, he would simply disappear.

There was only one way out – a desperate gamble that might save his life.

Before the televised press conference even had reached its messy conclusion, he left the room and hurried to his office where he opened his private safe and removed all his files, including the 'burn after reading' orders from Shurgin that he should have destroyed but had kept intact. This was intended to be his insurance against the contingency that Shurgin decided to eliminate those aware of his role in the Kondratiev affair. Now they would serve as another kind of insurance. He removed and shredded the correspondence containing his proposal to kill Terrence Stoddard, and stuffed the rest into an oversized briefcase.   Then he slipped out of the Embassy.

CHAPTER 61

Cozily ensconced in their suite at the Four Seasons, Ewan and Sasha laughed uproariously at the high definition close-up of Shurgin's face on the flat-screen television set. When the program switched back to the studio, the news anchor intoned that Shurgin was scheduled to fly back to Moscow that same afternoon.

"The bastard's running with his tail between his legs," Ewan exulted.

"He gave a pretty good answer to the accusation, almost word for word what we expected," commented Sasha. "He might get away with it yet."

"Not a chance. There's already too much evidence, and more is on the way."

"The U.S. Government might want to sweep it under the rug, too."

"You mean like the Warren Commission? The problem then was that they could lock away their findings and tell the public whatever they felt was safe. And, of course, the Soviets were free to plant false trails and conspiracy theories pointing away from themselves. That's one of the reasons Nosenko was sent over."

"Still ..."

"Vicky's press conference this afternoon will reveal even more that they can't refute. You saw the last page of the memo."

Strachey, Vicky, and Ewan had returned to the Four Seasons in the wee hours just as Amy was putting the finishing touches on the e-mail package she would send to every major news organization. While Amy comforted a still shaken Vicky, the other three had pored over the final page of the Andropov Memorandum and agreed on their final strategy.

There would be no contact between them and Strachey from this point on and nor with Vicky. Strachey insisted that it was more important now to protect Ewan and Sasha's anonymity. The CIA man had proven to be quite resourceful, even courageous, and Ewan had developed a grudging admiration for him.

Strachey took the two women to another hotel that morning where Amy would remain with Vicky until the final act. The CIA man still had a lot of work to do to set things up for what they had planned, and they decided it was too dangerous for Strachey and Amy to return to their own home until after Vicky's press conference.

"The Russians will just close ranks and deny everything or blame it all on Khrushchev and say they have nothing to do with the *ancien régime*," sighed Sasha.

"It doesn't matter what the Russians say or do. What matters is what the American public THINKS, as you yourself pointed out."

"I hope you're right, I really do, but I don't have a lot of faith in public opinion. What now?"

His face creased into a broad grin because what he was about to say would please her. "There's nothing more we can do here in any event. The rest is up to Strachey, and that means no more contact between us. Angus must miss us terribly. I think it's time for us to go home."

"Erin go bragh!" She gave it the proper Gaelic pronunciation of 'Erin guh braw.' "Home!   That sounds wonderful. When do we leave?"

"This evening.   I've booked a flight to Paris tonight. We'll have a nice dinner tomorrow at the Tour d'Argent with de Blottière. He deserves to have all the answers. We'll be home the next day."

*****

Across town at the J. Edgar Hoover building Special Agent Enoch Whitehall was not having a good day. Normally, uncovering a nefarious foreign plot on U.S. soil would warm the cockles of an FBI agent's heart. But the revelation of a successful foreign plot that was carried out forty-seven years ago was a questionable source of joy.   Perhaps it was best that a half century had passed. Had it become known at the time nuclear war would have been a real possibility. Now it might be better to suppress the information entirely. The FBI, after all, possessed the original of the Andropov Memorandum.

Director Mulvaney had caught major flak from the White House Chief of Staff which carried with it the onus of Presidential displeasure. The fact that the Director had followed the correct protocol was irrelevant.

And this brought into focus missing 'Intelligence Czar' Brian Tekla. The Secret Service guards reported he had left the White House that morning driving his own car. Wherever he went it was not home. Whitehall had agents at the Tekla residence with the man's wife, who was near hysteria.

He recalled Tekla's troubling evasiveness the previous morning when the body of his security man turned up. Whitehall's radar had pinged on that at the time, but none of this explained the arrogant S.O.B.'s disappearance.

Tekla had been a mere boy at the time of the Kennedy assassination in 1963 and could have had nothing to do with the bloodletting in Dallas. So what was the connection? Murphy's conviction that there was official Russian involvement in Kondratiev's murder had become a near certainty, especially if the FBI lab determined that the Andropov Memorandum was genuine. So was there more than just diplomatic substance to Tekla's known relationship with an SVR officer?

The case had everything: at least two murders, international intrigue, kidnapping, the attack at Viktoria Kondratieva's house and the resultant deaths in a gun fight of two as yet unidentified men. All hell was about to break loose. Even setting aside the question of the Kennedy assassination, Russian-sanctioned killings on American soil would unleash a firestorm of gargantuan proportions.

Whitehall was a seasoned investigator. He still did not have all the facts, but a picture was emerging nonetheless. He would complete his investigation and present his report, the contents of which could impact Russian-American relations for decades to come. What was done with it was above his pay grade, a fact for which he discovered he was grateful.

CHAPTER 62

In 1973 the United States foolishly agreed to permit the Soviets to build a new Embassy compound on Mount Alto, the third highest point in the District of Columbia. That from such a vantage point Soviet signals intelligence would enjoy an enormous advantage did not seem to have occurred to the Americans who negotiated the deal. They soon discovered their mistake, and it was not until 1991, after the collapse of the Soviet Union that the Russians were permitted to occupy the compound, which included living quarters, as well as diplomatic precincts.

After driving aimlessly for several hours, a profusely sweating Brian Tekla presented himself at the Embassy entrance demanding to see Lev Chertkov. Told that Chertkov was absent, Tekla demanded to see anyone from the SVR Rezidentura. He clearly identified himself to the startled guard as the White House Advisor on Homeland Security, the 'Intelligence Czar.'

After some delay he was permitted inside the Embassy where he formally requested political asylum. The Rezidentura staff tried in vain to contact Chertkov. Finally abandoning this effort, they sent a coded message to Moscow Center requesting instructions.

*****

At nearly the same time Tekla was clamoring at the door of the Russian Embassy, the man he sought turned his car slowly into a long, paved drive that culminated at a guard shack just off of Route 123 in McLean, Virginia. He handed the guards his passport and diplomatic identification and told them he was a high ranking SVR officer who wanted to defect to the United States. He said he carried with him documents of utmost importance to U.S. national security.

CHAPTER 63

Viktoria Kondratieva's press conference at the National Press Club commenced at five P.M., the perfect time to be picked up by the evening network newscasts. It was well-attended as the news services had been advised that her statement would be related directly to the so-called Andropov Memorandum and her late father's murder.

Vicky was accompanied by an attorney from one of Washington's top drawer 'E' Street law firms, an arrangement Strachey had set up. The attorney was an old friend of Terry Stoddard. Rather than place her in danger, she hoped that the truth she held would now become her shield. Nevertheless, she was ill at ease. She had never been an assertive person and never in her life appeared before an audience. The television cameras and bright lights added to her discomfort, but what bothered her most of all was what she was about to reveal about her father.

The attorney introduced her with an admonishment to the audience that she would make a brief explanatory statement, provide copies of a document, and would take no questions. He stepped aside, and Vicky approached the podium.

"My father," she began in a faint, tremulous voice, "was an officer in the KGB. He believed in and defended the Soviet system for most of his life. He was, in other words, a patriot. Thanks to his extraordinary abilities, he was singled out as a young officer for special assignments and received extensive training in the English language and American culture in preparation for a career as a so-called American targets officer. He achieved much in his career, eventually becoming the youngest KGB officer ever promoted to the rank of General.

"He spent many years in the United States in a variety of increasingly important assignments and enjoyed great success in running operations, including some of the most damaging penetrations of your Government. His success, yes, was due to his many talents as a linguist and an operative, but not only that. The fact that he enjoyed complete trust and support at the highest levels of the Soviet Government and the KGB also was due to a service he performed early in his career to which only a very few individuals were privy.

"In 1963 he was assigned to the United States under cover as a press attaché at the Soviet Embassy in Washington. Because he was unknown to the American security services at the time he enjoyed relatively free movement without surveillance. It was this circumstance that placed him at the center of one of the most spectacular successes of the KGB – the assassination of an American President."

The reporters in the audience were on the edges of their seats, some with mouths agape, and Vicky's voice gained strength as she spoke. The media pool camera operator zoomed to Vicky's face.

"One of my father's responsibilities at that time was to handle a KGB agent named Lee Harvey Oswald. In September 1963 my father travelled to Mexico City to meet this man and give him orders to kill the President. The assassin had been well trained in the USSR before his 're-defection' to the United States."

She told them everything: that Fidel Castro had long advocated the assassination of Kennedy whom he considered a mortal enemy; of the Soviet Premier's fury in the wake of the Cuban Missile Crisis.

"The man who in the end killed Oswald, Jack Ruby, was a long-time collaborator of Cuban Intelligence. He was a support asset who originally was to rendezvous with Oswald and drive him to Galveston where a fast boat waited to get him out of the country. When the assassin was captured, Ruby was ordered to kill him and assured that this would make him an American hero and a rich man.

"The rest is history, and all of this information is provided in detail in the document that will be provided to each of you this afternoon. It is the final page of the so-called Andropov Memorandum.

"My father was murdered to prevent the exposure of these secrets, and when I fled to Europe to a man my father trusted I was kidnapped by Russian agents for the same reason. Had it not been for the bravery of Lawrence Nelson and his wife who rescued me and took me in, I would not be standing here now. In all likelihood I would be dead too.

"My father, as one of the principle actors in the assassination, was the author of the original memorandum for KGB Chairman Andropov in 1967. It was one of the most closely guarded documents in the KGB archives, and my father was one of the few who knew where to find the single surviving copy when everything began to fall apart in the Soviet Union. He recognized its historical significance and did not want to see it destroyed. As for authentication, you will find his signature and date at the bottom of the page, along with the counter-signature of Yuriy Andropov himself.

"When my father saw what was happening to Russia and the kind of people who were taking advantage of the chaos to become powerful, his disillusionment led to his dismissal in disgrace from the KGB. The great irony of his life was that the country against which he had done battle for so many years in the end gave him asylum. He wanted to make the Andropov Memorandum public not to rake up the past, but because the poison is still circulating in the system, and he wanted to expel it. As you will read in the final page of the memorandum, the advance knowledge of the route of the Presidential motorcade in Dallas that made the assassination possible was provided by a KGB penetration of the CIA code-named 'Sasha.' His real name was Adam Tekla, the father of Presidential advisor Brian Tekla."

Vicky stepped away from the microphone as the room erupted.

CHAPTER 64

The Russian President sat motionless throughout the ten-hour flight. His famous stoicism was crumbling into ruins and when he was offered a meal he glared at the attendant so fiercely that the cabin crew gave him a wide berth thereafter. It was night in Moscow when they landed, and he was grateful at least that the darkness made him invisible as his car sped into the city to the Kremlin where he went straight to his office.

Every major American news network broadcast Vicky's statement in full to the American public that evening. In a very few hours the story was on television screens and the front pages of newspapers all over the world.

Shurgin immediately gave orders to issue a statement flatly denying the authenticity of the Andropov Memorandum and calling it a provocation of the basest variety likely concocted by the CIA.

Alone in his office he opened a chilled bottle of vodka and filled two shot glasses to the brim. He lifted one of the glasses and said to the empty space in front of him, "*Zhura,*" he used the Russian diminutive to address his deceased comrade Yuriy Ivanovich Morozov, "If only you were here. I could use your advice now."

In retrospect he was certain Morozov would

have advised against the actions leading to the Kondratiev debacle. If only someone had shot that hot-blooded old bastard, Khrushchev, the moment he broached the idea.   But Russia had been a different place in those days. The entire world had been different.

There was the nagging matter of Tekla who had followed in his father's footsteps to spy for Russia. Protecting that source had been an important consideration in going ahead with the Kondratiev murder.   But now the SVR duty office reported the presence of Tekla in the Russian Embassy in Washington, a sad attendant casualty of the affair. The second generation spy and agent of influence had served the SVR and before that the KGB well for many years, his entire life.   He might have survived this crisis, but his nerve had given out. Shurgin pondered what to do with him now that he had become a liability.

To reveal his defection would be to admit that there had been a contemporary reason for murdering Kondratiev and suppressing the memorandum. No. That could not happen. Tekla had to disappear if Shurgin were to retain even a shred of deniability. Like a glove, Tekla had concealed the Russian hand, but the glove had become soiled and must now be discarded.   His body would provide excellent nourishment for the flowers on the Embassy grounds in Washington.

The question was could Shurgin himself survive

the shitstorm that threatened to engulf him.

He might have guessed the answer had he yet known of Chertkov's defection.

*****

The Central Intelligence Agency is statutorily responsible for handling defectors to the United States. The Agency's Defector Relocation Service eventually resettles them and looks after them. The responsibility does not prevent the Agency from sharing information with other concerned agencies, however, and in the case of Lev Chertkov's admitted involvement in the Andropov Memorandum conspiracy, the FBI was in the interrogation room almost as soon as the Agency debriefers. Enoch Whitehall was the principal Bureau representative.

CIA Director Capriano reluctantly agreed to permit Strachey's participation in the initial interview with the defector. Despite the Director's displeasure over his unsanctioned involvement in the Kondratiev affair, he did this because it was justified by recent events and Strachey had shared his opinion that the Chain Bridge Massacre was a Russian inspired operation. Capriano was decent enough to believe Strachey deserved the opportunity to get a closer look at Chertkov. But it would be his final act as Executive Officer for the DNCS. Unsanctioned operations are serious breaches of CIA discipline and there would be consequences. In view of Strachey's past service Capriano needed time to think about it.

$$*****$$

They'd moved Chertkov to an interim safehouse, one of the anonymous McMansions in Fairfax, and he sat there at the table looking curiously indecisive. He demanded vodka, but got Coke instead. His confirmation that the missing Brian Tekla was an SVR agent came as an anticlimax after the revelation at Vicky Kondratieva's press conference.

"Tekla wanted to defect," volunteered the Russian. "He told me he wanted to go to Moscow."

Strachey knew that the FBI observation post had captured images of the White House advisor entering the Russian Embassy compound. As far as they knew, he was still there, but Whitehall mentioned none of this to Chertkov.

"How much did Tekla know about what happened to Kondratiev?" asked Whitehall.

"Everything. He ordered his man Buchalter to kill Kondratiev."

Whitehall's eyes flickered in his hatchet face as he considered this. "What about Cogburn?" he asked.

Chertkov answered this question easily. "The policeman? He was well paid to play the part of the patriot. Buchalter ordered him to stifle the investigation."

"So Cogburn believed he was acting under White House orders?"

"Maybe. Normally patriots don't require a payment of fifty thousand dollars to do their duty."

"Was Buchalter one of your agents, too?"

"No. He worked for Tekla. Buchalter was an ambitious fool who thought he was carrying out White House instructions."

"To kill a man?"

"Isn't it obvious?"

This might well be true, but Chertkov was cagey enough to avoid an admission that might be self-incriminating despite his defector status and despite the fact that it was evident that Tekla acted on instructions from the Russian.

Almost to himself Chertkov mumbled, "And nothing more would have happened had it not been for that damned woman and her friend."

"Woman?" The comment evoked Whitehall's immediate interest. The counterfeit Russian policewoman was still a mystery.

"The one that showed up at the Arlington police station claiming to be from the FSB. I knew immediately that she was a fake, and Buchalter ordered Cogburn to take her into custody and deliver her to him. I was there. Tekla told Buchalter we were cooperating in a liaison operation and that national security required that neither Cogburn nor the woman should continue living. We couldn't have anticipated what happened. The woman killed Buchalter, and the man with her nearly caught me."

"So you were there and you knew that two people were to be murdered." Whitehall said in a sharp voice, and Chertkov looked suddenly guilty. No, thought Strachey, it was more embarrassment at having to make the admission than guilt.

The Russian just shook his head.

"You say a man was with the woman. What man?" Whitehall asked, and Strachey pricked his ears. This was important for the safety of Ramsay and Sasha.

"There was a man with the woman. I saw him come out of the back of the farmhouse as I was driving away. It happened very quickly. All I can tell you is that he was tall."

Whitehall shot a look at Strachey, undoubtedly because he recalled Strachey's comment to Murphy about a Russian at the Buchalter shooting, and Chertkov's statement substantiated his story. But Cogburn had not mentioned seeing another man. Whitehall might think it had been Strachey at the farmhouse that night. It had to be obvious to Whitehall that the CIA man knew a lot more than he was saying, especially about the as yet unidentified players in the Kondratiev drama, but there was nothing he could do to make him talk.

Chertkov went on to describe how the SVR tracked Vicky Kondratieva to Brussels, her contact there with the Nelsons, and how the Nelsons had been tracked to Paris thanks to the intercept of a telephone conversation between Lawrence Nelson and Terry Stoddard. He had no idea how they had turned up in Washington, D.C.

"Tell me about the Chain Bridge bomb," said Whitehall.

Strachey watched the Russian intently.

Chertkov took a drink of his Coke before answering. "I know nothing about that. I thought it was Middle Eastern terrorists."

"Very convenient for you, though, wasn't it?"

"I suppose so."

Chertkov looked away from Whitehall when he said this, and Strachey knew he was lying. It was more than body language and instinct that told him this. By his own admission Chertkov had been the only SVR operative involved until the very end. He had detonated the device himself or ordered someone else to do it. Either way he was responsible for Stoddard's death.

Much to Strachey's relief the question of the

unidentified participants in Buchalter's death was overshadowed by the documents Chertkov brought with him. There were several messages decoded by Chertkov's personal cipher that purported to be direct orders from President Vitaliy Mikhailovich Shurgin to murder General Pavel Kondratiev. Chertkov confirmed their provenance.

Whitehall and the CIA interrogators recognized political dynamite when they saw it. Whether the Andropov Memorandum was authentic or not, the direct implication of Shurgin in a murderous plot on American soil was shocking. Whitehall later told Strachey he could not imagine the consequences when their report reached the President's desk. All the talk about "re-setting relations" between Washington and Moscow would fall apart like a wet tissue.

CHAPTER 65

"You can't keep something like that secret in this day and age," said Amy Strachey.

Five months had passed since the denouement of the Andropov Memorandum affair, and the four of them, Amy, Strachey, Ewan, and Sasha were enjoying the warmth of a roaring fire sweetly scented with peat in the living room of the Ramsay house in Cleggan, Connemara. Outside under a lowering sky a strong wind tossed whitecaps across the sea and winter rain pelted the landscape and lashed the windows.

Strachey was still on indefinite administrative leave and Amy was by this time very obviously pregnant. The Agency could well do without Strachey, but Amy was another story entirely, and Harvey Grant, the Deputy Director for Intelligence and Amy's boss, had settled into fierce opposition to any action that might result in her leaving the CIA, such as her husband's dismissal.

They were discussing the inevitable leaks to the media from the Chertkov defection. Multiple Freedom of Information Act requests to the FBI to release the results of the Andropov Memorandum analysis had yielded a cautious official confirmation of the document's age but nothing on the authenticity of its contents. Lawrence Nelson had written a book that meticulously made the case for the Memorandum's veracity, and strong public interest made it an immediate best seller. The damage assessment on Brian Tekla was ongoing, but there was no trace of the man himself.

Strachey opined, "The bureaucracy is much larger than it used to be, and the more people who know a secret the more likely it'll leak. It's certainly put Shurgin in hot water. I wonder where he is."

Shurgin's political career had been on life support over the intervening months, and when Chertkov's defection made it to the front pages, along with allegations of Shurgin's personal involvement in the Kondratiev murder even his power was insufficient to continue in office, and he resigned the Russian Presidency. Perhaps fearing revenge from those who had feared him for so long, he disappeared amid rumors that he had fled abroad. The arms treaty, though signed by both Presidents, had yet to win the approval required from the U.S. Senate, but with Shurgin no longer in the picture there were hopes it might survive.

"Shurgin still has tremendous financial resources from the old days safely stashed in foreign accounts," commented Ramsay. "He's gone to ground somewhere like some ancient dragon in a cave to gestate his revenge. We'll hear from him again, and when we do we'll know where to find him."

"You have something planned?" asked Strachey.

"We have unfinished business with him." Ewan looked meaningfully at Sasha who sat next to him with the Scottie, Angus, on her lap.

"Speaking of unfinished business," said Strachey, "I have a proposal for you."

CHAPTER 66

Handling defectors is a delicate and time-consuming business. Debriefing normally takes months, if not years and can try the patience of both the defector and his debriefers. In Lev Chertkov's case antagonism was a recurring theme. His fear of Shurgin forced his defection, but he retained a residual loyalty to the SVR, making the CIA's task difficult. Six months after surrendering himself at the gates of CIA Headquarters it was still a struggle to drag names and facts out of him, especially after he learned of Shurgin's disgrace.

The Agency possesses several facilities in the vicinity of Washington for the long term debriefing of defectors. This is for convenience's sake so senior officers would not have to absent themselves long from Headquarters to participate in interviews.

In Chertkov's case they selected a rustic house donated years earlier by a wealthy retired Agency alumnus, located not far from Front Royal, Virginia. Accessible by a single private road and surrounded by acres of private forest, the place had originally been intended for the week-end activities of a well-to-do family and their guests and comfortably housed Chertkov, two guards, and whatever debriefer might be assigned for the day. Front Royal was less than two hours from Washington, so the debriefers normally returned home at close of business. Strachey was quite familiar with the Front Royal debriefing facility, and no one was interested in the movements of a CIA officer on indefinite administrative leave.

Ramsay had warmed immediately to Strachey's proposal. Terry Stoddard had been a friend to both. While Vitaliy Mikhailovich Shurgin may have given the order there was no doubt that Chertkov was directly responsible for the IED that killed Stoddard. Ramsay's turn to exact mortal revenge on Shurgin would come eventually, but for now, it was Strachey whose point of honor demanded satisfaction.

He kept the house under observation for two days, just enough time to establish a pattern. The debriefer arrived mid-morning, and the sessions lasted until four or five in the afternoon when the debriefer returned to Washington. Afterwards, Chertkov and a guard took a walk around the grounds to take advantage of the remaining daylight before dinner.

On the third day Strachey arrived at the spot he had chosen on a heavily wooded slope above the house and a hundred yards away to make his preparations. A winter storm had poured over the Appalachians that afternoon and blanketed the countryside in white. Heavy wet flakes were still falling, swirling in the gusting wind creating conditions that were not ideal for what Strachey had to do. His tracks back and forth through the forest to his waiting vehicle would be easily discovered.

He opened the long case he carried with him. Nestled inside was an Izmash SV-98, a Russian sniper rifle that had seen its first use in Chechnya in 1998.   He had chosen the more expensive version that fired .338 Lapua Magnum rounds to insure greater effectiveness.   Before leaving his car, he'd fitted the muzzle with a suppressor that should conceal his location long enough for him to get away.   But the storm meant that his retreat now would cover three-quarters of a mile through deepening drifts of snow.

He mounted the Russian-made PKS-07 scope on the rail above the receiver, unlimbered the folding bipod, and stretched out prone behind the rifle, using the 7X scope to scan the house and its immediate surroundings. Then he waited, slowing his breathing, calming his heart, calling up lessons learned on deer hunts with his father in his native North Carolina.

The snow intensified, bringing with it silence and tranquility to the forest in which Strachey lay.   In contrast he was thinking of the rare sunny day in coastal Ireland when he had first laid eyes on Ewan Ramsay aka Harry Connolly and his wife.   He recalled his initial opinion of Ramsay as little more than a killer, a CIA man gone bad.   So much had happened since Terry Stoddard had entrusted him with that mission. The irony was that now it was he, Robert Strachey, who lay in hiding, waiting to kill a man. Was this the way it had happened to Ramsay – violence and death setting him on an unforeseen different path?

Ramsay had suggested many refinements to Strachey's original plan. Every article of clothing he now wore was of Russian manufacture or available for purchase in Moscow. The Mossad owed Ewan some favors and at his request they had acquired the rifle and ammunition through a cut-out from a Middle Eastern arms bazaar. The clothing and the rifle were sent to the United States via the Israeli diplomatic pouch and deposited in a public locker where Strachey had retrieved them.

The Mossad assistance had come with a price. Nothing could be left to chance, and capture was not an option. For such contingencies, the Israelis had thoughtfully included an L-pill, a fast acting suicide pill, with the shipment. The reasons for this killing would remain a mystery, even if it meant his death. If he escaped, the evidence would point to a Russian assassin.

He had not shared this with Amy who had done her best to dissuade him. It was their first real quarrel and Strachey still felt the guilt, could see her face and knew she feared raising their child alone. The sonograms told them they would have a son, and they had agreed he would be called Terrence in Stoddard's honor. But this was something he had to do, and it could be his only chance before the Agency decided to move Chertkov to another location.

To Sasha's visible exasperation, Ramsay had volunteered for the job arguing that it made more sense for him to carry out the mission than for Strachey, but he yielded to Strachey's stubborn insistence that the 'honor' belonged to him. Terry Stoddard had supported him in difficult circumstances, had invited him and Amy into his home without a trace of patrician condescension toward two people of modest background from North Carolina. Killing Chertkov would not bring 'closure' to Terry's wife and daughter, but justice would at least have been done.

He'd waited until near the end of their visit to Ireland to raise the matter because he knew his wife would object. In fact, gentle, perspicacious Amy had been stunned. "You intend to kill a man in cold blood?"

"Chertkov killed Terry and a lot of other innocent people that morning on Chain Bridge. He deserves to die instead of being resettled with a comfortable income to live out his miserable life at the expense of the American taxpayers. He's an animal, a rabid animal that needs to be put down."

It was the classic confrontation between female and male psyches: while the woman craved security and predictability above all, the man needed constantly to confront external challenges because if he did not he would begin to doubt his own self-worth and that doubt would fester until it destroyed him.

Strachey knew that Amy envied Sasha the comfort of being with her husband instead of suffering the anguish of not knowing if she would ever see him again, but he had given her no choice. He could still see the abject fear and look of abandonment on her face when he had left her three days earlier. He fervently prayed he had not seen her for the last time and worried about how the knowledge that he had killed a man would affect their relationship. He couldn't imagine life without her. He had not shared with her the bloodier details of last year's events in Spain. He'd killed men there, too, but then it had been in self-defense.

The debriefer left the house at five to return to Washington. Strachey pressed his eye to the scope's reticule. The winter sun was already setting, but the snow had stopped and the scope afforded him a clear high contrast view. He would take the Russian as soon as he stepped out of the house and squeeze off a few more rounds to pin the guards inside long enough for him to escape. The L-pill taped to the inside of his wrist was a constant reminder of the cost of failure.

Ten minutes after the debriefer's departure the front door opened. Strachey banished all other thought to focus his entire attention on the task at hand. The guard came out first, and he saw the man shiver when the cold hit him. Then Chertkov was framed in the doorway, still zipping his parka.

Strachey did not hesitate. He had adjusted the trigger to its lightest pull weight, and with the Russian's head in the crosshairs he squeezed it.

The Izmash coughed and bucked against his shoulder as it spat a heavy round that caught the Russian just above the right eye showering the startled guard with bone fragments, brain matter, and blood. As Chertkov's lifeless body sagged against the door frame and slid to the ground the guard dropped to a knee and scanned the forest as he fumbled clumsily beneath his jacket for his side arm.

Strachey placed two rounds in quick succession into the door frame just above the guard's head, showering him with splinters and prompting him to scramble back inside over Chertkov's body. From the interior of the house the guard returned fire blindly with his pistol, and the rounds smacked into trees forty feet from where Strachey lay. Strachey fired two more rounds high through the door.

Now for the hard part. Leaving the rifle where it lay he pushed himself backwards through the deepening snow into the trees until he could no longer be spotted from the house. He rose then and started back along the tracks he had made when he arrived, hoping the guards would choose prudence over the risk of someone taking another shot at them if they ventured outside.

If he made good his escape, the Russian rifle and its case would be found. His tracks in the snow would show the print of a boot of Russian manufacture. The logical conclusion would be that Chertkov had been tracked down and killed by his own countrymen, something for which the Russians were reputed. More perceptive investigators might wonder why a Russian assassin would leave such obvious clues to his identity, but it wouldn't matter.

Slogging through the wet snow even at a walking pace was arduous and the footing treacherous as he scrambled down the slope on the other side of the rise by now completely out of sight of the house; he half jogged, half walked as he made his way between the trees. Early winter darkness was falling now, and it became harder to find his way, but it would hamper pursuit, too. He couldn't tell if he was being followed, and the blood pounding in his ears made it difficult to hear.

Despite the Russian clothing, if he were captured or killed his body eventually would be identified. The L-pill obviated capture, but Amy would still have to live with the opprobrium and suspicion that would fall around her. He just couldn't allow that to happen.

He tripped over a branch buried beneath the snow and fell headlong down the slope. He had to grasp the ice-slippery trunk of a tree with both hands to regain his feet. He was suddenly drenched in sweat beneath his clothing. Gulping air in great ragged heaves, he forged on. *Not too far now*, he thought, *just a few hundred yards*. Several moments later the trees began to thin as he neared the road where the car waited.

There was still no sign of pursuit. No shouting, and more importantly no gunshots. But the area would soon be swarming with police and CIA security personnel. It was taking far longer than he had planned to get to the car and the minutes were stretching toward the agonizing possibility he might not make it.

He fumbled for what seemed like an eternity to open the car door and drag himself behind the wheel. He was still gasping for breath, and his vision blurred slightly. He started the engine, switched on the wipers, and drove unsteadily in the direction of his escape route, hoping the SUV he had rented in the alias supplied by the Mossad could cope with the snow now beginning to drift over the road.

Keeping to secondary roads he headed east and after thirty minutes of treacherous driving entered the city of Front Royal where he pulled into the large service station he had scouted previously. The station's restrooms had entrances separate from the main one which meant he could avoid being seen inside the station itself. He retrieved a plastic trash bag he had deposited earlier from behind the dumpster at the side of the building. The bag contained a complete change of clothing, as well as his true name documents, and when he had finished he stuffed the Russian gear into the bag and buried it in the dumpster before pulling back out onto the road. The snow was still coming down which made it more unlikely that anyone would be able to identify him.

He continued out of town via the John Marshall Highway, and the snow began to taper off as he drove out from under the weakening storm, finally ending altogether by the time he reached Markham where he merged onto the Interstate and picked up speed. An hour later he turned into the Hertz lot at Dulles Airport where he returned the rental SUV and rode the Hertz shuttle to the main terminal. From there he caught a taxi that dropped him at the Dunn Loring Metro station where he called Amy to pick him up and take him home.

He hoped she could forgive him.

CHAPTER 67

São Paulo, Brazil

The night air was still warm and moist from the sub-tropical heat of the day and the sky that vaulted overhead displayed unfamiliar constellations with names such as Lupus, Corona Australis, and Crux. But Shurgin was not admiring the stars nor listening to the night cries of exotic birds from near-by Ibirapuera Park. He reclined in a lounge chair on the veranda of his high-rise condominium, cloaked in darkness, brooding and nursing his wounds.

His escape had taken him to Brazil where a skilled plastic surgeon altered his appearance and agreed to keep quiet in exchange for an exorbitant sum of money. He grew a thick beard which he dyed black and shaved his head to improve the fit of the shaggy toupee he now wore.

There were many things he might think about: the revival of the *Voskreseniye*[1] network, the elimination of a certain *Russkaya Mafiya*[2] kingpin who resented his bid to regain control of the far-flung *vory v zakonye*[3] organizations, whether to

[1]   Rebirth, originally "Russian Rebirth," a powerful international organization created by Shurgin using funds stolen from the Soviet treasury and CPSU. It included elements of Russian organized crime and the intelligence services and served as Shurgin's clandestine political arm.

[2]   Russian Mafia

[3]   "Thieves in the code," a term describing Russian criminals, especially those who spent time in the Gulag.

retain or replace his financial manager in Monaco who had been using Shurgin's accounts to enrich himself. But all of these were eclipsed by a need he felt more viscerally.

He was physically safe, yes, and still rich. He wielded great power, but not the power of a nation-state. Despite advantages of which most men could only dream he had lost that which was most precious to him: control of the Russian Federation and with it the ability to influence world affairs, specifically to reduce the United States to second power ranks and build his beloved Motherland into the predominant world power. His gut would not allow him to forsake vengeance upon those responsible for his fall. Everything else was subordinate.

The key was the blond woman photographed by SVR surveillance at the Rue de Tournon address in Paris. He'd seen other photographs of her nearly two decades ago, sent to him by his colleague in Zürich where she was being held and interrogated. That had ended in disaster and the death of his colleague. Whoever she was, she had dogged his footsteps ever since and inflicted severe though not fatal damage on his organization. It would still require an effort to identify and find her, but she had been working with CIA operatives in the Kondratiev affair, and he would find her through them.

Lawrence Nelson was a possible link, but Robert Strachey, the former Executive Officer to the late

Terrence Stoddard, was a better choice. Strachey had worked with the blond woman and could lead him to her.

Strachey was easy to find, and he was a man with a family, with vulnerabilities.

It was only a matter of time.

END

AFTERWORD

I am not an advocate of any of the myriad and bizarre conspiracy theories surrounding the assassination of John F. Kennedy. I do, however subscribe to the belief that there was something amiss about the defection of Yuri Nosenko. The description of Nosenko provided in this book is completely accurate to the best of my knowledge. I attended a talk he gave at CIA Headquarters many years ago and my skin crawled. I made sure to take a seat in the back row.

Suspicion was quite rightly aroused by the timing of Nosenko's defection and his volunteered asseveration that the Russians had no complicity in the President's assassination. But these were neither the only nor even the most important red flags he raised. Nosenko claimed that through the entire calendar years 1960 and 1961 he was deputy chief of the KGB section that spied on, and recruited agents in, the American Embassy in Moscow. It was thanks to this post, where he had personally supervised all KGB work against the embassy's code clerks and its security officer that Nosenko learned the most important KGB secrets he reported to CIA. Unfortunately, despite the many official statements to the contrary, the information he provided was useless or, worse, intentionally misleading.

Nosenko changed his claims regarding his KGB career many times, and to this day none of his claims have been confirmed. As Tennent Bagley asks in his authoritative account of the Nosenko defection, "Why have at least four authoritative KGB insiders stated that Nosenko did not hold that position? They include a) the defector KGB Major Anatoly Golitsyn who visited that section during this period; b) a leading member of the section at the time; c) a top-level supervisor of KGB operations who had himself earlier held that exact position; and d) a later head of KGB foreign counterintelligence, Oleg Kalugin."[4]

More pertinent to the INCUBUS plot KGB veterans have repeatedly said that Nosenko was lying when he claimed that the KGB had evaluated and rejected Lee Harvey Oswald as agent material. Those were difficult and dangerous times, and the Cold War had only months earlier nearly become hot. What is certain is that Oswald had defected to the USSR, spent considerable time there, and married a Russian woman. That the Russians would be concerned that these facts could create the perception that Oswald was an agent seems reasonable. What might they have done to pour cold water on such a theory?

---

4   Bagley, Tennent, SPY WARS: Moles, Mysteries, and Deadly Games, Copyright © 2007 Yale University, ISBN 978-0-300-12198-8.

Whether Nosenko was a true defector or part of a Russian deception operation remains a subject of contention. A contemporary and undoubtedly genuine KGB defector, Anatoliy Golitsyn, believed that Nosenko was a KGB plant sent to discredit him. Golitsyn pointed out many inconsistencies in Nosenko's claims. At the same time an FBI agent code named "Fedora," later shown to have been a double agent, confirmed Nosenko's claim to be genuine.

Was there a secret the KGB wanted to protect that was even more important than muddying the waters about Oswald? Nosenko's apparently spurious claim to have been in charge of operations against the US Embassy in Moscow may provide a clue. Was his main mission to hide the fact that the KGB had made an important recruitment from among the embassy personnel? This does seem likely.

What is not in doubt is that the Nosenko affair combined with Golitsyn's claim that a Soviet mole had penetrated deeply into the CIA threw the Agency's operations against the Soviet Union into chaos. Careers were destroyed. It became imperative to get operations up and running again and to restore the morale of the badly damaged Soviet/East European Division. Nosenko was declared to be a genuine defector and legendary counter-intelligence chief James Jesus Angleton's reputation was ruined.

The story line of INCUBUS takes many liberties with these events and borrows from several Kennedy Assassination conspiracy theories.   Nevertheless, the true facts of the Nosenko defection remain unresolved to this day.

Michael R. Davidson

New Market, VA

October 2012

House Select Committee on Assassination

TESTIMONY OF RICHARD HELMS

FORMER DIRECTOR OF CENTRAL INTELLIGENCE

1978

Chairman STOKES. Thank you, Mr. Chairman. If I could just follow up at this point in an area that gives me some concern, that is, if I understand you correctly, I believe you said you still even today don't really know whether Nosenko is bona fide or not; further, it is your recollection you don't believe the agency ever arrived at that determination, particularly when you were there. Let me ask you this: If it were clearly proven that Nosenko's statements concerning Oswald were untrue, what significance would you attach to such a finding insofar as the broader question of his overall bona fides are concerned?

Mr. HELMS. I think, Mr. Stokes that is just the point. This is the issue which remains, as I understand it, to this very day that no person familiar with the facts, of whom I am aware, finds Mr. Nosenko's comments about Lee Harvey Oswald and the KGB to be credible. That ***still hangs in the air like an incubus***. I think, therefore, this tends to sour a great deal of one's opinion of all the other things that he may have Contributed to the knowledge of the intelligence community about Soviet affairs and Soviet agents and so forth.

I do not know how one resolves this bone in the throat. And therefore, if I sit here before you and say, Mr. Stokes, I believe that Mr. Nosenko is a bona fide defector and you can rely on everything he says, I am in effect saying now,

Mr. Stokes, you can rely on what he says about Lee Harvey Oswald. And I would not like to make that recommendation to you. That is where this thing lies and it is a most difficult question even at this late date.

Chairman STOKES. Then doesn't this raise a question, then, of a further part of the dilemma, that if he was not, bona fide, the only alternative, then, is what the CIA suspected, and that was that he might have been a KGB plant sent here for the purpose of deceiving the United States?

Mr. HELMS. That is correct.

Chairman STOKES. Doesn't that logically follow?

Mr. HELMS. That is certainly true, and that was foremost in our minds.

Chairman STOKES. So it leaves you with the conclusion, then, that if Nosenko was lying about Oswald, that Oswald would in fact be left as being an agent of the KGB?

Mr. HELMS. By implication.

The Author

Michael Davidson was raised in the Mid-West. Heeding President Kennedy's call for more young Americans to learn Russian he studied the language, and military service took him to the White House where he served as translator for the Moscow-Washington "Hotline." His language abilities attracted the attention of the Central Intelligence Agency, and following his military service Mr. Davidson spent the next 28 years as a Clandestine Services officer. Seventeen of those years were spent abroad in a variety of sensitive posts working against the Soviet Union and the Warsaw Pact.